# the idea of love

ALSO BY PATTI CALLAHAN HENRY

*The Stories We Tell*

*And Then I Found You*

*Coming Up for Air*

*The Perfect Love Song: A Holiday Story*

*Driftwood Summer*

*The Art of Keeping Secrets*

*Between the Tides*

*When Light Breaks*

*Where the River Runs*

*Losing the Moon*

# the idea of love

PATTI CALLAHAN HENRY

St. Martin's Press
New York

THE IDEA OF LOVE. Copyright © 2015 by Patti Callahan Henry. All rights reserved. Printed in the United States of America. For information address St. Martin's Press, 175 Fifth Avenue, New York, N.Y. 10010.

www.stmartins.com

The Library of Congress Cataloging-in-Publication Data is available upon request.

ISBN 978-1-250-04032-9 (hardcover)
ISBN 978-1-4668-3555-9 (e-book)

St. Martin's Press books may be purchased for educational, business, or promotional use. For information on bulk purchases, please contact the Macmillan Corporate and Premium Sales Department at 1-800-221-7945, extension 5442, or write to special markets@macmillan.com.

First Edition: June 2015

10  9  8  7  6  5  4  3  2  1

FOR SERENA,
STELLA, AND SADIE
WITH LOVE

*This is a good sign, having a broken heart.*

*It means we have tried for something.*

—ELIZABETH GILBERT, *Eat, Pray, Love*

# the idea of love

# *one*

---

In his mind, he was already writing her—the woman who stood at the patio table with her eyes closed and her face lifted to the sky. She was only a subject, or more precisely, an object. Her slumped shoulders folded inward and her beautiful mouth turned down. Did she know how obvious she was in her sadness? Right there in public, surrounded by syrupy sunlight and azaleas so garish they could be fake?

Could she be the one?

The towns blended together now. This one felt like the others, all dense light having to find its way through leaves and crowded branches. The briny water in rivers and tributaries, in basins and bays, rose and fell twelve feet or more with the shift of moon and Earth. Parceled plots of concrete-colored sand appeared and disappeared with the tides. And the marshes, winnowed out from one another, separated by swaths of blue-gray water, teemed with life. This town, Watersend it was called, felt the same as all the others, and different, too, because it was his last. He would stop here. So maybe he was noticing more, a kind of nostalgic impression where all towns blended into one.

The streets were old, probably original to the town's founding in the 1800s. They didn't force themselves into straight lines, but found their way through the existing landscape. Seafood restaurants and bars. Shops with names like Seashore Décor and Driftwood Sands. Coastal-themed hotels and homes. They all filled every one of these towns.

He focused on the woman across the street, her face lifted to the sky. This woman knew how to be still. She was otherworldly in the way he always imagined Southern women to be. Petite and fragile. While he stared, she opened her eyes and looked directly at him with a practiced air of "What the hell do you want?" She could have walked away, embarrassed, but she waited one more beat before sitting at the café table. He guessed her age about five years younger than his forty-nine.

The details that would go in his notebook: She was small, her hair a buttery yellow, melting onto her shoulders. Bangs fringed her forehead and were pushed to the left, curtains swept aside for that sliver of sunlight to fall into a room. Her face was round and full until her chin, which was shaped like a little heart—almost an afterthought. Her dress was a flowery flirty thing that tied behind her neck, old-fashioned, at least in L.A. terms. He didn't know her eye color yet, but he guessed it was blue. He wanted them to be blue. She was pale, but her cheeks held pink in them like a stain.

He exhaled. God, he was so cursed tired by now. All the highs of his earlier screenplays hitting it big thanks to bidding wars, with top stars and A-list directors jostling to make them. And then the lows, or more specifically two devastating lows. "Flops" they'd called the last two movies he wrote, and not behind closed doors, but in reviews heard on TV and at the cocktail parties of "friends" and printed in newspapers and magazines and online at a thousand different Web sites. Always online in the stories and blogs and especially in the comments below that you should never never read but you always do. "It's all in the execution" was the catchphrase in the movie business. *His* execution seemed likely if he didn't return with an idea for a great script.

He'd been traveling for two months now, wandering the southern

East Coast. He'd found a few stories from women who cried on his shoulder and told him their latest heartbreak. He'd listened to them all: the way they'd met, the way they'd parted; the meant-to-bes that turned out not-to-be; the waiting and the longing and the angst. (Oh, the angst.) And every last one of them believing her pain was unique. In the end, not one story was worth telling again, much less worth putting on paper. To all of these women, his name was Hunter Adderman and he was writing a book on Southern coastal towns. That's how he presented himself. That's who he was. At least for now.

Before he approached the woman, he glanced at his phone to see if Amelia had gotten back to him yet. Nope. He shook his head. How could he make it up to his daughter, if she wouldn't even answer his texts? He stuffed his phone into his pocket and then lifted his head again to watch the woman.

He approached her casually so as not to startle her. He had a feeling—he got those sometimes—a slight tingle in the palms of his hands that let him know that a moment carried more weight than it usually did. He ambled toward her as if he hadn't made up his mind where he was going. "Good afternoon," he said, and tipped his head in some stupid Southern gesture.

"Do I know you?" she asked. She looked him straight in the eye as if the answer rested there. Sure enough, her eyes were blue. He must have stared at her too long because she dug into her leather purse and brought up a pair of sunglasses, which she shoved onto her face with too much force. Her wedding band was simple. Platinum. Small diamond without extra adornment. Married.

"No, we've never met," he said. "But . . . well . . . I'm new in town and you look like you might know something about this place."

Damn. He should have thought this through. He usually did. He'd spot a woman and weigh his best opening line. He was getting lazy. No, not lazy. Desperate. He hadn't found the story he needed. And damn, maybe that story didn't even exist. Maybe they'd all been told to death. Nothing new in the world.

"Can I help you?" the woman asked.

Blake realized he'd been quiet too long, just standing there, looking at her, mulling over his failures. This would not work.

"This city," he said, trying hard to remember exactly which one he was in.

"Watersend," she said slowly, as if he didn't speak English.

"Yes, it's beautiful. Magical. A place where you could fall in love."

She laughed, but the sound seemed forced, unnatural.

"Sure thing. Love," she said.

He couldn't see her eyes behind the dark sunglasses, but she seemed to look past him, over his shoulder and into the park beyond. "You don't sound convinced."

She tilted her head and half smiled. "Do you always approach women this way?"

"No," he said, and took a step back. He'd screwed this one up without even sitting down. She'd looked so promising, too.

"Yeah," she said with a laugh and a little shake of her head, "I wouldn't try it again."

"Can I start over?"

"Sure." She looked up from under the fringe of her bangs.

Blake pointed to the empty seat next to her. "May I join you?"

"I'm waiting for someone," she said.

"Well, then maybe you could point me in the right direction. I'm here to do a little research about Watersend and I'm looking for someone who can acquaint me with the town."

"We have a visitor's bureau," she said. "You should have passed it coming in."

"I did," he said, and smiled in a way he'd been told was charming. "But I don't want to know what the brochures say. I want to know what someone like you would say."

"Like me?"

"Someone who lives here. Someone who knows the character of the place."

"And how do you know I live here?"

"I'm guessing. Hoping."

Finally she smiled. "Yes, I live here but I don't think there's much I can tell you."

"Can I ask you a few questions anyway? I promise it'll be quick. Can I buy you a coffee or something?"

She nodded toward the empty chair. "I guess. Okay."

He launched into his first question. "Can you give me one word to describe your town?"

She tilted her sunglasses down to look him in the eye. "Maybe a proper introduction first?"

"God, I'm so sorry," he said "I've been doing this for so long, I seem to have lost my manners along the way. Forgive me. I'm Hunter Adderman, from Los Angeles. I'm doing research on Southern coastal towns." The words came so easily, after weeks on the road lying to strangers about his name. He held his hand across the table.

The woman had a firm handshake. "I'm Ella Flynn."

Ella. It suited her, almost as if he'd named her himself. This was a good sign.

"Nice to meet you," he said.

"Doesn't seem like I had much choice."

"I can go bother someone else," he said, "but I'd rather not."

She clicked her fingers on the edge of the iron table. "Wet," she said.

"What?"

"You asked for one word to describe my town. Wet."

"How so?"

"Water. Everywhere you look: water. The bay. The river. The marsh. The ponds."

"That's nice," he said.

"Okay, is that it?"

Why couldn't he remember his next question?

"Could you excuse me for a minute?" he said. "I'll be right back."

"Sure thing," she said. "If you're looking for the men's room, it's at the far end of the café to the left."

"Thanks." He walked toward the café, with every intention of leaving by the back door.


Ella had never been one to confide in strangers or even to those she loved for that matter. Yet here she was talking to some man from L.A., bantering as if bantering was the thing she did best. Blah, blah, blah. He was so obviously a tourist it was almost embarrassing. He wasn't tall, but he wasn't short, either. His clothes were loose on him like it was the style, which it wasn't, at least not here in Watersend. If Watersend even had a style. His hair was wavy, and swept back off his forehead, longer than how most men around here wore theirs. He had what her dad called a five o'clock shadow, but cleaner, more deliberate. He wore black-rimmed glasses, the kind that had been dorky in middle school and were hip now. And even as he walked off, he had a little grin as though he'd heard a joke.

He returned quickly and settled back into his chair without comment. He leaned forward and smiled. The furrows on his forehead made a road map as if he'd been more places than she could imagine.

"So," she said when he just sat there. "You're visiting every single coastal town in the South? That will take a lifetime, especially if you keep including ones as small as Watersend."

"Not all, not really. I only choose the historic ones where battles were fought or lands conquered." He lifted his arm as if holding a sword, and he laughed, nervous and jittery.

"I guess that makes sense." Ella motioned to the waitress. She knew everyone who worked at this café. She came here often, to sketch, to have that third cup of café crème, and to pretend she was in Paris at Café de Flore with Sims, the man who had always promised her a trip to the City of Lights.

Darla came over to the table. "What would you like to drink?" she asked.

"Ladies first," he said, motioning to Ella.

"I already know what she wants," Darla said. "She's my favorite customer."

"Ah!" he said. "I should have known she'd be a favorite."

The compliment was fluffy, made of spun sugar and nothing more. Who was this man and what did he want? Surely there was no harm in having a drink on a Saturday afternoon. Where else could she go? Home to cry a little more?

"I'll have a coffee and a Bloody Mary," Hunter said, pointing to a nearby table where a tall glass looked tempting and sweaty, the celery stalk growing in the thick peppery liquid.

"Perfect combination," Darla said, and winked at Ella.

Darla dropped one menu on the table, on Hunter's side, and walked away, tossing words over her shoulder. "I'll be right back with your drinks."

"Have you always lived here?" he asked, his focus returning to Ella.

"About nine years. This is home now."

"Lucky you."

"Lucky me?" Ella shook her head. It was something he probably said in every town. Lucky you, he'd say. Tell me about living here. "So, why are you visiting all these towns?"

"I'm writing about them. That's what I do. I'm a writer."

"Oh," she said. "Like a tourist book?" She leaned closer to see his eyes, which were brown but not just brown—boring word. They were different shades of brown, like yarn, something rich with a little gold inside.

"Yes," he said as if it had just occurred to him that this is what he was doing. "Or no, more like a personality book but for tourists visiting, something to show them what the town is like, the personality along with the history."

This was boring. Why had she let this stranger sit with her? "Do you have more questions?" she asked.

"Yes," he said as if this whole idea were hers. "What is your favorite place here in Watersend?"

"The water. Always. I'm sure you've heard the same answer everywhere you go. Why else do people live on the coast? Right?" She sounded harsh and she knew it. Damn it to hell. It had been one of Sims's complaints: *Why do you always have to be so blunt?*

"I guess it's a dumb question. You're right." He looked away as if someone had called his name. "But you're the first person to really answer it that way. Usually someone gives me the name of the dock or the beach they love. The dive restaurant or the oyster shack they go to every day. But not so general, not just . . . the water."

"It came out rude, didn't it?" she asked. "I'm sorry. That happens to me sometimes. I think I'm talking nicely but something happens between my head and you hearing it and it's . . . all wrong."

He laughed. "You're funny."

"No." She shook her head. "I'm really not."

He leaned forward as if he needed to tell her a secret, the one thing in all the world she needed to know. "Yes, you are."

Darla returned with the Bloody Marys and a cup of coffee. She set them down, the glasses clanging against the metal table. "You want anything else?" she asked Hunter.

He nodded. "Yes, please. The spinach and feta omelet."

Ella hadn't seen him look at the menu. How did he know what he wanted?

"Anything for you?" he asked.

"No thanks. I'm not one bit hungry." She tilted her head at him. "How did you know what you wanted?"

"I ate here yesterday," he said.

She nodded. "Did you accost some other woman to tell you about Watersend?"

He laughed. "No. I just sat and observed. I watched everyone and tried to get a feel for what people are like here. You know, every place has its own personality."

"Personality," Ella repeated.

"We think it is just individuals who have personalities, but somehow people combine to make a place feel the way it does."

Ella took a long swallow of her Bloody Mary. Yes, extra pepper the way she liked it. "I wonder," she said to Hunter, the vodka softening the ache. "I wonder what comes first, individual personalities or the city. I mean . . . I don't know what I mean."

"No, go ahead. You're onto something."

"Well . . . do people conform to the city or does the city conform to the people who live there?"

"I have no idea. But it would seem that people choose a city for its personality, for its character. So maybe the city has its own life and we just choose."

"You're right," she said, realizing how very true this was. In a single moment she had chosen this city as her home and never turned back.

"What brought you here?" he asked.

"My college roommate. She introduced me to the place after graduation." It was vague enough to be true.

"Well, there are worse places to be," Hunter said. "Are your parents here?"

"No," she said. "My mom passed away ten years ago but my dad still lives in my hometown about two hours away." God, she hated that phrase, "passed away," but how else did you say it? Dead. Gone. Buried.

"I'm sorry you lost your mom. I lost my dad a few years ago." Hunter took a long swallow of his drink and his eyebrows lifted high. "Wow. Spicy."

"Oh, Darla must have given you the Ella Special. Yes, it has extra pepper and hot sauce. Maybe I should have warned you."

"You just don't look like a girl who would order extra spice."

Ella laughed. "What kind of girl do I look like?"

"I don't know." Hunter shrugged and looked away. "I'm sorry. I just meant . . ."

"That I don't look very daring? True, I suppose. Don't worry about saying it. I just like this drink that way. So you're right about me on the whole, I guess."

"Right about you?"

Ella took another swallow and her limbs loosened. The knot under her chest relaxed. Yes, it was nice to spend time with a stranger. She could say anything at all and it wouldn't matter. She had so many stories inside. She used them to stay calm or go to sleep or even to get through a boring shift when a bride spent four hours deciding between ivory and light ivory. Here she could be a ballet dancer. A call girl. What the hell difference would he know?

"So what else can I tell you about Watersend?"

"Well, I like to get to know the city by the person. So tell me a little bit about you."

"Trust me, the town is much more interesting."

"I'll decide if that's true," he said.

"Okay, fine. I'm here to prove you wrong. I was named after Ella Fitzgerald. My mother was obsessed with her. So embarrassing fact number one is out of the way."

"I think that's kind of sweet." Hunter leaned forward.

"Sickeningly sweet." Ella wanted to chug the rest of her Bloody Mary. Her tongue was itching for it.

"So what else about you?" he asked.

"I was born and raised in a city two hours away. I went to college close to here, Durban College. I'm sure you've never heard of it. After graduation, I wanted the big city, you know? Something so opposite of here that I could become a different person and start over . . ."

"Why would you want to start over?"

"Youthful fantasy." Ella stopped.

"What were you studying?"

"Fashion," she said.

"Are you still in fashion?"

"Yes, I'm a wedding dress designer," she said.

"Oh, what a great job. You must just love that."

"I do." She said this like a woman who knew how lucky she was. "With all the destination weddings and engagements in a coastal town, I'm plenty busy."

"Yes, Watersend does seem romantic. And with this little café and the umbrellas and park, it's like Paris almost."

"But not quite."

"You've been?" he asked.

"Yes." Her voice went soft, downy, as if recalling a real memory. "Tell me about you," she said.

"Me? Boring."

"We all think we're boring. And maybe we are to ourselves."

"I write travel books, history books, coffee table books that people buy and look at once and then use as decorative stands for the Waterford crystal bowl they won at the golf tournament."

He was funny, this Hunter from L.A. It felt good to laugh.


It was like he'd tapped water from stone. He was in now.

"So did you get engaged here like the rest of the world?" he asked.

"Yes. Not very original is it?"

"Love is always original to the person in it. It feels like no one in the world can feel the way you do. Like you've discovered the word itself." He'd said this one sentence so many times he could feel the words rounding out in front of him before he spoke.

He could tell she agreed by the way she softened, by the way she looked away as if trying not to cry. "Yes," she said in a whisper.

He wanted more. Her response hinted at a good love story. But how did he ask? He sat silent; sometimes this worked. If you gave the other person space, they wanted to fill it up as if it were an empty bowl.

"I'm sorry," he finally spoke. "I'm being personal."

"Thank you," she said. "But I don't want to talk about my personal life. Okay?"

A swell of frustration filled his chest. "Okay," he said. "I understand. I really do."

"Listen, it was a pleasure meeting you and I wish you the best of luck on your book, but I need to go now." She took a bite from the celery stalk before dropping it back into the glass.

"Can I call you?" he asked. His food hadn't even arrived and she was about to leave.

Her eyebrows dropped into the cutest Y, like a little road to her nose. "Why?" she asked.

"Because I'd love to ask you a few more questions. I'll buy you dinner if that's bribery enough."

She nodded. "I guess so."

He pulled out his cell phone. He'd have to trust that she would give him the real number, and not lie to him as he had to her. "What's your number? I'll just enter it in my phone."

"Here." She pulled out her own cell. "I'll call you so I'll have your number, too."

"Great idea," he said.

That's how he got Ella's number. That's how he felt like maybe, just maybe, something good was finally going to happen. He knew about peaks and valleys. He knew all the philosophical ways to look at failure, how the word *crisis* was just another word for change. He'd heard it all. Bullshit. He didn't need failure to learn something new. He had liked everything in his life exactly the way it had been.

Still, he liked this Ella here and he would call her. He'd wait so as not to freak her out but then he'd call.

"Wait," he called after her.

She turned and lifted her sunglasses. "Yes?"

"I thought you said you were waiting for someone."

"I lied," she said.

He smiled. This girl had nerve. "I'd love to meet your husband, too. Ask him a few questions about the town from his perspective."

"You can't," she said.

"Oh?"

"He's dead." She paused, and then walked back to the table. "I'm sorry. That was rude. He's passed on."

Blake stood and reached for her arm, but then dropped his hand. "I am so sorry. What happened?"

"Drowning," she said.

"Oh, God," Blake said.

She nodded. "It was so unnecessary. He was trying to . . ." She closed her eyes as if she could see it all again, a reenactment. "My hat flew off and I reached for it. I wasn't thinking. It was all instinct, you know? I lost my balance and I fell out of the boat. Sims dove after me, but it was the motor . . . it hit him in the head. There was nothing to be done. It happened so fast. And it was all for a hat, a stupid wide-brimmed hat, the kind you see in every beach shop." She opened her eyes then, and Blake saw the tears collected in them. "I'm sorry, but I have to go now," she said.

He readied himself to console her, but she turned away, her purse draped loosely over her shoulder. A broken V of white birds slung through the sky and rounded a corner as if to follow her. Blake's palms tingled. This was it. This woman, she had the story. He knew it. And he had to be careful.

# *two*

---

It was *that* kind of day. The sky a bowl of blue, dotted with birds. The air so warm it caressed the skin. And everyone smiling, taking photos, and holding hands.

Which how-to-get-over-your-loss book had told her to live in the present? Ella had consulted so many that they all blended together. *Notice. Be present. Stay centered.* She tried. She really tried. She focused and noticed the statue in the middle of the fountain, the way the angel seemed to lift its wings to the surrounding water. And beside the fountain, the pink petals that dotted the putty-colored sidewalk. There were benches, too, curved iron ones that circled the angel and the pond.

A man and a woman sat together on one of the benches. They were huddled together, almost burrowed into each other. Two as one. He stroked her hair. She wound her fingers through his belt loops, draped one pretty leg over his lap.

Of course she was jealous of this couple. Their world went on even as hers had halted. This was as close as she'd come to acceptance, and the small victory warmed her. But as triumphs go, it was short-lived.

Walking closer to the bench, Ella felt the ground shift beneath her. It was an earthquake. Something biblical. Nothing less than devastation.

Sims. Betsy.

Her husband. Her best friend's sister.

Good job, Ella, for your full presence and attention in this world. That's what you get for noticing every detail. Every rotten detail.

The affair. What else to call it? To Ella, there had been nothing out of place. Not so much as a hint of anything amiss in their love.

Their marriage had been easy and peaceful, the way it should be when two people settle into something that passes from infatuation and passion to love and domestic harmony. They knew which coffee cup to use and who picked up the dry cleaning on which days. They each had their own side of the bed, each with books piled high on the nightstand: history and biography for him; fiction and health for her. She fed the birds. He bought the birdseed. They didn't fight.

Their sex life had been good. The magazines all said that infrequent sex was the biggest sign of an affair. But not in their case. They made love. A lot. More than her friends. She knew this because other women talked about their dwindling sex lives, about how they pretended to be asleep when their husbands came to bed, or felt too tired for anything but the couch and TV. Ella never bragged that she and Sims made love a few times a week, that they tried to be creative, inventive even. They'd been married for over seven years and still she would thrill at a look he'd give her over the table, a sly touch when they were in public. She thought of him when he wasn't around. She spoke his name when she was alone.

But while she felt settled, somewhere along the line Sims had felt like he was settling. Big difference.

Ella left the park, moving away from Sims and Betsy as quickly as she could without drawing attention to herself. She found a bench at the exit of the park and slumped there, her face in her hands, once again going over the excruciating details of the day she found out about

Betsy. She did this often, reviewed those moments, as if she could change one thing about it and everything else would change also.

Ella had been at the kitchen table when her world had shattered. It was her favorite place in their home, the rounded space where sunlight fell into the room from both sides of the house. Ella had painted the walls a blue so pale they looked almost white, until dusk when the evening gray pulsed in through the windows.

This had been Sims's house before it was theirs: a diminutive cottage facing east with a front garden that had been ruined by neglect until she arrived. The house was covered with cedar shake shingles weathered to gray. It had wide wood floors that she'd refinished during their first year of marriage, board by board, lovingly by hand.

Their home wasn't fancy, but it was a reflection of Ella and Sims, their partnership and deep love. Everything, every piece, had been chosen together.

A porthole mirror hung in the hallway, as did an antique map of South Carolina. Next to the map stood a hutch made from an old boat hull. Sailboat paintings were everywhere, mismatched and hung without frames: a vivid reminder of their sailing life. Ella and Sims bought them at garage sales, flea markets, and art shows. They displayed the paintings among treasures they had gathered at festivals: chipped vintage plates with anchor motifs; blue-striped linen and grain sack pillows; folk art from local artists; crab-shaped pottery; and one of her favorites, a bubble glass jar she'd found on the beach and turned into a lamp.

Sims had come home flushed the evening of the Debacle, as she had come to think of it. He was listening to music on his phone, singing along to "Jack and Diane" by John Mellencamp back when he was John Cougar and a lot more fun. He didn't see Ella when he came in, she could tell that much by his distracted smile and far-off gaze. It was an empty house as far as he thought. She sat at the kitchen table sorting through sailboat sketches she'd found at a flea market, enjoying the few minutes of watching him unaware. So cute, her husband in a good mood, sweaty from a workout or a sailing excursion, she didn't know.

It was this flushed quality, the way he engaged fully in everything, which first attracted her to him. He was athletic and clean-cut, always looking like he should be wearing a suit. His hair, which now was starting to gray at the temples, had been dark without variation. His eyes were beautiful, with lids that fell low and dreamy, always looking like he just woke up. His chin was a perfect rectangle, like something drawn. She'd told him so on their second date. He'd laughed. And why not? He was relaxed in his body, comfortable as if there was no one else he'd rather be.

There he was, moving about the house, singing to John Cougar and oblivious to her presence, which should have been her first hint. That's hindsight for you: twenty-twenty.

When he saw her, when he looked up, he startled. "Oh," he said.

She laughed. "Oh! Back at you. What's up?"

His face changed so dramatically that she thought maybe he was having a heart attack or something. "Are you okay?"

"No," he said. "We need to talk."

Nothing good has ever followed the phrase "we need to talk." Ella knew that. It was how the teacher pulled her aside about her grades. It was how she broke up with every boyfriend. It was how her dad told her about her mom's death. Weneedtotalk.

Ella tried to postpone the inevitable, whatever the inevitable was. "Look. I found these vintage sailboat prints. I'm framing them for the marina," she said.

"That's nice," he said without looking. His gaze was twitchy, his pupils large enough to make his eyes appear brown instead of dark green. He pulled out his ear buds and placed his phone on the table. He took her hands in his. The gesture felt stiff, wrong.

"I was hoping I would never have to say this to you. I was hoping it would go away, that it would fade, that it wasn't real."

She knew what he was going to say.

He was dying.

Stage four something or other. Months to live. Maybe weeks. This explained the absences and the appointments. The loss of appetite. The sudden withdrawal and exhaustion at night. The whispered phone calls and quick hang-ups.

"God, this is so hard for me to say. I'm . . ." Sims didn't finish.

"It's okay. It's okay. We'll beat this." She started to cry, the tears gathering.

"Baby, listen," he said. "Ella. I need you to listen."

"I'm listening, Sims. I'm here. We are not giving up. We will face this together."

"Ella," Sims said. His voice was strong now. Resolute. "There is no 'we' anymore. Not you and me anyway."

"I don't understand."

"I'm in love. . . . I'm so sorry." He tented his fingers on his forehead as if to balance the weight of his statement.

What was he saying? Of course he was in love. They were married. He'd told her he'd loved her years ago, on a dock with a handful of black-eyed daisies from his neglected garden.

"I'm confused," she said, because she was.

"With Betsy."

Then she understood. Everything. He wasn't dying. He was In Love—capital *L*—with her best friend's sister. He was flushed after being with her all day. The understanding came with a series of images, like a spliced film running too fast through a projector.

The rest of the conversation was a blur, a mash-up of questions and accusations.

How long?

When did you start sleeping with her?

How many times?

Bastard.

Have you been with her in our bed?

Divorce.

Separation.

Love.

Hate.

She threw up—she remembered that part well—then fell asleep on the couch while Sims placed a cold washcloth on her face. As if he cared. As if he still loved her. It was dark when she woke up. He was gone. The ground caved in again, just like when her mom had died. She'd been walking along, staring at the sky, and then had fallen into a black hole. She'd barely survived the first time. It took everything she had to crawl out, and when she had finally seen daylight, Sims had been standing there.

Now he wasn't.

Blake sat on the hotel bed because the couch looked like someone might have died on it. What else would have caused that dark stain on the middle cushion, that dent on the armrest? It was the only hotel in town. He refused to stay in a bed and breakfast, somewhere charming where the host would chat to you over breakfast, asking what your plans were for the day and what you thought of the place.

So there he was, at a third-rate hotel that charged first-rate prices. What the hell did it matter as long as there was a minibar, room service, and a bed? He always asked for extra pillows.

Blake used a digital tape recorder. He'd always hated typing. When he tried to make his fingers move across a keyboard, his thoughts were robotic and stiff. But speaking into a tape recorder—that was magic. It used to be, anyway. He'd dictate his ideas from the day, then send the recording to his assistant to type up. She would add these notes to the STORY CONCEPT files he'd been keeping these past months.

"Hey there, Ashlee," he said. "I'm in Watersend, South Carolina. It's as pretty as a picture, which is such a bullshit platitude but still true. I have some ideas I'm going to need you to transcribe. I'll call you later tonight. I miss you . . . hope you've had a great day and all that."

He stopped and rubbed at his eyes. How many times had he told himself not to get involved with his assistants? About as many as he'd told himself not to have the fifth JD. Next time, he'd hire someone ugly.

He cleared his throat and took a swig of Jack Daniel's from the tiny plastic bottle from the minibar.

Pitch Fourteen

Damn, had he already gotten to fourteen without a trace of anything good?

**LOGLINE:** *TITANIC* meets *MESSAGE IN A BOTTLE. A beautiful young widow must learn to love again after her husband dies saving her life in a boating accident.*

TREATMENT: A woman loses the love of her life when he saves her from drowning. She meets him—it's not quite love at first sight, but it's close.

Ella, the main character, was meant to have a magical life. She is petite and has golden hair. She has a quick wit, and yet as soon as she speaks she becomes shy, withdrawing like the words scare her when they come out. She thinks she can never love again. She believes in The One. Soul-mate stuff. She is naive and beautiful. How can she ever love anyone again when the man she loved died saving her? He saved her for a life without him—a cruel irony.

OPENING SCENE: a windswept ocean with a small boat being tossed around like a toy. Fades to present time . . .

NOTE: (There has to be an obstacle or two. Consider obstacles.) They have adventures, wild outdoor adventures. What brings them together is what also destroys them. Is he willing to sacrifice everything for her? (What good is love without sacrifice?)

Blake stopped and took a breath. This might work, but he needed more. So much more. He lifted his extra cell phone, the one with the "Hi, this is Hunter Adderman" voice mail. He pulled up Ella's number. It was too soon; he'd appear desperate if he called her now. He'd scare her off and he was starting to feel like this could be something.

When he stood, the carpet was crisp under his feet. He was glad he was wearing socks. It felt like they'd washed the rug and left the soap, like his hair felt when he was so hungover that he forgot to rinse out the shampoo. He tried not to think about what went on in hotel rooms.

He bent over and opened the minibar: M&M'S in a tube; granola bars; orange juice; tiny bottles of rum and vodka. No more JD. Shit. It was only JD for him. Anything else made him feel like hell the next day. Well, Jack could kick his butt, too, but only if he forgot *not* to have the fifth one. He counted backward in his head. How many mini bottles had been in the fridge? Two. Definitely only two. And didn't two mini bottles count as only one drink?

Rental car keys in hand, Blake patted his back pocket to make sure he had his wallet before walking into the hallway. The aroma of carpet freshener and Clorox hit him and he shivered. God, to be back in his house in L.A. His tea olive trees would be in bloom right now, filling the yard with fragrance. But if he went home, he'd lose home. A conundrum for sure. What he wanted was what he would lose if he didn't find the story.

A story. *The story.*

He climbed into the Ford Taurus. Who the hell bought a turquoise car? It was the last on the rental lot and he had been desperate. Again.

The bar he'd found the first night here was a few blocks away. A pub. Exactly what he needed until he'd let enough time go by before he texted this Ella.

Everything here seemed softer with the sun filtering through the oak trees and the moss dripping like the South's version of the icicles they'd never see. When he'd first arrived in the South, another town, one he can't remember now, he'd reached up to touch the hanging moss. It was coarser than it looked, rougher on the palm than it appeared. What an odd thing it was. Spanish moss, it was called. Shrouding the streets and alleyways, it was a curtain, a beard, a veil. He grabbed his cell phone and dictated that description into his recorder.

The pub was dimly lit. He stood still for a moment to let his eyes adjust. Mirrors on the back bar returned his reflection and he saw himself squinting. He turned away from the image. He looked tired. Sad. And he hated that.

He sat on a barstool and ordered from a thin waitress in a black T-shirt claiming that Guinness was the answer to life. "Jack Daniels, straight up. A double," he told her. This would put him at four if he had two at the hotel. But they were spread out over time, so maybe they didn't count.

He scanned the room, twisting around to see a group of women seated at a round table. Six of them. Or was it seven? All coiffed and wearing cute sundresses and wedged heels, and not a man in sight.

Blake drank his JD slowly—it warmed him inch by inch—and watched the women. Surely one of them had a story. When women got together, what did they talk about? Not baseball scores or football stats or the crisis in the Middle East. If women were huddled together at a bar and all dolled up, it was time to talk about love.

"I'm going to sit at a table," Blake told the bartender. "I want to get something to eat. Can you transfer my bill over there?"

"Sure thing," she said. "Someone will come get your order in a minute."

He sat down next to the group of women and pretended to be interested in the menu.

Blake was right.

They were talking loudly about men and love, and something they revered as fate. And they were oblivious to everything around them. Lucky him. As conversations go, it was hard to follow. He had to get past nicknames and loud laughter. He focused without looking at them, trying to catch the disconnected phrases that dropped like clues in a scavenger hunt.

*He told her he loved me but she won't accept it.*

Clucks of sympathy. Curse words for the male of the species.

*Well, he has been a dream. I'm not kidding. It's like telling the truth freed him up. We've been fine. I mean, I feel bad for her but . . .*

*If she'd wanted to keep her man she should have gotten her life together.*

There was one voice that dominated the conversation—a woman who had a new love. Her lover had left his wife for her. And it was all so romantic, full of flowers and letters and poems, angst and waiting and finally—*true love.*

God, what an old story. As if this guy wouldn't leave her at some point for the *next* good thing. She, the one talking with such self-importance, told the girlfriends about how it was to move into his house, to have everything she ever wanted. How true love is *always* worth the wait. Blake turned his head slightly and lifted his chin in what he hoped was a subtle gesture, to see which woman was talking. It was the dark-haired one with the bright red lipstick and the low-cut sundress.

Cosmopolitans and white wine were the drink of the night, obviously. Except for this woman who drank liquor—Scotch, maybe. Another woman with copper hair and gray roots caught Blake's gaze and he looked away in what he hoped was a casual gesture. She didn't buy it.

"Can we help you?" she asked.

All six women stared at him. "Pardon?" he asked in a smooth voice, lifting his JD to take a sip.

"You were looking at us." The woman with the copper hair pointed at him and wagged her finger in feigned admonishment.

He had two choices here: deny and move tables, or tell the truth and try to charm them. "How could I not stare at you? My God, you ladies light up the room. And me from out of town? I'm not used to such beauty all gathered together. We don't have women like you where I'm from."

They laughed, all of them except the dark-haired woman who had snagged her married man.

"So forgive me for staring but I don't rightly see how I couldn't unless you blindfold me," he said.

"Or you move tables," the dark-haired woman said.

"Shush," another said. "That's rude."

"No," Blake said. "That's funny." He looked directly into her eyes but he couldn't see what color they were from where he sat. Too dim. "You're right. I could just get up and move."

"Yes," she said, but this time the word had a little laugh behind it.

He picked up his drink and nodded. The copper-haired woman spoke again. "Where are you from that you don't see women at a bar? Alaska?"

"I didn't say I don't see women. I see them everywhere. All the time. Hordes of them trying to look good. I live in L.A. But nothing like all of you."

"Really? God, I've always wanted to see L.A.," the dark-haired woman said. "You're probably in the movies or something, aren't you?"

"Kind of," Blake said. This time he would tell them who he really was, and what he really did, because it would impress them. He was taking a chance here, but he wanted to be in on their conversation. Nothing good came without risk. Or so went the oft-repeated senti-ment. He'd used it once, in his second movie, the pivotal moment when the character needed to make a tough decision.

"How do you 'kind of' be in the movies?" one asked.

"I write them. I'm not in them."

"Oh." This came from a blonde who had just spilled some white wine on her blouse, oblivious to the stain growing on her right breast. "Name one." She rolled her blue eyes with the too-dark eyeliner.

"*Love Interest*," he said.

"Oh, my God," voices screeched and overlapped.

"Really?" the dark-haired woman asked.

"Yes, really."

"So you know Tom Hanks?" she asked.

"Yes, he's a friend." Blake was in his element now.

"Sit," the dark-haired woman said. "Tell us everything you can about movies. The most we can brag about is that Forrest Gump drove through Watersend on the way to Savannah."

"And not even Forrest." He pulled up a chair and laughed. "Just Tom."

"Whatever," the blonde said. "Forrest to us."

From there, the conversation took its usual turns. These women didn't really want to know about him or his screenplays; they wanted to know about the stars and the way movies were made and if he lived in a huge house overlooking the ocean. Yes, he did.

After a while, and slowly, one by one, the women looked at their cell phones and groaned as they exclaimed that their husbands were waiting at home, that their kids needed to be put to bed. As luck would have it, as it hadn't been lately, Blake was left with the woman who had just stolen another woman's husband. *True love* for sure.

"So." She leaned forward. "Only we remain."

"Yes," he said. "So . . ." What the hell? He might as well get right to the point. "Is your love story like a movie?"

"Oh, yes," she said with such emphatic hand gestures that Blake thought she might hit herself in the face. "I loved him the minute I saw him. I'm not kidding. He was standing in the kitchen at my sister's house and I walked in and stopped in my tracks. I stopped." She held up her hand in a stop motion, palm facing Blake. "And so did my heart. Just like that, I knew."

Did she know how stupid she sounded? Really? Her heart stopped? She loved him the minute she saw him? Blake took another swig of his drink. Was this the third or fourth? Probably the third. Tonight he could have a fourth because this woman was about to tell him a story.

There might be parts he could use. "Go on," he said as he motioned for another drink.

"Well, it totally is like a movie because the minute he saw me he knew, too." She leaned forward and whispered, "But he was married."

"That complicates things," Blake said.

"Yes, it does. So we've had to work through that. You know, find our way to be together."

"Find your way?"

"Well, I guess that sounds kind of cheap, but I promise it's not. He had to find a way to tell his wife, and that wasn't easy because she's really fragile. I didn't want to be the one to hurt her, but love . . . you know, it's just so, so strong."

God, who did this idiot think she was fooling? Blake looked at her again. She'd seemed so pretty from across the room. Maybe because she'd been surrounded by other pretty women or because the lighting was dim or because he was on his second JD. But she wasn't pretty at all. She was desperate and harsh. Her lipstick bled into the lines around her mouth and her hair was fried as if she'd put a curling iron in it one too many times. "Yes," he said with a sigh. "Love is just so strong. That's why I write about it."

"Why," she said with a whine that made her sound like a four-year-old. "Then *why* does it ruin so many lives?"

"Because it's powerful." He was on autopilot now. Words said without meaning, a language used in a foreign land, a second tongue. The waitress set another glass of JD in front of him and he took a long slug.

"Powerful. Life changing. Exactly," she said, and then looked at her phone. "Oh, shit. I gotta go. I didn't realize how late it was. He'll have been waiting for me for twenty minutes."

"It was nice to meet you," he said, and nodded at her as she stood up, wobbly and grabbing the edge of her chair back.

"You, too. I can't wait to tell him that I met someone super famous."

"You okay to drive?" he asked.

"Oh, sure I am. I've only had one drink."

She walked to the front door, and after she opened it she stood there long enough that when she left he still saw her outline, a wobbly halo of dust mites, in the entry. The door slammed shut and he leaned back in his chair. For a moment she'd looked as though she might be changing her mind about leaving and come back to sit with him. He was really glad she hadn't.

He glanced down at his own phone and saw one message from his daughter, an answer to his text asking, *How are you?* Her answer: *Just fine, Dad.* He exhaled his disappointment. He was getting nowhere fast with Amelia and being gone this long was not helping. The rest of the text messages—six of them—were from his assistant. *Call me. Where are you? Great idea. Seriously great idea you sent me. Are you okay?*

Blake texted her back and apologized, told her he missed her and would call later, although he knew he wouldn't. He would sit in this bar until he took a cab back to the hotel to pass out.

# *three*

---

The dog was barking again: The sound was so loud, so full of misery that Ella imagined a small dirty animal living with a sweaty fat man who forgot to feed him. That dog needed to stop barking. God, for just five minutes.

Ella dropped down on the couch, a sagging brown corduroy number that had been left there by the previous tenant. The room appeared in front of her like a still from a bad movie. A thick black cable snaked across the floor where it hooked up to the back of the TV. A wooden coffee table had magazines stacked in a lopsided pile. A bed, unmade with white sheets and a watered-down blue bedspread, was across the room and against the wall. And in the tiny kitchen, her one good pot sat on the chipped counter, like a gleaming jewel at a garage sale. This is what the landlord deemed "furnished."

She'd come here to Crumbling Chateau after Sims had handed her a suitcase with what he thought she might need—a couple of dresses, pjs, yoga pants and tops, underwear, T-shirts. That was four months ago. Now she had most of her clothes and a few kitchen necessities because Sims had been oh so generous and left them with the manager. He hadn't even had the courage to face her.

Ignore him.

That was item number twelve on her growing list of "how to get over a breakup." *Ignore him.* It came from a *Cosmo* article. A "thirty-day detox" they called it. "Getting On with Getting Over Him."

1. *Let yourself cry* (all too easy).
2. *Show him that you can survive without him.* (Yeah, good luck with that.)
3. *Find a hobby* (other than getting over him).
4. *Remember the things that annoyed you* (and wish there were more).
5. *Erase his text messages.* (Nope. Not yet.)
6. *Get a pet.* (Does a tortured mutt in the apartment below count?)
7. *Pursue your career with new vigor.* (Does sketching dresses count?)
8. *Spend time with girlfriends.* (Sure, if they hadn't deserted her.)

Blah. Blah. And blah.

Accept.

Move on.

Abandon hope all you who enter here.

Who knew how to get over a breakup? Not Ella. Not *Cosmopolitan*. Not a single book she'd read so far. Number one was still the easiest. *Cry.* That she could do.

It was almost impossible to imagine how she'd ended up here. But she could explain it to anyone who asked. Which not many had. Not really. So she'd gone a little crazy. Anyone in her situation would have done the same.

Sims had one other obsession besides sailing. (And obviously now Betsy, his *true love.*) Baseball cards. He'd been collecting them since he was six years old. He had boxes and boxes of them, labeled by year and by team. If he had ever agreed to sell his collection, or even a few selected cards, they could upgrade the house. But that wasn't the point. (He'd told her this again and again.) It was the having of them that mattered. The finding and keeping and collecting and acquiring. The ownership.

When she tells this story to the few people who ask, she says that she didn't know why she settled on the baseball card collection. "Really," she would say. "I was out of my mind with grief. I didn't know what I was doing."

But that wasn't true. She knew exactly what she was doing.

On the day of the Debacle she got up from the couch, removed the washcloth from her forehead, and threw it across the room. It landed with a damp thud. She was hurt. Angry. Betrayed. And she wanted Sims to feel the same way.

She took a box. And not one at random as she would later claim. She chose the most valuable one. No sense in doing things by halves.

The streetscape was dark that night. Thick cloud cover. No moon. She knew the way to the construction site at the end of the cul-de-sac. She had listened to the backhoe and jackhammer for months now while a neighbor renovated his house. The hideous Dumpster, red and black with graffiti she couldn't read, squatted right in the middle of the driveway.

Destroying those cards—tearing some, tossing some in the Dumpster, setting light to others—had been more fun than she would admit to anyone. The way the cards caught the wind and fluttered like birds, the precision with which a few of them slipped under the Dumpster like they were hiding. She ripped a handful in half without looking at the names and photos of the players she obliterated. She threw one on the ground, digging her heel into it until she made a hole in Roy Campanella's head.

If she'd asked herself in the moment why she was doing it, which of course she didn't—reason can't interrupt revenge—she would have said that she needed Sims to experience something of the ugly pain he had caused her, that he needed to lose something that meant everything to him, even if it was just some cold statistics on a set of cards.

But the thrill hadn't lasted. By the time she'd walked home, she was sick with what she'd done.

"Where are they, Ella?" Sims had asked in a broken voice. He was standing at the front door, cell phone in hand.

"In the Dumpster at the end of the road."

Sims ran into the house and grabbed the monstrous industrial flashlight, the one they used when storms knocked out the power. He bolted to the end of the road and called Betsy to come help him.

The police came the next day, and with them, the restraining order. Her outburst—the Debacle—came under the heading of malicious damage to valuable private property. Since her name wasn't on the deed (nice one, Sims), she could actually be "kicked out." Ella didn't even know this was a thing, being kicked out of your married home. Now she knew. If your name wasn't legally part of it all, you weren't the "owner." And if you weren't the owner, you could be removed. She could get a lawyer and fight the inequity of it all. And she would. Seven years of married life was worth something in the courts, after all. But that would have to come later. After the humiliation. After Crumbling Chateau.


When she was younger—much younger—she would have thought this apartment to be a romantic place. Plaster walls and a tiny kitchen, vintage appliances and crooked hardwood floors . . . she would have loved it. In her twenties she liked shabby chic. Function? Safety? Who cared? Now she wanted the stove to work and the floors to be level and the air conditioner to exhale frigid air instead of dust. Hell, she'd be happy if the rain didn't seep in under the warped windowsill.

There were so many things she'd believed when she was younger—like how she'd have children by now. But that hadn't happened. They still didn't know why—Sims said he didn't want to know why; he didn't want to place the blame on either of them. We're in this together, he'd said after years without a pregnancy. No blame. We have a great, great life.

Now alone in the apartment, she checked her cell phone again. It was old habit, looking to see if Sims had texted her. Of course she wouldn't hear from him. He was in love, the very real kind of lasting love. Or so he said. As if the love they shared had been some sort of knockoff.

There was only one text. Her father.

*Hi, bunny. Just checking in. How are u?*
*I'm great. How are you?*
*Been fishing. Now for a nap. Just wanted to say love you.*

Ella wanted him to stop calling her "bunny." That was her mom's pet name for her. But how could she tell him to stop? He'd lost his wife and then his only daughter went and moved away and never looked back. They carried on with their relationship with perfunctory texts. Her dad didn't even know she was in this apartment, alone. He didn't know much at all because Ella had moved away and stayed away, an ember of blame burning just below the surface of their relationship. Hell, he'd been on that boat: couldn't he have saved her?

Ella had never discussed these things with her dad because to do so would be futile—what happened had happened and there was nothing new to be done about it. Her dad had married after six years as a widower, moved on with his life, and Ella was trying to do the same. Obviously not doing so well at it at the moment.

Ella tried to force herself to stop thinking about her mom, about how much she needed her. But it was like trying to slow a hurricane. Even ten years later, Ella still felt the acute emptiness of her mom's absence. Ella needed to find distraction; she moved from the couch to the kitchen, where a folding card table with wobbly metal legs was set up. Its faux leather top was dotted with pen marks like moles on skin, and it had a hole in the top right corner that she'd patched with duct tape. She spread her wedding dress sketches across the table.

As a child, Ella designed new wardrobes for all her paper dolls—not one of the outfits they came with was good enough. Even then, as now when she was drawing, Ella would find a calm she couldn't access at any other time. Sometimes she would start to work on a wedding dress and her hand would fly across the paper as if compelled by some unknown force. Not today. She drew for more than an hour without coming up with anything. Nada. Zip. Nothing. Still, she sketched and scribbled, until a little figure became clear on the corner of her page. It was a funny-looking character and he was wearing a deer stalker of all things. Like Elmer Fudd when he was hunting Bugs Bunny. A hunter. Hunter.

She laughed.

What had she been thinking? She would not pick up when Hunter called. If he called, that is. Because . . . why would he?

But *if* he called, she would tell him the truth. Listen, she'd say, "I made up a few things. I'm not who I said I was and if you need information about the town, you should stop at the visitor's bureau." That is *exactly* what she would say.

She glanced again at her cell phone but the screen was blank except for her screensaver: the Eiffel Tower. Then she did exactly what she'd told herself she wouldn't do anymore: she read old text messages from Sims. The good ones. The *I love yous*. *Home soon. I miss you.* She kept those texts. She'd deleted the others, the ones that in hindsight were so obviously cover-ups.

*Crisis at work, home late.*
*Meet me an hour later than planned?*
*Sorry, something's come up. I'll explain later.*

The sadness came again, a punch to the heart. There was nothing to be done, just ride it out. Just cry, like she'd been doing for months.

God, this grief felt so heavy. Who knew sadness had such a weight to it?

She'd read all the self-help books. *After the Affair. Women Who Love Too Much. Codependent No More.* Whatever. *Take care of yourself,* they all said. Righto. This was the time friends should surround her, but silence was all she heard. She understood, sort of—most of them had grown up with Amber, Sims, and Betsy. What were they to do? Call her, that's what. Take her out, bring her a bottle of wine, offer a kind word. Something. Anything. Be a friend.

Finally her cell phone buzzed to interrupt the latest cry fest—Hunter.

*Lunch?*
*What about it?* She texted back.

*Let me try again. Can I take you out to lunch in an hour?*
*Sure. But I can't go for long. Work is crazy busy.*
*Got it. Where should I pick you up?*
*I will meet you at the same place in an hour.*
*k*

This would be the last time she'd meet Hunter. There was no reason to keep talking to him, but one last time couldn't hurt, right?

Blake wanted to see where Ella lived, but he didn't want to push it. He'd never spoken to a single woman on this journey more than twice. He knew his limits, he always had. Until now.

He must have lost count of his JD the night before. His mouth tasted like cat litter, or what he imagined cat litter to taste like. His head felt too big, too wobbly on his shoulders. God, he hated hangovers—they ruined entire days. He could still act young. (Or so he told himself.) But the day after, he felt all of his forty-nine years and more.

His cell phone buzzed and his assistant's name appeared over and over as if his phone was in a spasm. *Ashlee. Ashlee. Ashlee.*

"Hello, baby," he said, the words sliding off his tongue. He'd never called her baby before.

She laughed too loud for his hangover. "You're silly," she said. "What's up with the cutesy name?"

"Don't know," he said. "It just came out. So what's up? I only have a second."

She sighed, long and loud, exasperated he knew. "You always only have a second. That sucks so much," she said.

"You sound five years old. You know I'm busy out here trying to get . . ."

"I know. I know. I just *missss* you."

"You, too."

"You know that story idea from Newport Beach?"

"I get my cities mixed up," he said.

"Well, the one about the woman who was pregnant with her husband's brother's child and she didn't tell him, and then the baby saved their marriage and . . ."

"Stop." Blake rubbed at his temples and squinted against the almost-too-perfect day. "I know that one."

"Well, I've really started to dig into that idea. You know, I started writing it."

"You started writing it?" He wanted to moan.

"Yep. I thought, why not? Maybe when you get back you'll like where it's going and we'll have less work to do."

"Ashlee, honey, I don't think I want to write that one. I think . . . this one is better."

"Which one?"

"The one here in Watersend. The one I dictated to you yesterday. That one."

"Oh. Well, I like the other one."

"Okay. You do whatever you want. I'll be home in two days."

"I thought you were coming home tomorrow."

"I need another day."

"But we have that party. We worked so hard for that invite and now . . ."

"You can go without me," he said.

"No, it says Blake Hunter and guest."

"Ashlee, I have to go."

The sidewalk ended and Blake found himself staring at the bay. He never understood why they called it a river here. The water looked alive like the current had a heart and was beating fast and hard. He sat on a bench, to write that down—"the river has a heart"—when he realized that maybe he didn't have one at all, a heart that is.

His Moleskine was damp on the edges from a glass of water he'd spilled the night before. He dug around for a pen at the bottom of his leather satchel, worried he'd lose the thought, that it would disappear into his hangover, where he'd never retrieve it again. And it seemed important, like it had something to do with the story of this woman, Ella.

He had to trust that it would come together. Until recently, it always had. He scribbled in his notebook and then stood to walk toward the café, texting Ashlee:

*Sorry for the disconnect. I lost service. Xo More later.*

Blake adjusted his glasses (he was glad he remembered to wear the fake glasses for their second meet), and walked toward the café. He glanced around with what he hoped was panache. There was Ella sitting at an outdoor table and looking straight at him. Damn. He hated the thought of someone catching him unaware.

She was even cuter than he remembered. Her hair was in a pony-tail, curled at the edges in a flip that bounced in the slight breeze. Her bangs were pinned back with a bobby pin. She looked like a teenager. She smiled, but it wasn't a full smile. She didn't stand or speak as he approached her table, and for a terrible moment he thought she might not remember him.

"Hi, Ella," he said.

"Hello, Hunter." She motioned to the chair across from her. "How are you?"

"I slept like hell. How about you?"

She laughed. "I'm good. I guess you must be sick of hotels by now."

"The sad part is I'm getting used to them. But I'll be home in a day or two." He sat across from her. "Thanks so much for meeting me. I promise not to take up too much of your time."

"No problem."

The same waitress, Dana or Dylan, he couldn't remember, approached their table.

"Morning, Darla." Ella stood and hugged her friend. Blake couldn't help but feel slighted. He'd received only the vague finger wave and a motion to sit.

"Omelet?" Darla asked, and looked to Blake.

"Perfect," he said.

They sat in silence. Blake, who was never at a loss for words, felt off-center, his mind padded and spongy.

Ella spoke first. "You're really lucky. This is one of the most beautiful springs we've ever had."

"It is lovely."

"Doesn't spring always seems so glorious after the bareness of winter? When it bursts open, I always think it's the best we've ever had."

Damn, he wished he'd been taping her.

She shrugged. "Guess I'm rambling. Tell me what you really want to know. I don't want to waste your time, either. I can point you to the tourist office and there are some really wonderful horse-drawn carriage rides that you can take. We like to call ourselves the Front Porch of the Low Country."

"Yes, I saw that on a billboard. But I'd rather talk to you."

"Okay," she said, "but I don't really understand why."

"Because you seem like you *are* the city." He was amazed at his ability to lie. It was a skill he hadn't realized he'd cultivated.

"That's nice, but trust me, there's much more to this city than I can explain. Places and restaurants and bars I've never been."

"Yeah? I went to Mulligans last night."

"Ah." She laughed. "There you go. That's a place I'd never go to. How many divorced or unhappily married women hit on you?"

"None. They were too busy complaining to one another."

"And that, my friend, is why I never go to Mulligans." Ella swirled the straw around inside her iced tea. "Okay. I better earn my drink, I suppose. But I don't know where to start. How about asking me some questions? That'll be easier."

Blake launched into his topics for the history book that didn't exist. Founding year. Battles. Best beaches and boardwalks. He'd been using that list in the last cities and even he was starting to believe that he was writing a book. They ate and talked, sipped iced teas until they were done and Ella asked, "You don't take notes?"

He dug his fork into the remainder of his omelet. "I remember what matters most and write it down in here." He pulled out his Moleskine and dropped it onto the table. "But I don't like to write while I'm talking."

He needed to be careful with this one.

Her hand slid across the table. She picked up the notebook and opened it to the middle. Blake, on instinct, grabbed it back. His fork clattered to the ground.

Ella held up her palms in surrender. "Sorry. That was rude of me. I didn't . . ."

"No, it's okay. You can look at it if you want. I don't know why I grabbed it like that." He held it out to her and took the chance that she wouldn't want to see it.

"No. I wouldn't want anyone looking at my sketches. I should have known better. I don't know what I was thinking." She waved her hand toward him. "Hold on to it."

The restaurant grew busy around them. Every table was full. Couples holding hands and oblivious to the outside world; young moms in workout clothes with their babies in fancy strollers; a white-haired man alone with coffee and a newspaper. On those tables, small Mason jars were full with gerbera daisies, Queen Anne's lace, poppies, and wildflowers. Blake absorbed the setting. It felt like a movie scene to him, something that needed to be saved. The air was almost like washed linen blowing across his face. The sunlight filtered through the branches, moss and leaves, patterns created on faces and sidewalks. He sat still, and absorbed the moment.

"A drawing," he finally said, and tore a piece of paper from his notebook. "Try one for me."

Ella lifted her hand to her cheek and brushed away something invisible, then looked away. "No . . . I'm not . . . I can't just do it on the spot like that."

He handed her a pencil from the bottom of his satchel. "Then show me one of the designs you've already done. Something simple."

The paper fluttered on the table. It would have taken flight if she didn't put her hand on top of it. She grabbed the pencil from his hand. On the paper, slowly a thin silhouette appeared and then a skirt flowing from the waist. She didn't talk. The tip of her tongue rested in the right corner of her lips, settling there while she drew. She removed her sunglasses and squinted at the drawing, twice making a small noise in the back of her throat, like a whimper.

"Nice," Darla said as she leaned over Ella's shoulder.

Ella's hand flew from the side of the table to cover the sketch, and with a swipe, she knocked over her glass of tea. A tawny liquid spread across Ella's drawing. She jumped up with a half shout, half laugh. Darla grabbed a napkin and threw it over the mess. "Oh, no. Did you ruin the drawing?"

"It's not good anyway," Ella said. "I was just messing around."

Darla looked to Blake, who threw his own napkin over the mess. Ella picked up the drawing and shook it. Her dress, it moved around her small body like it was dancing on her skin. She would make the perfect character; not only would he use her story, but so much about her, the way she moved, the way she dressed, the way she—

"Hunter?"

He startled out of his reverie. "Yes?"

"You ready to go?" Ella asked.

He looked to the left for Darla. "I'll go inside and pay. I'll be right back."

"She'll bring it out," Ella said, but he was already gone.

He entered the café and took a deep breath, winding his way back to the men's room where he quickly wrote some notes. He wanted to remember how this all looked. How it all felt. He used to believe that he could remember every detail. Now he knows that the sooner he writes it down the better the screenplay will be. And this—after all this time—was finally something worth remembering.


The first lie about Sims's death had just slipped out. It had been a defense against the truth, a soft-padded denial of reality. This one? About being a wedding dress designer? It had been all too easy. Hunter didn't need to know that she sold shoes, cleaned the backrooms, and entered orders for her boss-from-hell. Ella dried off her sketch with a napkin. It wasn't the best she'd ever done, but she liked the way the pattern on the waist migrated down the skirt.

And the drowning. Anyone who knew her would have known that she was telling her mother's story. The drowning that had been accidental.

Ella's mom had fallen off the back of the boat reaching for her hat, which had blown off in the wind. It was so simple, Ella's dad told her, like it wasn't real. She reached into the air, the boat running at full speed, when she slipped and fell into the water. She didn't seem to make a splash, her father had said. Just disappeared into the wake. The hat floated away and Ella's mom didn't come up for air. The autopsy showed that she'd slammed her head into the engine as she'd come down into the water. She had been knocked unconscious almost immediately. She never knew what hit her. Ella never knew what hit her.

Sims's death was such a blatant lie that Ella was going to have to stop talking to Hunter. She could only take this so far. And there was no way to back up now.

Hunter exited the café, squinted against the sun and put his Wayfarers on. He looked like the L.A. guy he was. She wouldn't tell him that he'd fit in much better if he wore a pair of khaki shorts and a Vineyard Vines button-down. His jeans and black T-shirt were good with her. She'd had enough of preppy-Savannah-false-aristocrat to last the rest of her life.

A shrill laugh echoed across the café and Ella's stomach rolled over in what was becoming an all-too-familiar way. Ella knew that laugh from the time she'd been on the back porch drinking lemonade with Amber and Betsy a long-ago afternoon. She'd made that lemonade herself, squeezing each lemon by hand. Oh, to do that to Betsy's little head. Maybe this was the "anger stage" she'd heard so much about.

Ella turned slowly. If she didn't disturb the air, maybe they wouldn't see her. But her eyes found them just as theirs found her, all at once and with wide surprise. She froze, as if in a dream where she couldn't move. A really bad dream. There was Sims, his hand on Betsy's back, his mouth open in surprise.

They pulled in closer to each other and Betsy placed her arms around Sims, a move of ownership. Ella's world was in turmoil, a twisted metal car accident. But she knew how to save face. She turned away from them and sauntered—she would not run—toward Hunter. "You ready to go?" she asked.

"Ella," Sims called her name. She heard it. So did Hunter. He stopped.

"Someone is calling you," Hunter said.

Embarrassment would come later, a sick aftertaste in the back of her throat. But for now, she needed to get out of the café. She put on her best shaky smile. "Oh, I'm not in the mood for him. He's . . . kind of annoying. Keep walking."

"Okay," Hunter said. Not quite a statement. Not quite a question.

"He's an old friend of my husband's and I don't want to hear any more condolences. I'm done with false reassurance, with prayers and love being sent my way."

"I get it," Hunter said. "When my dad died I got more texts and e-mails and letters with 'prayers' than I'd received in my whole life. I know they meant it, but the words started to sound candy coated."

"Yes," Ella said, "exactly."

They rounded the corner and, brave face or not, Ella was starting to feel sick.

"Are you okay?" Hunter asked as she dropped to a bench. "I thought you had to go to work."

"I'm fine." She patted the bench. "So this park square is one of three in the town. The elementary school kids come here from half a block away. Sims and I had picnics here about once a month during the good weather, just to watch people and sit in the sun."

Hunter sat next to her. "I'm so sorry. It must be terrible to see him on every corner."

Oh, he had no idea.

"Do you all have kids?" he asked. "I didn't even ask . . ."

"No." She shook her head. "We couldn't."

"I'm sorry."

"Seems like you're having to say that to me a lot," Ella said.

"Sorry about that," he said, and then laughed. "Comes too easily I guess."

"Do you have kids?" she asked him, twisting to face him.

"I do. A fifteen-year-old daughter."

"You have a fifteen-year-old daughter? Oh, God. You're in the thick of it for sure."

"What do you mean?"

"I was once a fifteen-year-old daughter," Ella said.

"Ah, so is this normal? The kind of father-daughter standoff that hits at this age?"

Ella closed her eyes for just a moment, imagining those days when she'd been so close to her mom, when her dad had tried so hard to be a part of their closed circle. She opened her eyes and looked at Hunter. "I don't know, really, if it's normal. But I know that you just have to keep being there for her."

"Are you close to your dad now?" he asked in a voice that sounded full of hope.

"No," Ella said. "But it's different. Very different."

"How?"

"It's complicated."

"Ah, it's complicated. Meaning, you don't really want to talk about it. Got it," Hunter said.

"Thanks," Ella said.

"Well, now for the business part of our conversation." He pulled out his notebook. "Tell me more about your city."

"Back in the day, whatever that means, the town was originally one square mile sitting on a bluff. They say we started the secession movement." She spread her arms wide. "So this was the place where defiance was the definition. But still we are so small that both our movie theater and our bookstore closed."

"So if a tourist came here, what would they do?" he asked. While she'd been talking, he had taken out his black notebook and scribbled in it.

"I don't know. Maybe go out in the boats from the marina. Paddle boarding and kayaking seem popular, too. We have a slave relic museum. Then there is the art—we have about five studios."

"A slave relic museum? What the . . ."

"I know. It's odd . . . especially if you're from L.A. It probably seems barbaric."

"I have to see this. Now."

"Really?"

"Yes. It's the first interesting thing I've had to write about in a while. Take me?"

"Well, it's only a block away. We can walk there. But wouldn't you rather run by the city hall and get information and all that? I mean, don't trust me on dates and facts. There's a library with old documents and—"

"I will definitely get all those things, but before I get the facts I'd like to see the city from your vantage point."

She shrugged. "Okay."

They walked side by side. Twice their hands brushed each other as their arms swung. She tried to see the town from his point of view, that of a stranger who had never walked these sidewalks or seen these houses. The town was like a painting, she'd once said to Amber. She wondered if Hunter saw it this way. The brick sidewalks buckled in places where the oak tree roots pushed upward, groaning against the mortar. White picket fences really did surround the yards; the gardens were riotous in their need for attention. Rocking chairs and hanging ferns dominated the front porches, almost a parody of a Southern street. Every fifth house or so was decrepit, falling in on itself with the weight of neglect. Cars squatted in those yards, grass growing underneath the metal carcasses as if for protection from a lawn mower that didn't exist. Someone would come along and buy this house, see it as a fixer-upper, and the structure would turn into a home, join the ranks of the others with kids in the front yard on plastic play toys, dogs barking, and small boxed herb gardens for the green generation.

They rounded a corner and Ella pointed to an empty building, a painted white brick structure with a crumbling sign hanging sideways: FOR LEASE. Above the white brick structure a marquee had three words on it: *You've Got Mail.* "That was the last movie that was here. We keep hoping someone will turn it back into a movie theater, but for now . . ."

"What is it now?"

"Well, all the seats and equipment were sold in the bankruptcy, so now it's just an empty building. Sometimes it's used for parties or high school concerts, but you have to stand or bring in seats."

"Can we go in?" Hunter walked to the door and pulled at the locked doors, which made a rattling sound, groaning against being touched.

"Do you know anyone to ask for keys?" he asked.

"I do."

"Will you?"

"Sure. It's really pretty inside. There's beautiful millwork and stars painted on the ceiling." She walked away and then looked back at him. "You coming?"

Hunter remained in front of the movie theater, his forehead against the glass, trying to see inside. He looked so young, a little boy wanting to sneak in. He tried the door one more time and then walked to Ella.

"I adore movie theaters," he said. "Everything about them. The smell, the chairs, the sticky floors, the hushed waiting."

"Me, too," she said, "but I have to drive a half hour for that. Sometimes I go alone, just to sit in the air-conditioned quiet and eat Milk Duds and popcorn."

"Raisinets for me," he said.

She stared at him for a minute. What an odd creature. He looked the part of the writer, with his glasses and rumpled hair, his notebooks and satchel. But he seemed interested in everything but what he said he was writing about.

They reached the slave relic museum and the sign, handwritten with a handless clock image, said CLOSED.

Ella made a noise in her throat. "Sorry. I don't really know the opening hours. It's not somewhere I go. In fact . . . I've never been."

Hunter touched her arm and then pulled away quickly. "No big deal. Just to know it's here is enough to write about." He shook his head. "The South. It's a funny thing sometimes. Even though I grew up in the South, it was definitely not Southern."

"Where did you grow up?"

"South Florida," he said. "The Everglades. The snake and alligator part of the South. But definitely not *Southern* like this, with the history and plantations. It's not the same."

"Yes. It's different. . . ."

"Your husband," he said.

"Yes?"

"Was your husband from here?"

Ella didn't know what to say, how to describe a dead man who was still alive. This was absurd. They could run into him any minute—not that he'd be strolling through the slave relic museum—but they were standing in the middle of town. "Yes." She stopped. If she kept going, she'd trip over her lies.

"Tell me about meeting him," Hunter said.

He looked at Ella through those black-rimmed glasses. "I didn't want to love him," she said. "He was all bravado and smoothness, all wonderful and hip and cool. And my boss."

"Yes?" he asked in this quiet voice that made Ella want to tell him everything.

"His family had always owned the marina," she said, walking slower now and glancing sideways at Hunter. This was more fun than she'd had in months and yet it also felt wrong. Yet she continued. "He had a big sailboat and I was hired to work on it, a 'stewardess' if that's what you want to call it. The rules were strict: absolutely no fraternizing. It was grounds for firing. I needed the job. Badly. So I lived in an eternal state of longing. Constantly passing him in the tiny passageways or on the docks." Ella closed her eyes as if she could see what never existed. There'd been no sailboat. No yacht. Only the docks and some rental boats. But she'd talked her way into the story this far.

"How long did this go on?" Hunter asked.

It had been so, so long since someone asked about her life that she dove back in. "A year or so," she said, and looked at Hunter. "Have you ever been in love for that long and just known you were supposed to be together but also knew there was just no way? That it was impossible?"

"I don't think so," he said.

"You'd know," she replied.

"So what finally happened?"

"He offered to teach me to sail. We'd come back to port and we were unloading the boat. His girlfriend ran off to the spa because she needed an emergency mani-pedi and a blow-dry. We were there, just standing on the edge of the boat, the wind blowing . . ." She paused and looked away. "And that was that."

"Love arrived," he said

"Yes. Love arrived."

# *four*

---

FADE IN:

EXT. DOCK OF WEATHER-BEATEN MARINA IN SMALL
HARBOR. DAY.
Late afternoon. Slightly tackily dressed, silly woman saunters off, leaving her boyfriend, NAME TK, to finish tying up boat with female crewmember, WOMAN. Departing woman seems indifferent, ignoring his good-bye.

WOMAN and MAN TK—who is clearly the boss—work together easily and efficiently, though he is continually indicating what she should do; this is new to her, clearly. His hand brushes hers when handing her a rope and he jerks back as if electrified. WOMAN pretends not to notice, but smiles.

WOMAN breaks tension by laughing at little boy on dock who is chasing seagull.

MAN
Do you know how to sail?

WOMAN
No. That's bad, right?

MAN
Bad? Why bad?

WOMAN
(laughs)
Well, I DO work on a sailboat.

MAN
(laughs)
Good point. Do you want to learn?

WOMAN
Yes, I just haven't had the chance.

MAN
You've got the chance right now. How about it?

WOMAN
(friendly smile)
Great! Do I get overtime?

MAN
Not until you can tie a clove hitch and steer by the North Star.

Blake shut his notebook and leaned back on the hotel bed. He felt peaceful for the first time in a very long time. It could have something to do with the slow Southern pace of the world he'd found himself in, or Ella's delicate voice. But no matter. He would relish the moment for what it was: happiness.

The day nudged into evening. He thought of what hell the past year had been. It was nice to feel good again, if only for a moment. He'd spent the entire afternoon with Ella and told her more than he meant to about himself and his life. If she suspected he was up to something, or lying about his job, it wouldn't take more than a quick Google search to discover that a man named Hunter Adderman had never written a book about anything, ever. But she had seemed so trusting, so accepting.

So he'd told Ella that his father died and that he had a fifteen-year-old daughter. He would tell her nothing about his L.A. life, his ex-wife. . . .

His ex, Marilee, hated him. It wasn't exactly a mystery *why*. The bigger mystery was that they had ever loved at all. Love. It was supposed to be the *be all* and *end all*. Wasn't that what his movies were about? How he made a living? But in the real world, the world where people lived and ate and slept and made love and worked . . . well. That was a different matter. Love was just something else to muck up, something else to fail at or with. It was the hammer to the heart.

This was his new life philosophy. Yet, if they hadn't loved each other, what had it all been about? Status? Survival? His ex could probably answer this. What was therapy for if not to help her process her hatred of him? Okay, so he deserved her disgust. In the black-and-white world of deserve or not-deserve, he was getting his due. He cheated on her. There wasn't a dainty way to say it. He drank too much JD on the night of his movie premiere three years ago and slept with a rising TV starlet who had been cast as the main character's best friend. She'd been known for her offscreen hijinks as much as her drama. He couldn't even really pretend it was a mistake because he'd wanted to sleep with her since he met her. But he'd resisted. Until that night. Oh, the paparazzi didn't care about him, but unfortunately they most definitely did care about her.

There were photos.

Even if Marilee did love him still, which she said she didn't, she couldn't stay with him. Didn't he understand that there were pictures out there—in magazines, on their friends' computers, out in the big wide world? How could she stay?

He'd wanted her to stay. He'd wanted to sleep with the actress, but he hadn't wanted to lose his family. As Marilee said when she kicked him out, "You can't always get what you want . . . but—"

He didn't stay to hear the end of it. He knew the Rolling Stones as well as the next guy.

Ella walked up the back stairwell of the Crumbling Chateau, running her hand along the brick wall to guide her because the overhead light was out—again. The dog, the damn dog from the apartment below, was yapping—again. Ella paused in front of the door on the second floor. She'd do it. She'd tell the guy to shut that damn dog up when it barked at all hours and minutes of the night. What was wrong with people?

The door opened just as she lifted her hand to knock. She looked straight into the apartment and saw a small white puff running in circles. It was an apartment just like Ella's but different, full and cluttered with furniture and flowered patterns, rugs and books, and knickknacks. Everywhere knickknacks. Where was the stinky old man and the dirty dog? A woman appeared in the right side of the doorframe. "You scared me," she said. "I heard you out there in the hallway."

Her snowy hair spread in every direction like a compass. Her face was lined in the way happy people's faces were, an unidentifiable pattern. She was short, five feet tall at the most. She held her hand up to her face and smiled. "But you don't look so scary after all."

Ella's anger about the dog and the barking stopped in her throat. "I live upstairs," was all she said.

"Well, how nice. I thought I heard footsteps the past month."

The woman wore a floral dress appropriate for a fifties dance. She held out her hand. "I'm Mimi."

"I'm Ella. I just moved in about a month ago but I won't be here that long."

Mimi laughed and it was a tinkling sound. "Oh, dear. I said the same thing years ago. Just a transitory place. You know, until I decided where I really wanted to live."

Ella smiled. She couldn't help it. This woman deserved a smile. "It's nice to meet you." The dog, the one that never stopped barking, wasn't barking. Ella looked past Mimi into the apartment and pointed. "Yours?"

Mimi motioned for Ella to step in, which she did. The apartment smelled of chamomile and lavender and buttered toast. Framed pictures and books were stacked everywhere, in corners, on tables, underneath furniture and against walls, double deep on bookshelves.

The couches and chairs were plush, overly plump, as if in opposition to Mimi's tiny self. Mimi motioned to the kitchen and Ella followed. "Would you like a cup of tea?" she asked.

"No, thank you," Ella said. "I was just on my way to . . ."

"Oh." Mimi's face fell. Her disappointment was palpable. She leaned down and picked up the dog. "This is Bruiser."

Ella, despite her best intention to hate the dog, reached forward to scratch his head. Her fingers sank into his downy hair and she felt the fragile bones underneath. "That's a funny name for a tiny dog."

"Irony. It's one of my best qualities."

Ella laughed. "Okay, yes, I'd like that cup of tea but I won't stay long."

"I'm sorry about the barking. I really am. Bruiser has sort of a condition that irritates his vocal cords and he feels he has to bark all the time. Or that's my theory. The vet has no idea what is wrong with him, and wants me to put him down because he is obviously miserable. I can't. We could remove his vocal cords, but that seems so . . . barbaric."

"It's okay," Ella said. And it was okay. Knowing why this little guy was barking seemed to make all the difference.

"It's not, but it's nice for you to say so, dear." Mimi put Bruiser on the ground. "He's not barking now because I gave him a sedative, but it won't last long. Beware."

"Forewarned," Ella said.

Mimi placed a kettle on the stove and hummed under her breath, a song Ella recognized but couldn't name. "So how did you come to live here?" Mimi asked.

"To Crumbling Chateau?"

"I like to call it Manderley," Mimi said.

"From *Rebecca*!"

"The very one. I like to think that everything has a past. Even a place as downtrodden as this. So, what brings you to Grumbling Gateau?"

She liked this Mimi.

"My husband left me," Ella said. "I had a day to find a place to live. This was open and cheap. A short story, I'm afraid."

"Ah, exactly why I came."

"Your husband?"

"No!" She waved her hand in the air. "Never had one of those. I had a bookstore here in town. It closed and I needed somewhere fast and cheap. That was twelve years ago."

"I heard we once had a bookstore. Where was it?"

"In the town square, two doors down from the defunct movie theater."

"Why did it close?"

"Oh, for all the reasons bookstores close these days. I couldn't make enough money to keep it afloat. They mourn when it's gone but don't help to keep it. I hear it's the same everywhere. But it still was a great loss to me."

"I'm sorry. That's rough." Ella sat on a kitchen chair and watched Mimi prepare the loose tea leaves, scooping them out of a tin and placing them in an infuser ball, which she dipped in and out of the boiling water until she seemed satisfied with the timing. She placed a cup in front of Ella. "Milk? Sugar?"

"Milk would be nice."

Mimi opened the refrigerator. There were two bottles of water, a container of strawberries, and a quart of milk, which she handed to Ella.

"Yes, everyone went to my store when they were kids but not when they were adults. Everyone just stopped coming." Mimi shrugged. "Everything changes. It's a law of life."

"A law of life." Ella took a sip of her tea and her eyebrows shot up in surprise. "This is delicious"

"Rose petals. That's the secret." Mimi smiled.

"So you moved here after you closed the store?" Ella asked.

"Yes."

Ella wanted more. She wanted to know how this woman got over such a setback and still stayed this damn happy. She wanted to know how she lived in a place like this when she'd never planned on such a life. She wanted more than a "Yes." Ella prodded. "So you like it here?"

"It's a great place to live, what with the convenience to everything and the big windows. This was once the most beautiful building in town."

"It's not anymore," Ella said.

"Well, there are so many great things about it. I mean, look out my window—if you crank your neck to the left and then lean against the glass, you can see the river. Plus the market and almost anything you need is within walking distance. And this building." She knocked on the floor with a stomp of her soft shoe. "Sturdy as a rock."

"A crumbling rock," Ella said, and smiled. "Okay, I get it. You obviously can see good in anything. I just keep thinking about my house and my stuff and all I've lost. It's hard to think about . . ." Ella stopped. She didn't want to unload her misery on a stranger.

"I know." Mimi said as if she really did know. "So where were you coming from this evening that made you finally knock on my door?" Mimi asked.

"I guess it was a date. But not really. A pretend date like when I made my Barbie doll go out with G. I. Joe to the Barbie camper for a picnic. Nothing real."

Mimi laughed so loudly that Ella startled, spilled a little tea on the table. "What wasn't real about it?" Mimi asked.

"He thought I was someone else."

"Now this is the most interesting part of my day or year maybe."

"I met this man and he wanted a tour of Watersend. Because he was a stranger and I thought I'd never see him again, I told him what I wanted to be true instead of what was true."

"But then you saw him again."

"And again."

"Oh, my, this is good."

Ella shook her head. "Your definition of good is quite warped."

"Yes, dear, I know that. It always has been. Don't stop."

Ella wanted to laugh. She felt it in the back of her throat, but she stopped herself. She leaned forward and told this stranger what she'd done, like the confessions she imagined Catholics made to the priest on the other side of the partition. Now she knew why they did it— not just for the forgiveness, but for the release.

"You're quite a woman," Mimi said. "You've gone and imagined a new life."

"No, that's not it," Ella said. "I made it up. I can't believe I did that. And I kept going. Even though I said I'd stop, I didn't. He leaves tomorrow so . . ."

"Well, it sounds fun to me," Mimi said. "And can't you see that you're trying a new story? A different life?" She leaned forward and tapped the table. "Go live that one. I mean, without killing your husband, of course."

"He'll come back to me," Ella said. "And then—"

Mimi shook her head. "Trust me on this—you can't sit around

saying 'and then.' You can't wait for someone else to give you permission to chase your life."

Ella felt the panic of loneliness well up behind her chest, but she smiled anyway, because that's what she'd always been taught to do. "You are so sweet to invite me in and let me tell you my crazy story, but I need to get on home. I just wanted to . . . meet you."

"Well, it's nice to know where the footsteps are coming from."

Bruiser started up again. Mimi scrunched her face. She glanced at the dog and then at Ella. "It's bad, I know. I'm so sorry. I don't really know what to do about it. I can't keep medicating him all day long."

"It's okay," Ella said. "Really. It is." And she meant it.

Ella walked to the door and Mimi went with her. They stood side by side as Mimi opened the door. "I'd like it if you came by anytime you want. I really would. I make a mean pound cake and I do like to drink bourbon now and again."

"Bourbon and pound cake. Sounds like it could be the cure for everything wrong in my world."

"It just might be," Mimi said before shutting the door.

# *five*

---

Ella had a goal. She wanted to design wedding dresses at Swept Away, the premier wedding boutique in the Low Country. But that seemed a long way off. Ella had been at Swept Away for six months now, hired by the owner, Margo, with the understanding that she would rotate through every department to learn the wedding trade from the ground up. Ella didn't have any formal training. She was going to take classes at the University of South Carolina satellite campus when the next semester started up. But first she had to pay her dues on the showroom floor. It was an apprenticeship of sorts, and Ella worked hard for the privilege.

Margo Sands (yes, that was actually her name) opened Swept Away with her daddy's money. She wanted a hobby, she said. But the joke was on her. The salon had become so successful that her hobby had turned into a real job with real responsibilities. In fact, Margo herself had turned into something of a superstar in the bridal world. She was a tyrant who wore white every day like she was the Tom Wolfe of the wedding world. Small boutiques were popping up in towns across the coast, trying to imitate Swept Away. Margo hated all of them. Actually

Margo hated just about everything: gum chewers; cloudy afternoons; tall brides; short bridesmaids; country music. The list was endless and varied. And Ella was sure the list included her. But she so desperately wanted to be a designer, she persevered.

Ella believed that if a woman with a degree in accounting can turn into a wedding dress designer, then so could she. It wasn't just Ella. Sims, too, had encouraged her. One night, sharing the same pillow, their legs tangled together and her hand on his back, Ella had told Sims about this lost dream of becoming a designer. He'd whispered, "It's okay, sweetie. I understand. We all need to pursue our dreams. I'll be fine at the marina." Of course Sims had encouraged her to follow her passion. He needed her out of the way so he could follow *his*.

If pressed, Ella would admit that Margo was a fairly good designer. A natural in fact. The dresses they stocked were mostly from other designers, but when a girl wanted a one-of-a-kind wedding gown she'd imagined her whole life, Margo would help her draw it, before passing it along to their seamstress, LuEllen, to work her magic. Ella had taken her design ideas to Margo more than once. (It was fourteen times, but who was counting?) She would look at Ella and smile, as if at a small child with a broken shell she had picked up on the beach. "That's sweet," Margo would say.

Back to the shoes, back to the shoe department for Ella. Which was where she was today, Thursday. Ella stood in the middle of the shoe department arranging boxes into a pyramid. She wiped off the chairs and arranged the peonies in milky vases on the coffee table. She'd already decided, sometime in the middle of the night, that if Hunter stopped by the store, she would tell him the truth. She would. Definitely.

Ella wondered what Hunter would think of Swept Away. He might feel it was silly. Men often did. Especially the way that each department had a whimsical name: Tide the Knot for invitations and announcements. Sea-Blush for veils and headpieces. And for the dresses, Tides of Tulle. (Ridiculous, since most of the dresses didn't even have tulle.) And Sole Mates, where they stocked twenty different styles of shoes, all covered in white satin that could be dyed to bride specification. A chart like the periodic table of elements hung on the wall, and the brides and bridesmaids would stare at it as if they were studying for an exam. Did they want "deep rose" or "ambiance"? "Blush" or "passion"? And was "allure" a half shade lighter than "bashful"?

Ella had learned a long time ago that bridesmaids don't like to be told what color shoes they must wear. If a bride wants blush pink, chances are the bridesmaids want siren red rose. If the mother of the bride suggests ocean wave, the maid of honor will counter with marsh green. As if any of it would make a hell of a difference in the end. Today the drama concerned color swatches. The bridesmaids were rebelling.

This bride—Tilly—had twelve bridesmaids. Twelve! Absurd. Ella didn't even know twelve women to call for lunch, much less line in pink dresses with shoes to match. Three of them, a trio of blondes, had been sent to finalize everything on a girls' weekend with Silly. Er, Tilly. They'd spent the last two days in the store, and the nights drinking sugary pink drinks at the Shore Thing Bar two blocks down. This was the third day and they were sunburned, cranky, and hungover. The shoe situation seemed their final straw.

"Tilly," one of the blondes called out.

"What?" she snapped.

"We hate these shoes," the other blonde said.

Margo appeared. Margo always magically appeared at the slightest conflict.

"Ella, darling," Margo said as she reached the shoe section in what seemed like a single step.

"Yes?" Ella smiled at her boss.

"Which shoes has the bride chosen?" Margo directed her question not to Ella, but to the trio.

"These." One of them held up the open-toed strappy shoes with the highest heel in the bunch.

"Oh!" Margo cooed. It actually sounded like she cooed. "Those are one of my very favorites." One thing Ella knew about Margo: everything the bride chose was one of her favorites.

"Of course it is," the girl said, "because it's the most expensive. Don't you have flip-flops or something simple?"

Ella held her breath. This was the part Margo hated, the part where someone wanted to buy the least expensive thing in the store. Yes, Swept Away did have flip-flops, white with charms that could be attached to the strap.

Ella jumped in. "Your dresses are so diaphanous and romantic, let's use something less clunky than flip-flops, something airy, like maybe these?" Ella held out a shoe with a kitten heel and thin white leather straps that wrapped around the ankle.

"I like those," the third blonde said. She turned to her friend. "Anna, do you like these?"

Anna, the tallest blonde, stepped forward. "I do, actually. Much better."

Margo raised her eyebrows in approval.

Tilly let out a little whine. "But you can't dye those to match the dress," she said.

"But you can get jeweled flowers in any color you want and attach them to the straps at the ankle," Ella said. "A subtle addition without going over the top."

"Okay," Tilly said. "I guess I have to compromise on some things. Right, girls?"

They groaned, then laughed as one.

How was this girl ever going to get married? Ella wondered. She was practically sewn together with her friends. Had anyone even mentioned the husband-to-be? This wedding seemed to be all about the girls. It had nothing to do with the man who would be at the end of the aisle. And what did it matter? Ella thought as she went to the backroom to grab the tray of charms. Tilly's husband would probably cheat on her and Tilly would be alone in some crap apartment over a yapping dog.

No, not this girl.

Girls like Tilly didn't end up in crap apartments. They ended up with a group of friends who took her to Paris to get over her heartbreak while her lawyer made sure she got the house and all the assets.

Ella couldn't imagine a happy ending anymore. It was a curse.

She returned with the charms and held them out for the girls to choose. They played with the flowers until finally Ella pointed to one that was the exact color as the dresses. "This one is called blush, the same as your dresses."

"Then that's it!" Tilly said. One more decision made, one more thing to cross off the list.

The group wandered into the Tides of Tulle, separated from the rest of the store by a long white curtain. Margo sat on the chaise snuggled in the corner of the shoe section. "Good save there, Ella. Thanks."

"No problem."

Margo stretched one foot and raised the other to move a box away, but kicked at Ella's satchel instead. The linen bag fell over, spilling its contents onto the cream throw rug that had to be taken to the cleaners at least once a month. Chapstick, car keys, a stained scrap of paper, two pens, and a cell phone fell out. And what was the one thing Margo picked up? The stained scrap of paper. The one with the drawing of the wedding dress.

"Oh, I'm sorry. I didn't realize your bag was down there."

Ella reached to retrieve her purse's contents. "No worries."

Margo looked down at the sketch and the world slowed, the bridesmaid's voices sounding like a warped recording, an LP left out in the sun. She squinted at the drawing, picked it up to turn it left and right, even holding it up to the light. "You drew this?"

"Yes." Ella held out her hand, reaching for her drawing.

Margo looked up. "You really did? Like this isn't from some magazine or Web site?"

"No. I like to draw . . . at lunch."

"At the café? I see you there almost every day," Margo said.

"Really?" Ella hadn't noticed Margo there, ever.

"Yes. I'm usually rushing past and I'm jealous of the way you can just sit there enjoying the day, enjoying the sun and being quiet. I'm always in such a rush."

"Well, I don't run a store." She smiled at Margo and finally dropped her hand.

"Do you mind if I keep this?" Margo asked.

"Yes, I kind of do. I mean, I really like it and . . ."

"Then can I Xerox it?"

"Why?" Ella bent over to pick up the remaining contents of her satchel.

"Because it's beautiful. And who knows? Maybe someday it will come in handy."

"Oh. Okay, I guess."

Margo stood up and wandered back to the office area where her name was written in shells on driftwood over the door. MARGO SANDS. OWNER. DESIGNER.

Ella placed the shoes back in the boxes and organized the display area as if Hurricane Tilly hadn't come through only moments before. She wrote down the orders and put the paperwork in the order box in the backroom. It wasn't until she arrived home, when Bruiser started barking, and she realized she was out of wine, that Ella remembered the sketch. She dug into her purse just to make sure it wasn't there. That's when she saw her phone light up. Hunter.

Four texts from him—*What are you doing tonight? Are you free for dinner?*—and her apartment suddenly seemed dingier than usual. It felt old and musty and sad, what with the aggressively peeling paint and slanted floorboards. And empty. The kitchen faucet dripped one small drop every few seconds onto her breakfast dish and coffee mug. She turned on the tap and squirted soap into the sink. She scrubbed the plate and cup and dried them with the single white cotton towel. She did these things while thinking about her kitchen at home. Her pile of blue-striped Turkish dish towels. Her Vietri dishes in the just-right cream pattern. Her dishwasher.

"Stop!" she told herself. It was enough, pining for all that was lost. She had to take action. Get moving. Do something about it.

Her phone buzzed. She took three steps to cross the sparse room and pick up her cell. Hunter: text five. *Last chance . . .*

Enough was enough.

She shouldn't have started lying to him. Telling him "stories" as her mother had once called lies. If she had just told him the truth, she'd be able to go out with him to dinner right now. It would be better than sitting in her apartment, if nothing else.

A walk. She would take a walk. That was something.

The elevator in the apartment frightened her with its groaning and stretching, so she always took the stairs. The last thing she needed was to be caught inside its metal cage. When she had groceries, she would place them on the elevator and then race to meet them on the third floor where the doors would open with her packages. Only twice had someone been on the elevator when it had stopped. The first time it was an old man eating her granola from an open bag. The second time a young child was staring at the groceries in confusion.

She walked down the dark stairwell and reminded herself, again, to call her landlord about the missing bulbs. Ella thought about stopping in, saying hello to Mimi, but she wanted fresh air. Hell, she wanted a fresh life.

The evening was humid, a watery intimacy she could swim through with the hope of forgetting who she was and how she had landed in this life she didn't recognize. How did people stop thinking about the things they didn't want to think about?

Could she have been more inventive in bed? Cooked better meals? Done Pilates? Read articles in the *New York Times* to discuss over dinner? Bought more bohemian clothes like the girlfriend wears? Or ask more questions about his work? "How was work today, honey? Did you rent a lot of boats? Sleep with any of my friends' sisters?"

In the back pocket of her jeans, her cell buzzed again. Hunter.

*No problem about this evening. Get some rest. Talk soon*

She answered.

*I changed my mind. Meet me at Fifth Avenue, a block from the Sunset, in fifteen minutes. Walked halfway there.*

*Great!*

What else was there to do? Obsessing was getting old.

Blake saw her before she spotted him, which he liked. Ella sat on a bench at the far end of the park, her head back as if on a hinge. She stared up at the evening sky.

"What are you doing?" Blake asked as he reached her side.

"Every night at about this time, the birds come in. Hundreds of them in little flocks of ten or twenty. White birds with hidden black wings. Like magic." She lifted her head and smiled at him. "Sit down. I'll show you."

Her skirt, a mess and mingle of flowers, spread across the bench. He moved the fabric aside to sit next to her. Her top was a simple white tank that didn't compete with the skirt. There he was, dammit, narrating in his head, when he should be enjoying a lovely night with an equally lovely woman. He wanted to stop. He didn't want to stop.

He leaned his head back, his neck cranking with the stiffness that came from weeks of travel in crappy rental cars, pillows made of foam, and sagging mattresses. It felt good. God, he wanted to go home. The back of the metal bench dug into his neck like strong fingers. He rocked back and forth, just an inch or two each side, trying to work out the knots in his muscles.

It was twilight, the "magic hour" as they called it in Hollywood, everyone's favorite kind of light to film in because it softened everything. But it was hard to catch. This light, right here, made him wish he had a crew, a camera, and mostly, a good love story.

The clouds were motionless, the few that there were, as if they'd been painted in permanent repose. The sky, which all day had been washed-out blue, was now navy. In his peripheral vision he saw a purple sunset, seeping down, soaking the sky.

"Here," Ella whispered.

"Here what?"

"Here they come—"

She didn't need to finish her sentence because he saw them, the undersides of them at least: a flock of thin white birds flying in broken V formation. Their underbellies rounded and their wings spread wide and hardly moving, they were gliding, skating on air. They flew as a group to the dense tree next to a pond. One by one they settled on branches above and below and next to one another as if they had assigned spots. They folded their wings and bowed their heads, acknowledging the day's end.

"How do they all know when to come?" he asked. "They're flying in one after the other. Flocks of them."

"I have no idea. I've thought about looking it up. Why is it they come at dusk? Where is it they've been all day? But part of me doesn't want to know. Part of me likes the mystery of it all."

"Yes," he said, and he knew he would look it up. He didn't like the mystery. If there was something to be known in this life where so much was unknown, he wanted to find it out.

Finally, Ella lifted her head and turned on the bench, one leg tucked under her bottom. The breeze, full of sea, blew her hair around as if from an offscreen fan in a photo shoot. She smiled and he wanted to take a picture, to capture her just like this. He held his phone up and tapped to take a picture.

Ella held up her hand. "No . . ."

Blake lowered the camera. "It's a great picture." He lifted the phone again and tapped the camera, prompting the sound of a shutter.

"Delete that," she said, laughing.

"No way." Blake shoved the phone back in his pocket.

"Take a picture of the birds, not me," she said.

"What kind are they?" he asked.

"Now *that* I know," she said. "White ibis."

"Sounds like a goddess name," he said.

"I said the same thing when my mom told me the name. I was like ten years old and I said . . . that." Her words rushed out easily and quickly and she seemed embarrassed, turned away. "I feel young when I see them."

Blake took in a long breath like he was about to jump off a diving board into the deep end. "I do, too," he said, exhaling.

"You do what?"

"I feel young, watching those birds with you."

The silence that followed was long and quiet, full of nature's secret sounds of life. On the dock a block away, two seagulls crowed.

"Why do seagulls always sound like they're crying?" he asked.

"What do you mean?"

"Other birds call and chirp and squeal, but seagulls always sound like they're crying their tiny hearts out."

"I think you're right," she said. "But weird, they were my mom's favorite bird. She read a book when she was younger, a book about a seagull and she's always loved them since."

"*Jonathan Livingston Seagull*," he said.

"Yes."

"You were very close with your mom, weren't you?"

"Yes," Ella said. "There were a few years when I was twelve and thirteen years old that we weren't, but I guess that's normal. She just always . . . understood me."

"Tell me about her," Blake said.

"That's so hard. I always have a hard time describing someone. I lose the details in the big picture. I'm not good at it."

"Try," he said.

"She was beautiful and smart. She laughed too loud, and talked too soft. She had freckles on her face, but more on her left cheek and that drove her crazy. She mixed up her words, got them backward. So if she was trying to say 'Four Star Hotel,' she might say 'Whore Far Stotel,' and not even notice it . . . she'd just keep talking." Ella smiled and then shook her head. "She was fun. She was kind." Ella stopped. "I know I talk about her like she's still here . . . still alive. But she is for me sometimes."

"She sounds like someone I'd have liked to meet."

Ella nodded "Who wouldn't? But she'd embarrass me because she called me 'bunny,' even around other adults."

Blake laughed. "Cute name."

Ella held up her hand and shook her head. "Don't even think about it. I'm not kidding. Do. Not. Do. It."

"Okay. Okay. Well, let's get something to eat," he said.

"I'm not all that hungry. Is just a drink okay with you?"

"Always," he said.

Ella kept quiet even as she walked next to him, her arms swinging with each step, her skirt lifting inches above her knee with every breeze. She slipped a rubber band off her wrist and put her hair in a ponytail. He wanted to release her hair, watch the wind catch it in its hands and twist it around. For a moment, he was jealous of the air and sea, how they could touch her hair, wrap themselves into its tangle and waves.

He wanted to say something to make her talk. So he lied. Again. He hated it but still he did. "It might be interesting to include the white ibis in the book. I need to find out more about them, why they flock that way to the trees at night."

"But if it's really a history book, you know, comparing past to present, I doubt the birds have much to do with that."

"Unless . . ." He paused. "Unless they've always been the same. Maybe it's one of those things that doesn't change, even as the town and environment does."

"Maybe," she said. "But everything changes. Everything."

Blake stopped. She didn't notice he wasn't keeping up until a full block later. She finally turned around. "Come on," she hollered.

He stood still, not knowing why, staring at her. Everything changes, she'd said. Everything. It wasn't some profound statement, so why did he feel like it was? And why the hell was he trying to make everything in his life stay the same? Trying so hard.

"Hunter?" she said, and there she was, at his side. "Are you okay?"

Hell. She didn't even know his real name. He hated himself, that metal-tasting tingle on the edges of his tongue that he'd identified as self-hatred. He'd tasted it for months after the photos appeared in the magazines, in his wife's e-mail, on his friends' desks.

"I'm fine," he said. "I was just . . . thinking about what you said. About change."

"What did I say?"

He stared at her for a moment, just a small slice in time. He could have opened his mouth and said something authentic, something true. Instead he mumbled, "Nothing. Let's go."

He walked ahead of her—she had to take a couple of long steps to catch up with him—and then they were in front of the bar. It was a ramshackle place that seemed to be made of sticks and duct tape. A flashing sign, missing the U, stated s_NSET. Strings of lights were hung crisscross and sideways, overlapping and drooping down. Someone had thought that enough twinkly lights would hide the decrepit condition.

"I know it doesn't look like much," she said. "But it's really good. Our best chef works here if you're hungry."

Blake raised his eyebrows. "Oh, really?"

"I know. Best chef in nowhere Carolina doesn't give you a lot of hope but trust me, okay?"

He felt the sinking-chest ache of his betrayal as he said, "I trust you."

The crowded bar smelled of bodies and beer. Ella sipped white wine while he tried to make his JD last. There wasn't much talking because there couldn't be. A band played Beatles cover songs while drunk, sunburned patrons yelled to one another, straining to be heard. And in the back corner, a Ping-Pong table. Two clearly drunk girls were pretending to play and yet mostly chasing the ball under the table and into the corners, bending over so they could display their lace underwear.

"Ella," Blake said. She didn't answer; her eyes were across the room, watching a couple kissing in the corner. "Ella," he said louder.

Her eyes moved lazily toward him as if he'd just awoken her from a dream. "Yes?"

"Want to play Ping-Pong?" He pointed across the room.

"Only if you want to get your butt whipped," she said. "I'm good."

"Well, let's see if that's true or not." He motioned to the frazzled waitress who wound her way through a group of high-fiving men.

"One more?" she asked.

"Yes," Blake said. "And you?" he asked Ella.

"I'll have what he's having," she said. "A double."

"You sure?" he asked.

"Very," she answered. "I'll go secure the Ping-Pong table."

She wound her way through the crowd, winding past people without speaking. One woman, a tall brunette with a goblet of beer, tried to stop Ella, but Ella pushed past, ignoring the woman, who proceeded to lift her middle finger behind Ella's back. If it had been a guy, Blake would have had to throw a punch. But he knew better than to get in the face of an angry woman. You only try that once.

The waitress returned with the drinks. He tossed too much cash on her tray and she smiled. "Thank you."

Blake carried the drinks toward the Ping-Pong table, where Ella was negotiating with the panty-flashing girls. "Just one game," she said. "And then it's all yours for the night."

They wouldn't budge. They just stood there staring at Ella with dark, drunken faces. "No," one of them finally said, as if it was a word she had to dig deep to find.

Blake approached the women, put on his best smile. "Hey," he said, trying to sneak in some semblance of a Southern accent. "Can I buy you girls a piña colada for one turn at the pong table?"

They giggled. Actually freaking giggled. "Sure," the tall one said. "I'm Pamela. And this is Angela."

"Your names kind of go together," he said. "How cute."

"I know, it's like we should have a TV show."

"For sure," he said. "A reality show."

"I told you," Pamela said to Angela.

Blake handed the JD to Ella but addressed the girls. "Go tell the waitress two drinks on me. By the time you two finish, we'll be done," Blake said.

The girls sauntered away with their giggles and high fives.

"Brilliant, Hunter. Brilliant." Ella clapped and bowed. "Were you an actor or con artist in another life?"

"Sort of," he said, and picked up the paddles. "Which one do you want?"

"Red," she said. "Good-luck red."

"It is?" he asked.

"It is now." She was seriously adorable.

For a few minutes they hit the ball back and forth, friendly and slowly. They didn't talk and this was nice, just hanging out with her without thinking so hard about what to say, about the facts that might give him away.

Ella missed the last hit and scrambled off to find it, leaning down to catch it from a warped floorboard. She returned to the table. "Okay, any bets you want to place?"

"Sure," he said.

"Your call." She tossed the ball up and caught it in her palm.

"If I win, you have to tell me a story from your childhood," he said.

"Deal. And if I win?"

"You won't," he said.

"If I win, you . . ." She paused. "If I win, you have to tell me a story about you. Anything, but I have one rule."

"What is that?"

"It has to be embarrassing."

"That's a cruel bet." He bowed. "You're on."

It was hypnotic the way they hit the ball back and forth. He didn't want to make her miss a hit because he wanted to stay there for hours, just letting the ball go between them, spinning and then returning, rotating like the Earth in space, bouncing and then the satisfying thwack of ball on paddle.

The little white ball, so neat and perfectly timed to return to him, flew past his paddle as it twisted downward into a deep dive. "You!" he hollered across the table with a laugh. "You put a spin on it."

She smiled and he knew he'd been had.

The game ended with a score of 21–3. And he was fairly sure Ella gave him the three. The piña colada girls had been waiting, sipping their frothy drinks and cheering on Ella as if they were all part of a sorority.

Blake didn't so much mind losing to Ella, which was odd because he hated losing at anything. Watching her with her tongue stuck firmly in the lower right corner of her lips, her wrist twisting in instinct to the angle of the ball, he even forgot to drink his JD.

They gave the table up to the girls. "This way," Ella said, and pointed to a stairwell. "Goes to the roof. It's a great view. The perfect place to cash in on my bet."

The sun had set and the moon, a dented balloon, rose above the water. Waves, high and full of spray, a ghost cloud of water, battered the docks. Boats swung, drunk and still hitched with ropes, against the buoys.

It was as crowded on the roof bar as downstairs, but Ella led them to a corner where she lifted her face to the breeze and sighed. "Nice." She took his drink from him, taking a long sip.

"Whoa," Blake said, and placed his hand on her glass. "Slow down. That is definitely not a chardonnay."

"Really?" She looked at him, raised her eyebrows and then took another swig. "Or are you just avoiding paying off your bet?"

He moved closer so he could hear her. But only so he could hear her. "I don't have any embarrassing stories," he said.

"Right. I'm sure. As we like to say in the South, 'Don't let the truth get in the way of a good story.'"

"Okay, let me think. . . ." Of course he had embarrassing stories. Shameful ones. Devastating ones. But he wouldn't tell those. "I once invited a dead person to our house." This story, the one he was about to tell, was true. He wanted to tell her about the time he looked like such a fool that his wife left him alone in the pew, red-faced, standing with his daughter, who probably wanted the floor to open up and take her.

"You did what?" she asked with laughter.

"So let me set the scene," he said.

"Go ahead." She might have slurred a little, but how could she not after slamming down that double JD?

"Well," he said, and moved a little closer. "We had these dear family friends named Deenie and Frank. We did everything together. Vacations. Kids' graduations. If we believed in godparents, I would have been their children's godfather."

"Okay . . ." Ella looked into the empty glass. "What does this have to do with . . . ?"

"I'm setting it up for you."

"Got it. Good family friends. You know them really well. You're close."

"Yes. Very close."

"So then?"

"Frank's father passes away. Mr. Cameron. That's his name to me. He was very formal. A pipe-smoking intellectual who I played poker with a few times. The funeral was in Saint Stephens. A huge, multi-steeple church with stained glass windows casting crucifix shadows everywhere. This is Mr. Cameron's funeral."

"You can tell you're a writer," she said.

"What?"

"The way you say things. You know, like that thing about the shadows? You can tell you're a writer."

"That's kind. Thank you." He turned away for a moment. "Anyway, we went to the funeral. My wife, Marilee, and my daughter, Amelia, and I. We sat behind Deenie's parents—well-dressed, lawyer types who were both in the entertainment industry, always on the lookout for style and fame, always talking to the right people at the right time. Well, Deenie's father, Carlos, leans over to shake my hand. He says, 'Good to see you. Even under these terrible circumstances.' We make small talk about the weather and the kids and then he says, 'Saw your house in *Architectural Digest* last month.'"

"Your house was in *Architectural Digest*?" Ella raised her eyebrows.

"That's not the point."

"Okay . . ."

"So Carlos says that and then tells me, 'You know, I'd always wanted to take Marcus to visit that house.' I nod, solemnly because solemn is how you should be at a funeral. I reply with sincerity. 'Feel free to bring him by any time.'" Blake paused and shook his head. "And then it hit me, in the stunned silence of my wife and my daughter, and in the nauseated expression of Carlos, Deenie's father, that I had just invited the man in the coffin at the front of the sanctuary—*Marcus Cameron!* I had just told the leading entertainment lawyer in L.A. to bring his dead friend, his son-in-law's dead father, to my house."

"Oh, my God." Ella burst out into such rowdy laughter that people stared. "That is the best. Seriously the best story I've heard in a long time."

"It's great if it's not you." Blake took her elbow and squeezed it, not to steady her, but to touch someone who could laugh that freely.

"How did you get out of that one?" she asked.

"I apologized. What else was there to do? And then I sat alone at the funeral because my wife was embarrassed and my daughter saw her best friend, and I was mourning the loss of a man whose first name I didn't even know."

"You're a nice guy, Hunter."

"Thanks, Ella."

"I think I need to go home," she said, and closed her eyes. "Everything is sort of moving in circles."

"Let's get you home," he said.

He guided her through the crowd and out the front of the restaurant. "Let me drive you home in my fancy turquoise rental car," he said.

She shook her head with such force that he thought she might fall. "No. I'll get a cab."

"It's not a big deal," he said. "It can't be out of my way."

"No." She motioned to a cab parked a few feet away. "Thanks, though."

The bright red cab with the words BEACH TAXI on the side pulled up. "Hey, Billy," she said. "Take a girl home who accidentally drank too much?"

"Sure thing, Ella. Get in."

Ella turned to Hunter. "Thanks for the fun and so sorry to kick your ass."

Blake was still laughing as the taxi drove off.

# *six*

———————————

Her tongue had been replaced with a sheet of sandpaper. Her head felt heavy on her shoulders. What the hell had she been thinking? She knew better than to drink hard liquor.

Ella gripped the steering wheel of the car and turned the air conditioner one notch higher. The bridge was backed up as she tried to get to Bluffton, where she'd told Hunter she would meet him to show off the best farmer's market in the area. They'd texted that morning; he was concerned, wanting to know that she'd made it home safely the night before. She didn't tell him about the headache or nausea, just pretended that all was well. He seemed like the tough kind of guy who never suffered from a hangover. She didn't want to seem fragile. This fake Ella was strong and could drink Jack Daniel's while beating him at Ping-Pong. Oh, righto.

She didn't want to run the risk of running into Sims again at a café or riverside store, at the park or Good Day Grocery, where they both still shopped. She would show Hunter the town next door, the place she went when she needed to feel far away, even if she wasn't. Sims had always promised to take her somewhere far away: Paris, Rome, romantic names of cities that now seemed like characters in a novel, not at all real.

The dock where they had agreed to meet was empty. Ella walked down to the water, sat at the edge of the wooden plank with her cell phone in her hand. A man and a woman passed by on a kayak. They moved slowly so as to barely make a ripple in the water. They waved at her and she waved back. Her cell phone sat faceup on the dock and then it happened—Sims's face appeared with the word *hubby*. Yes, she'd left it like that because he was still her husband, if only on paper.

She allowed herself, for one false moment, to pretend that he was calling her to say hello, or better yet, to say that he missed her and that he needed her to come home because he'd made a terrible mistake. He loved her and her alone.

She picked up and used her happiest (fake) voice. "Hello?"

"Ella, we need to talk."

"Okay." She pulled off her sandals and reached her toes down into the water, scooting farther to the edge of the dock.

"You keep promising me that you'll get a lawyer so we can get this going. You can't just ignore the papers. You can't. You lied to me."

"*I* lied to *you*? Isn't that your ground to cover?"

Ella closed her eyes; her stomach knotted up. She'd done it again, even as she'd told herself a thousand times not to. She'd been sarcastic and rude when she could have been nice. This wasn't going to win him back.

"You feel good about getting in those stabs, Ella? Does that make any of this better?"

"No."

"Have you found a lawyer yet?"

"A lawyer for what?"

"This is how you want to play it?"

Ella swung her feet from the dock, back and forth, back and forth, like she once had as a child. When she'd felt free, when she'd believed that life was full of possibility. She opened her mouth for another sarcastic comment, something to catch him off guard, but what came out was this: "I miss you."

Shit. Had she really said that? She wanted to take it back. Oh, God, how she wanted to take it back. She closed her eyes because whatever he said would hurt.

"Don't," he said. "Don't make this worse, Ella. Do not make me feel bad."

"I have to go," she said. "Now."

"Ella," he said quietly in that voice that made her melt, in that voice he used right before they made love.

"Yes?" She was hopeful for something kind, even as her mind, her guardian mind, screamed at her, *Don't even hope; do not hope.*

"You have to accept that this is happening. The divorce is happening. Please let's make it easy on each other. Sign the papers. Get a lawyer."

"Sims . . ."

"I heard you were at Sunset last night with some guy."

"What?"

"Drunk," he said, and she heard the disgust in his voice, the loathing.

"No," she said with the lurch of the lie in her stomach curdled with the whiskey.

"Listen, Ella, let's end this civilly, okay?"

"I need some things from home. It's not all yours . . . and I need . . ." She stopped because the end of the sentence was *I need you.* She refused to say it one more time. It changed nothing—the truth that was supposed to set you free? It didn't.

"Soon. As soon as all the paperwork is done, you'll get all of that. But what's the use in giving it to you now if I have to come take some of it back?"

"Because you have to have at least one decent bone left in your body. Because you loved me."

"Okay, Ella. Okay."

"Or did you?"

"Did I what?"

"Ever really love me?"

"Do you want to torture us or move on in life?" His voice was so dull.

Where had he gone? Who was this? Ella felt the tears well up in the back of her throat, in the places of panic and fear. She'd messed up the conversation with her desperation and her need, with her idiocy. Why couldn't she be cool so that he'd know he lost the best thing he ever had? That's what all the books said to do; she'd read them. Be a "bitch"; have your own life; show him you're too busy for him. But here she was again showing him how much she needed him.

"I have to go," she said. "I'm meeting someone."

"Me, too."

Ella hung up and let the tears fall. If she didn't cry, her throat would hurt with the effort and she'd get a headache. Let the tears out and they dry up.

Something new for the list: *accept that this is happening.*

Great.

Why would she even want him back? The lies. The pain. And yet here she sat wanting him back more than she wanted anything else. It didn't make sense. Love didn't make sense.

"Ella?" Hunter called her name.

He was early. She wiped at her face but he was at her side before she could hide the tears.

"Hey," he said. "I thought I'd come check this place out before you got here but you beat me."

She looked up at him and smiled, readjusted her sunglasses. "Hey."

He sat down next to her and took off his sunglasses. "You've been crying. Are you okay?"

His question, one no one had asked her in so long, set the tears loose again. She remembered a time, a long, long time ago, when she'd fallen off her bike, scraped her knees and face on the pavement. She'd been so brave in front of her friends, jumping back onto the bike and pedaling home, but as soon as her mom came into the kitchen and saw the blood and scrapes she'd gasped, "Oh, Ella-bunny, are you okay?" And Ella had busted out sobbing so hard and wretched that she almost threw up. And this, right then, with Hunter gently asking her if she was okay, felt the same. There was nothing to do to stop the tears. Nothing.

She dropped her head onto his shoulder. This was ridiculous. She had to get a hold of herself. But she couldn't. She didn't. He patted her back, making small noises that sounded like clicking. His shirt, it was wet where her face was buried into the soft fabric.

"Did something happen?" he asked.

The question wasn't funny, not one bit, but it hit Ella the wrong way—sideways, where sadness flipped to hysteria. She started laughing. "Happen?" she asked, and leaned back to wipe her face, try to cover her tears.

"Is that funny?"

She shook her head and tried to stop the cry-laugh combo. "No. Not funny at all."

Hunter looked around. Ella thought he must have been planning an escape. She was obviously loony.

Then it happened again—the lie coming so easily, so quickly, brisk in its alacrity. "This was where my husband and I came when we wanted to be alone and away from all the hustle of Watersend. This was . . . our spot. I shouldn't have told you I'd meet you here . . . I wasn't thinking."

"Oh, God, I'm so sorry." Hunter placed his hand on her knee, squeezed it with compassion, or what she thought was compassion.

"Thanks," she said. "I'm so sorry you have to see me like this. I don't even know you."

There were, as she'd discovered, myriad ways to distract yourself from a broken heart, but none that worked. So why not try this? Lying to this man about her love life was as close as she'd come to feeling better in a long, long time.

He didn't have to figure out how to bring up her love story; it was soaking there in tears on his shirt. He walked right into it as if by magic.

"I don't think I'll ever love anyone again. Ever."

"You will," he said. "I know it doesn't feel like it now, but . . ."

"No. It won't happen again. He was the only one."

"The only one," Blake repeated. If he could ransack the story from this woman, if he could get to the gold of this tale, he would call it *The Only One.*

"Why here?" he asked. "Why did you two always come here?"

Ella dropped her head onto his shoulder again. It was nice the way she did this, placed her head on him to rest. His hand went to her hair without any thought.

"It's quiet. See?" She pointed and then waved her hand. "It's a full panorama here. You can see forever. Over there is the Oyster Company. We used to get fresh oysters on the boat and then roast them in the backyard with friends. Over there—" She pointed to the right. "That leads to the sandbar where we'd anchor. Friends would join us and we'd drink warm beer. We'd stay until the tide rolled in and there was nothing left to sit on. The water would take whatever remained on the sandbar. I bet there are a thousand coolers floating through this river." She laughed. Or maybe it was the start of tears again.

"Where are those friends now? Have they been a help at all since he . . ."

"Died."

"Yes," he said.

"No. Of course they were all there for the funeral and the memorial. They were there at the beginning, bringing food and fancy cards and all that, but not since. A couple of them have called to say hello or dropped an e-mail to say 'thinking of you.'"

"That's it?"

"It's a couple's world out there."

"A couple's world." Blake needed to remember that phrase.

"Yes," she said. "That's how it feels. The Morrisons' dinner party. The Yanceys' boat round up. Game night . . ." She lifted her head and ran her fingers through her hair. Her hand caught in a tangle and she absently worked her fingers through it while she talked. "It's not that they don't want me around. At least I hope that's not it. It's more like they just forget. They forget that I'm still here because he's not. So when he left, in many ways, he took me with him."

"I know. I've been through divorce," he said. "Friends divide. They say they aren't choosing one over the other, but they always are. They can't help it."

Ella lifted her sunglasses and wiped under her eyes, clearing her face with that smile of hers. "Okay, enough about that. I'm sorry." She jumped up. "Come on. I'll show you around. I know that you have to get back to L.A. today, right? Or is it tomorrow?"

"I've changed it till tomorrow."

"Great. Let's go."

Her countenance changed that quickly. Her face lit up and she shook out her hair. She wore another one of those little flowered sundresses. Or maybe it was the same one. This dress hinted at the body underneath, enough for him to make an adequate guess.

"Where do you want to go first?" she asked.

"You decide."

"Well, really it matters more what you want to write about. I mean, I'm guessing each town gets only a couple of pages or something. So what's most important?"

"Today isn't about that. Today I'm just here to enjoy. Okay?"

"Farmer's market first," she said. "Then we can stop in any of the shops you want."

The street was blocked off with orange traffic cones and streamers announcing the local vendors. The crowd was light, and everyone carried more than one brown paper bag of produce. Blake stayed at Ella's side and they picked out tomatoes and green onions, ate kettle popcorn, and drank hand-squeezed lemonade. A banjo player played a song Ella seemed to love, one he'd never heard, called "Down to the River to Pray." She dropped a five-dollar bill in his case. She waved to a couple of people but never stopped to talk or even say their names. It was nice, this peaceful afternoon. Blake wanted to film it, construct a montage of the bright red tents and silver-white corn stacked in rows, the puddles at the edge of the sidewalk with white petals floating like miniature lily pads. Ella. Most of all he wanted to film her. The way she moved. The way she'd look over her shoulder. The way she'd smile.

The thunderstorm came without warning. There must have been a few black clouds or a breeze that smelled of electricity, but he hadn't noticed. Now he knows that he was only seeing Ella, the way her dress moved around her hidden body, how her hair lifted and settled with the breeze. How her shoulders pulled forward slightly so that her collarbone formed the loveliest little space at the base of her neck. These were the details he gathered.

They ran from the thunderstorm, ducking into an art gallery. Lightning tousled the clouds without reaching down to earth. "My God, where'd that come from?" he asked.

"That's how it is around here," she said, shaking her wet hair.

Blake looked around at the gallery full of folk art: a mermaid made of shells and driftwood on metal; a sunset painted on warped wood; puppets carved from coconuts and a vivid watermelon on canvas. But the thunderstorm was the real show, and Ella and Blake stared out the front door at the leaves trembling in the slanted rain, the spiderwebs catching the drops and holding them, the Spanish moss dropping in clumps from the wind.

"See?" she said. "You just don't know when life will catch you unaware."

Blake lifted his arm and dropped it onto her shoulder. He pulled her close to him before he even knew what he'd done. Ella went stiff and he dropped his arm.

This was the definition of an awkward moment.

Blake faltered. "How long do you think the storm will last?" Dear God. That was the best line he had? Next he'd be asking, "Are your people from around here?"

Ella pulled out her cell phone. "Let me check the radar. I have this app. . . ." She stopped talking midsentence, covered the phone with her hand but not before Blake saw the word "hubby" on the screen.

She looked up to him and opened her mouth, and then looked away. "That's really embarrassing," she said.

Blake held his breath. She was remarried? Already? It wasn't true about one true love and never loving again? His mind circled—a spiral with crazy side trips. Thunder sounded far away and then close, a double clap of dueling storms. "Hubby?" he asked.

"Yes." She spoke so softly, a hint of speaking.

"I don't understand. How could he show up on your screen?"

"The thing is," she said, "sometimes I call his old number to hear his voice on the answering machine. I didn't know they'd given his number to someone new already and when I called today, they called back wanting to know why I called—" She trailed off.

"Oh."

"It's embarrassing. But it's all I have left of him—his voice. And now, not even that. I don't want to talk about it," she said.

"Okay, so what do you want to do? You pick. Anything," he said.

"A movie," she said. "They have a theater here, the one I was telling you about. And during the afternoon they play favorites that aren't in the theater anymore. Dollar-movie day."

He smiled. Could this get any better?

She had to stop with the lies. Now. Hunter knew enough about her to find out who she really was, who Sims was and continued to be. It wasn't hard these days what with Google and Facebook. What if Hunter visited the marina? That alone would make her out to be a liar. It was time to end this charade. Maybe she'd just flat out tell him. Just rip off the deceit Band-Aid and tell him.

A movie was a great idea. No talking. And that meant no lying. And what was she doing with this guy anyway? Surely she could find other distractions. But a movie? Now there was a great distraction.

They sat side by side with a tub of buttered popcorn between them.

"Don't you love this movie? I mean, have you even seen it?" she asked.

"Yes, I've seen it," he said.

"Do you like it?"

"I do like it, but I've seen it more times than I can count."

"Well, once more won't kill you. The storm will be gone by the time we get out." Ella settled back in her chair, pried open the Milk Duds, and settled in for *The Mess of Love*. "And then we'll finish our tour before you have to leave tomorrow."

It was the perfect romantic comedy. At least that's what it had been praised as for the last ten years. It had made the "Best of the Year" lists when it came out. Unrivaled. Yet Hunter seemed bored, checking his cell phone and leaving twice for the bathroom.

She glanced at him during a funny bit about the best friend mixing up the boyfriends and Ella saw him mouthing the words, a soundless narrative. She leaned closer and whispered, "You sure know a lot about this movie for not liking it very much."

Hunter took another handful of popcorn. "I've seen it a bunch of times," he mumbled.

Then it ended with a long street, shimmery gas lanterns creating a circle of light where the characters meet and kiss in front of a theater marquee. They live happily ever after, frozen on film. Still Ella and Hunter sat there, taking turns reaching into the popcorn bucket. Onscreen, the outtakes scrolled: the actors flubbing their lines; the actress tripping on her dress; the dog peeing on the set and the kids running and screaming. The credits rolled by on the split screen, also.

"I love seeing the mess-ups," Ella said. "It makes the movie more fun to see."

Hunter shrugged. "I think it takes away from the fantasy that was just shown. Who wants to know that the actors are someone other than who they just played? Who wants to see them as real people?"

"I do," she said. "Most people do, I think. It's fun to know. It's like a secret peek behind the curtain."

Hunter made a small noise, like a cough, and stood up. Ella placed her hand on his arm. "One more minute."

"Okay."

"And look at these jobs rolling by, Hunter. It's kind of funny. The credits go on forever. Do they have to mention anyone and everyone who ever, even for a minute, had anything to do with the movie? Like the guy who once brought you a sandwich?"

"What do you mean?"

Ella pointed at the screen where the actress was ruining a scene with laughter and names scrolled on the left side. "There. I mean, what is a 'best boy'?"

"The assistant to the gaffer," Hunter said.

"And what's a gaffer? It's like a secret language for movie makers."

"A gaffer is the guy who is in charge of the electrical department."

"Or woman, right? Gaffer—it sounds like the guy in charge of killing someone who mucked up their lines."

Hunter laughed and shook his head. "The name comes from the men in England who used to carry a gaff to turn the lights on."

"You sure know a lot about movies," she said.

"Kind of mandatory when you live in L.A.," he said, and shrugged. "Let's go. Okay?"

"Okay." Ella took one last glance at the screen. "And a 'key grip.' What is that?"

He took her hand and pulled her toward the aisle. "I have no idea."

On the way out, Ella dumped the dregs of the popcorn into a trash can. "You know," she said, "the movie has a perfect ending, but it's never like that in real life. No one waits under the marquee." She pointed upward at the theater sign. "You know, for that huge moment. Love isn't so dramatic like that. Grand gestures." She spread her arms wide and ran to the gas lantern, stood underneath it. "They don't really happen."

He caught up with her. "And even if it did happen in real life. Look—" He pointed up. "The damn lantern would be out of gas and he'd look like a fool."

"A fool," Ella said, and the flood of shame washed over her, again.

"It's a funny word, isn't it?" he asked. "Fool."

"Yes, it's the very idea of it that's funny, too. But the idea of something and the real thing aren't the same."

"Like love," he said. "It's more of an idea than a real thing. It's something that wants to be bigger than it is. Maybe it's just an idea we carry around until we don't."

If what Hunter said was true, if love was just an idea they carried around, then why the weight of sadness? "Wait," she said. "That can't be true. I love my mom. That's a real and true thing. That is not an idea. When I lost my mom, when I lost my husband, I lost more than an idea."

"Then there should be a different word," Hunter said. "We don't have enough words for love. We can't keep using it to describe everything from hamburgers to best friends to spouses to moms. It's not the same damn thing."

Ella laughed. "It sounds to me like love sort of pisses you off."

Hunter smiled. The corners of his mouth reached up high, and his eyes crinkled, but his lips never parted. He seemed to fight the smile, and his face wouldn't let him. "Yes, sometimes it pisses me off," he said. "It's too casually said, and too casually used."

"Let's see if we can go an entire day without using the word," Ella said. "Want to try?"

"Easy for me," he said, and then he drew closer, so close that he could have kissed her.

# *seven*

---

Ella couldn't wait to tell Mimi about her afternoon, how all of a sudden she was having an adventure. It might all fold in on her—it probably would—but it was something for now.

Mimi answered the door before Ella's fingers tapped on the wood. Ella laughed. "How'd you know I was out here?"

"I hear it all." Mimi winked. "Not really. Just heard footsteps heading my way. I hoped it was you."

"It's me," she said.

"Come in. Come in."

Ella stepped inside and Bruiser ran straight for her, jumping as high as he could, which was about mid-shin on Ella. He barked. Of course he barked. His tiny little paws swept across Ella's legs. She leaned down and tucked her fingers behind his ears, scratched his head and greeted him in a baby voice she'd never used before. "Hey there, Bruiser. How was your day?"

"He's had a rough one," Mimi said. "I wish they could figure out what's wrong with him. If you'd met him last year you'd love him better than you do now."

Ella smiled. "Let's take him to a different vet."

"I've tried three. It's a mystery."

"Then let's try four."

"I just don't have the money for that. Plus, it really isn't fair on the little guy. He hates the vet."

"I'm sorry," Ella said. "I really am."

"It's fine, darling. Others have worse problems than I do. A barking dog isn't enough to kill me. At least not yet."

"God, I hope not."

"Well, you look like you've had a glorious day. All sun-swept and smiley. Tell me about it."

"I met Hunter at the farmer's market and just had fun. That's all. But I'm about to run to the grocery store and I thought I'd see if you needed anything."

"I don't need a thing. Now sit down and let me get you that promised pound cake. I made it fresh this morning just in case my wish came true and you stopped by again."

Ella laughed. "You need bigger wishes."

"Oh, I have those, too." Mimi walked to the kitchen and took down two delicate plates. Painted pink and crimson flowers circled the outer edge of the china. Mimi hummed to herself as she cut a slice of pound cake, yellow and thick with a thin brown crust like baked bread.

"That looks so good," Ella said.

"Sit down and enjoy." Mimi placed the china on the side table next to the blue chintz chair. Ella sat down and picked up the plate.

Mimi took a bite of the cake and closed her eyes while she finished. "I will never grow tired of this."

Ella took her own bite and savored the buttery texture, the melted crust on her tongue, the sugary aftertaste. "I will never ask how many calories are in this. Ever. Because it doesn't matter, I will eat it anyway."

"Thatta girl." Mimi took another bite and then placed her plate on the coffee table. "Now tell me more about Hunter."

Ella recounted the day, and she loved talking about it. She loved telling Mimi every detail.

"Well," Mimi said. "It sounds like you're having a great time. You do know that eventually you will run into Sims." She clapped her hands together. "And I do wish I could be there for that."

"I know. I know. I have to stop. I have to tell Hunter the truth. He's leaving tomorrow so I won't keep this up, but . . . oh, you must think I'm a terrible person."

"Far from it, my dear."

"It's not the best way to deal with a broken heart, but it's seemed to help these last few days. I've tried everything else. Almost. I have a whole list of things to do to get over it and I've tried all of them."

"Well, I've heard it said that the best way to get over someone is to get under someone," Mimi said.

Ella's laughter came with a burst, pound cake still in her mouth. "God, Mimi. I'm not sleeping with him."

"Why ever not?" she asked.

Ella shook her head, then wiped her mouth and leaned forward. "I love Sims. After my mom died, he came along like a miracle. I've loved him ever since."

"Ah, the hole in the soul created by death."

"What?"

"That place where someone is lost. You just up and stuffed Sims in there."

"I did not replace my mom with Sims. That's not even possible. I just love him. I'm keeping busy until he wakes up and comes back to me. I mean, I know what I'm doing is just a silly distraction to stop thinking about losing the one thing that seems to be everything. Like your bookstore—I'm sure it meant everything to you. How did you get over losing it?"

"Well . . ." Mimi settled back into her chair. "I don't think there is a way that any human can get through life without at least once feeling like you have lost everything that means something. More than once usually. If there is such a person who says they haven't, they're the luckiest person in the world. Or a liar."

"So what do you do when that happens?" Ella asked.

"I'm not so sure there is something to be done. It's something you be."

"I don't get that at all. I'm being for sure, but here is what I'm being—mad. Sad. Humiliated. Lethargic. Pissed off. And I don't want to be any of those."

"Well, those things first."

"Now you're going to tell me that the next step is accepting it. I know. I've heard it. I've read it. Acceptance."

"You don't want me to say that?" She smiled that damn coy smile. Ella wanted to be angry with Mimi, wanted to roll her eyes, but she couldn't. There was some kind of wisdom wrapped up in her laugh and her quick retorts and possibly in her pound cake.

"Accepting the unacceptable," Ella said. "That's what you're asking me to do."

"I never said you had to do anything like that, but if you could find a way to do that, my, wouldn't you have all the answers in the world?"

"Exactly," Ella said. "And I feel like accepting it means saying that I'm okay with it this way. That I want it this way."

"Nope. I think it means—and what do I know—but I think accepting it means you recognize that you can't do anything about it. You can't fix it. You can't change someone's heart. You can't make someone love you."

"God, Mimi, I feel just so much better now." Ella flopped back on the chair and dropped her head onto the cushion. She took the entire wedge of remaining pound cake with her, stuffing it into her mouth, eating it whole.

"I don't have what you're looking for, Ella," Mimi said. "But I know this—*you* have what *you're* looking for."

"And what is that?"

"You don't really think I'm going to tell you, do you?"

"And why not?"

"You don't get off that easy, missy. You expect me to give you the question and the answer, too?"

"Mimi, you sure you weren't a philosopher instead of a bookseller?"

"Fairly sure."

"Okay," Ella said. "I'm game."

"That's my girl!" Mimi replied. "So do you know what it is? That thing you're looking for?"

"It's the pound cake," Ella said around the huge bite in her mouth. "That's what I was looking for."

Mimi laughed. "You know, something else always happens. Something. And then there is always something you can do, say, create, read, breathe, eat, make, laugh, and then—who knows what—something always happens next."

"Not always something we want," Ella said.

"Not always but sometimes it is."

"You are infuriatingly optimistic, Mimi. Hell, haven't you ever loved someone so much that you thought you'd die without them?"

Mimi closed her eyes and one tear, a long trail of some lost sorrow, nestled into the folds of her face. "Yes," she said. "I have."

"What happened to him?" Ella asked.

"She. It's what happened to her. My daughter." Mimi's voice cracked, fractured.

"Oh." Ella jumped up from the chair and stumbled over the corner of the flowered throw rug before she knelt at Mimi's side. "I'm so sorry."

Mimi patted the top of Ella's head. Bruiser barked. "Thank you," she said.

"What happened?" Ella asked.

"She was four years old. A rare case of viral meningitis in the days when we didn't have a doctor here who knew exactly what to do."

"Your husband . . . your family. It must have been terrible."

"It was. But there wasn't a husband, or I guess he was a husband. Just not mine." Mimi took in a long breath. "I don't talk much about this because it's so long ago. Someday you'll say the same, how long ago it all seems. But I was just out of high school and fell in love with a married man. I didn't know he was married and I loved him, so maybe I just didn't want to know. But by the time I found out that I was having his child, I *did* know he was married. So I never told him. I couldn't make him choose because there wasn't a choice—he already had a family. I never told my family who he was either. No one has ever known. Not even now. When she died, when my Rosie died, I lost my heart and I thought for good. I escaped into a life of books. I built that life and it was a good one. I never married. I never had another child. Books and friends filled my life and still do."

"Oh, Mimi."

"That's enough for now, sweetie. It really is. I need a nap."

Ella stood and looked down at the old woman. How old was she, exactly? How long had it been since she suffered such an unimaginable loss? "Thank you for telling me, Mimi. I wish I knew something better to say. Something more than 'I'm sorry.'"

"Oh, stop. Now go enjoy your little fling and come back for more cake later."

"It's not a fling." Ella shook her head. "And I need to stop. It's wrong."

"Oh, the dualism of youth." Mimi smiled. "Everything is so black and white for you. Go enjoy some in-between for once."

Ella laughed, and she wished, fervently for the first time in a long time, for something other than Sims's reconciliation. Instead she wished she'd known Mimi forever.

. . .

It was torture, pretending he didn't know every line of the film, every camera angle and lighting mistake. That he didn't know what lines littered the cutting room floor. Blake still abhorred the fact that his favorite line had been nixed. ("I want to come home to you.") And, God, how he hated that actress who had slept with everyone on the set while playing the innocent on screen. He wanted to talk about all of it with Ella, and that was the problem. He wanted to *share* it with her.

"That part," he'd wanted to say. "That part was when the actor had a hundred-and-two fever and pushed through, but got everyone else on set sick."

Blake had acted like an ass, and he knew it. Getting up, checking his phone—he'd been rude. He didn't know how else to be in that situation.

Now his hotel room was frigid. Shit. Icicles should have been hanging off the ugly mauve curtains. He'd left the air conditioner on high. He clicked it off and tried to open the window before he realized it was a fake knob. The window was permanently shut. He dropped onto the couch and pulled out his notebook. He didn't feel like dictating today and he most definitely did *not* feel like talking to Ashlee and hearing about the dinner party or the movie preview or any damn thing. He also, oddly, didn't want Ashlee knowing any more of this story. He just wanted to write down ideas. One by one. A scene list. Yes. It was coming together. He probably didn't even need to see Ella again—his imagination was churning and returning.

NOTES:
Scene where she and her love (let's use the name Flynn for now—good, solid name) are feeding the birds and one of them lands on her shoulder, and she screams and laughs only to have Flynn accidentally hit and injure the bird in a quick move to

95

help her. They take the bird to the vet and discover there is nothing to be done: the bird dies.

Blake smiled. Yes, good scene. It can happen quickly, just to show their bond over the littlest things in life. And to foreshadow a death to come, the fragility of life.

He wrote in his notebook for another hour, dumping ideas he could go back to and look at later, scenes he could sift through. When he'd finished, he opened the minibar and poured himself a JD. He'd asked the front desk to double-stock the bar. After the warmth settled into his chest, he checked his cell phone. It was brimming with text messages and missed calls. He settled back into the couch with drink number one and sifted through his messages. Ashlee. Ashlee. Ashlee. His mom. Ashlee.

Great.

He threw back the drink. He wouldn't count this one; he drank it too fast to count it. The texts from Ashlee started off with kind questions.

*How is your day?*
*What's going on?*
*Any notes for me to dictate?*

And descended into

*Where the hell are you?*
*Are you alive?*
*If you're not dead, I'm going to kill you.*

He typed to her in return.

*Hey, sweetie, I'm good. All is good. Just really busy and getting words down on paper. I'm not dead and please don't kill me. Xo*

She answered immediately. She missed him. She loved him and wanted him to hurry home.

Ashlee was like a changing weather system, unpredictable like the thunderstorm today. It was part of what had drawn him to her in the first place. But it was getting tiresome, the flashes of anger followed by the cloying sweetness. Blaming him for a bad day and then seducing him in the next breath. Berating a waitress and then hugging her when they left the restaurant. Before he'd left for this trip, he'd told Ashlee that he loved her. Why the hell had he done that when he didn't love her at all? "Whoops, didn't mean it." Yeah, as if that would work.

He'd been desperate when he left. His world had been coming undone, unraveling in ways he'd never anticipated. He'd grabbed on to Ashlee like a raft, and he'd climbed on up. Even if he didn't love her, he didn't want to hurt her. At all. He wanted to undo the damages he had done. But that seemed impossible.

His agent was ignoring his calls.

His ex-wife hated him.

His daughter wasn't speaking to him.

Amelia, his daughter. She was the one he missed the most. She was the one who broke his heart. Yes, Marilee shattered him with her hatred, but his heart, only his daughter could break that. The ache he felt when he thought of her, which was a million times a day, helped fuel his need for JD. Marilee had poisoned Amelia, told her everything. Who the hell tells a fifteen-year-old girl about the misdeeds of her father?

Well, *People* magazine for starters. After that, his ex-wife.

It had been like a plug pulled out of a tub, the way his daughter's love disappeared. Instant. All of a sudden and with sucking force. It wasn't hate that remained, it was worse—disdain and disinterest. No matter what he did or bought or sold or said, Amelia was resolute in her loathing.

There was only one thing he wanted to fix more than his career: his relationship with Amelia. He'd tried. For a year he'd tried. He wouldn't give up, but here in Watersend, he would try to fix something he had some control over.

The worst part of it all was that he'd made all these mistakes during the best part of his life. He'd done the damage when he thought he was flying high, living the life, being The Man. He'd been invincible and strong, not once seeing the havoc he wreaked with every step he took. Too oblivious in his own glory.

He picked up his cell phone and called Ella before he even realized what he'd done. Her voice, soft, answered, "Yes?"

"It's Hunter."

She laughed. "I thought I'd heard the last from you."

"No. I just realized how much of your precious time I'd taken up and I thought I should thank you before I leave tomorrow. Can I take you out to dinner?"

She hesitated, silence, and then a little cough. "Sure."

"Great. You pick the restaurant."

"Okay." She was quiet for a moment, and there was running water in the background. A shower? A sink?

Blake looked outside. No, it was rain. "Do you have a window open?" he asked.

"What?"

"I hear the rain. I wish I could open the window here. . . ."

"Yes. It's pouring."

"So, what restaurant?" He wanted her to say, *just come here with my open window and the rain and I'll cook for you.*

"How about the Patio? You'll like it and it has a great view of the park."

"Perfect," he said even though it's not what he meant.


The restaurant was packed—spring Friday night. But Ella had called in a favor and reserved a corner table. It was stupid, choosing Sims's favorite restaurant. She was tempting the fates. Messing with the gods, her mom would have said. And you can only do that so many times.

Ella arrived early so she could take a breath and scope out the restaurant. She didn't recognize anyone, so she settled back in her seat. Hunter walked in and spoke to the hostess, who directed him toward Ella. "Over there," she said.

Hunter smiled and waved as he wound his way through the tables to the back corner. He leaned over to hug her. "Glad you didn't have plans," he said. "I know it was last-minute."

"Oh, I had plans," she lied. "I just changed them because I know you're leaving tomorrow."

"Oh, okay." Hunter sat and unfolded his napkin, placed it in his lap. He picked up the wine list. "What are you in the mood for tonight?"

Ella leaned forward and smiled. "Malbec. You?"

"Ah, first a real drink. Then wine."

They talked about the small things, nothing important; the weather and the architecture of the restaurant, and the waitress's pretty smile. They ordered their food—salmon for her, steak for him—sharing their side dishes until they'd emptied the first bottle of wine and ordered a second.

"Are you getting excited about going home?" Ella finally asked him.

"I am. But I have some messes to clean up when I get there."

"Tell me more about you. Why are there messes at home?"

"I did some people wrong and I need to fix it," he said, and twirled the wineglass on the table, his thumb and forefinger around the stem of the glass.

"We all mess up."

"Yes, but then we all have to find a way to fix it, too. And I've been gone for months. I'm happy about going home, but there are . . . things."

"What is home like?" She closed her eyes and smiled. "I mean, is it totally different from here? What does it feel like?"

"It's beautiful. As beautiful as it is here, but not in the same way."
He smiled at her and she saw the crinkles around his eyes deepen. He
really was handsome in a craggy sort of way.

Silverware clattered to the floor somewhere across the room and
Hunter startled. They'd been quiet for a few minutes and he must have
gone off somewhere in his mind. Ella laughed. "Where'd you go?"

"Huh?"

"In your head. You were so far away." Ella cut into her salmon,
but didn't take a bite. She really wasn't hungry at all. "What are you so
worried about?"

"Let's see. I can list them. A daughter who isn't speaking to me.
An ex-wife who hates me. An assistant I need to fire. And break up
with. And—" Hunter held up his hands. "That's enough right there,
although there's more."

The warm feeling under her heart was so unfamiliar that at first
she thought she was embarrassed. But it wasn't embarrassment. She
was happy to be talking to him about real things. "I'm sorry," she said.
"That is a mess. Maybe you should just not go back?"

"Sounds nice but I've tried the running-away thing. It doesn't fix
itself just because I'm gone. If it would have, it would have by now."

"And your daughter?" Ella leaned forward thinking of Mimi's
daughter, of losing a daughter in any way.

"She hates me, too," he said.

"Why—?"

"Because I was selfish. Stupid. I made a mistake. . . ."

"We all make—"

Hunter held up his hand with a sad-type smile. "Don't say it. I
know what you're going to say and it's not going to make me feel any
better. Yes, we all make mistakes. But mine are screwups more than
mistakes."

"What's the difference?" Ella asked.

"One that does real damage to someone you love." He closed his
eyes. "Yes, that's the definition."

Ella repeated his words. "'One that does real damage to someone you love.'" She took a long sip of her wine. "Yes, that's a screwup."

"See?" Hunter hit his forehead with his palm. "I'm an idiot and I don't know how to fix it."

"You say sorry. You say sorry until you can't say it anymore. You can do that, right?"

"Tried that," he said, and made a check mark in the air.

"Can I ask what it was?"

"I cheated on my wife, a very public thing."

"Yes, that's . . . bad." Ella didn't even try to hide the hit in the chest that those words gave her. *I cheated.*

"I know. It's bad." The dining room grew louder; a quartet played in the far corner. Hunter reached across the table and tapped the top of Ella's hand. "I shouldn't have told you. Now you think I'm a terrible person. Which I guess I am."

She really liked this man. She liked his brown-gold eyes and his sense of humor, his quick retorts and fun questions. And yet was he any different than Sims? A cheater? She obviously didn't know anything about men. Or life.

"Betrayal," she said, and leaned forward. "It changes everything. The lies. The deceit. She must have felt like such a fool. Why the hell would you do that?" For a moment in her anger, Hunter became Sims, a man choosing to betray his wife. Ella dropped her fork on her plate and it clanged, an exclamation point.

His eyes, focused on her, were damp with the beginning of tears. "I don't know why I told you. It's a terrible truth. I could try and explain, offer you the reasons it happened. Not the excuses because there aren't excuses. But there were reasons. My marriage was bitter and sad. But it doesn't really matter because when you put the facts on paper, when you say them out loud, it's sordid, it's cliché, it's hurtful. I know."

"Couldn't you have just told her that you weren't happy? That things were changing? Why lie and sneak around and make hushed phone calls and hide e-mails and pretend to work late?" Ella's voice rose and she couldn't stop it. She wanted to, but the words were pouring out as if they'd been waiting. Why? She always wanted to know *why*.

"It's like you were there for all of it." He exhaled and looked away. "I don't know, Ella. I don't know why. It was awful. I'm sorry. I feel terrible. I can't fix it. I can't go backward. You hate me." He paused as if all those sentences exhausted him and then said, "I shouldn't have told you."

"I don't hate you. I just don't understand." She fought back any kind of emotional display. Hunter was not Sims. She was judging without understanding.

"I'm trying to understand. I really am. Sometimes I think my ex was relieved that I did that. That I cheated . . . because now she has a real reason to hate me. But the worst part is that I don't know how to make it up to my daughter."

"I don't know if there is a way to make it up to somebody. I don't think that's what forgiveness is about," Ella said. She knew exactly what Sims would have to do to make it up to her: apologize, run back to her, admit that he made a mistake, and then prove his love by being there, staying there. "I think maybe the only way to make things right is by being present, by really being there for her. Going to her and not allowing her to push you away. Run back to her. Don't give up."

"I'm not talking about my ex."

"I'm not, either. Your daughter . . ."

"Yes, I don't think my time on the road has helped things at all. I send e-mails. I've sent presents. I've called and texted."

Ella shook her head. "Not what a girl needs. I mean, it's nice to get those things, but being present is more important. Being there, next to her."

Hunter leaned back in his chair and smiled. "I can definitely try that."

"I just know what I needed when someone . . . I mean, *if* someone betrayed me."

"Your guy. He wouldn't have ever done anything like that, would he? Cheated on you. Embarrassed you."

She shook her head, unable to answer.

"What do you think made—" Hunter asked.

Ella cut him off. "I don't want to talk about it anymore. Please. You can ask me about Watersend or tell me more about your life. But not me. Not me anymore. I'm tired of me and I'm tired of being sad."

"Ah, that has to be progress."

"Yes. So, tell me, why didn't you like that movie today?"

"I was just preoccupied." Hunter cut into his steak, stared at it as if it was the most interesting thing he'd ever seen. "I think it's one of the director's best. But I liked *Driftwood Summer* better."

"It was okay," Ella said. "It was so sappy and romantic. I saw what was coming from the first two minutes. And I was not once surprised. Sometimes those kinds of movies are good. Like *When Harry Met Sally*. You know she's going to end up with him, but you're surprised along the way by how she ends up with him. Not this one. It was two hours of my life I won't get back."

Hunter moved in his chair, and then he busted out laughing. It was a quick burst of noise.

"It wasn't that funny."

"It was," he said, and wiped at his eyes while he turned to the table. "It really was. I didn't realize you were such a movie critic."

"I'm not. I just like a good story. That's all. I don't get what's so funny."

"You." Hunter took in a long breath and put both his hands on the table, palms up. "Give me your hands."

She did.

"You are adorable. And funny. I'm sorry things have been so rough for you. I'm sorry for a lot of things."

His hands were strong and soft, and he wound his fingers through hers. The touch of another human made her feel weak, her chest full and warm. If she didn't still love Sims, she would actually have a crush on this man she barely knew (who cheated on his wife and lived three thousand miles away). She pulled her hands from his. "Thanks, you're sweet."

"You see," he said. "That's the problem. I'm not."

"That's not true. You really are."

Hunter's face changed then. His eyelids fell to half-mast. "I'm glad this was my last city," he said. "I'm glad I met you."

"Thanks," Ella said, and felt the too-much wine flowing through her thoughts, softening its edges, blurring the truth and the lies.

With vivid detail, Ella saw Sims across the room just as the waitress brought the check. Maybe she knew she would. Maybe she came here wanting to see him. But whatever she had wanted when she made that reservation, well, she didn't want it now. She didn't want Sims anywhere near Hunter or the false life she'd created. Sims looked up from his dinner and caught her gaze. Betsy, her hair up in a bun, had her back to Ella. Sims looked away quickly as if Ella's gaze burned.

"Let's go," Ella said to Hunter, and smiled her best smile.

They were halfway across the room when Hunter tilted his head to the left. "That woman over there," he said. "Don't look yet, but I met her at a bar the other night."

Ella didn't have to look; she knew. He'd met Betsy. Ella's heart thumped and rolled. "And? Was she trying to pick you up?" Ella tried for light and breezy, missing it.

"No, not me. Not anyone. She was with a bunch of women and went on and on about this guy. How they were made for each other. How they were . . . meant to be. She thought she was living the ultimate love story of all time."

"Because stealing someone's husband is the ultimate love story?"

"Ah, you know her."

"Only in passing." Ella rolled her eyes. "As if she has any idea what love is." Ella glanced around at Sims and Betsy, leaning toward each other, holding hands. "Let's go," she said again.

"I haven't really had this much fun in a long time," he said. "I'm sorry we have to go."

"Well, let me take you to my favorite little bar." Ella slipped her arm through Hunter's and hoped that Sims took at least one glance, one furtive glance her way.

Hunter walked with Ella under gas lanterns and over cobbled side-walks until they entered a small bar where a musician sat in the corner tuning her guitar. "I love this place," Ella said. "I never see anyone I know and this girl is always here singing on Friday nights."

A strum of guitar chords from across the room, a screech from a microphone. Hunter placed his hand on the small of Ella's back. He followed her into the room and stayed connected, his palm against the cottony fabric of her sundress. She found a table in the corner and they sat and ordered drinks—he a JD and she sparkling water. "We won't stay long," she said. "I know you have an early flight. I just want to hear her sing a couple of songs."

"What's her name?" he asked, and not because he cared but because all of a sudden he found himself nervous and short on words.

"Willa. Isn't that the best name? She's really good. She comes over from Savannah."

"Did you used to come here with your husband?"

Ella shook her head. "This is where I come alone. It's my place. I've never come here with anyone. Until now."

"Why?"

She shrugged. "A girl has to have something that's just hers, right?" She smiled at him and he felt his heart do something unfamiliar: it rolled over. Her hair fell in loose curls to her shoulder and he wanted to touch it. No, he wanted to write about it.

He'd thought this was the place where he could get more information out of her, but instead he stared at her with his mouth gasping for air like a fish. He looked stupid; he could feel it and there was nothing he could do about it. He couldn't take this any further. He'd lied so terribly there was no going back now. He had to leave.

Bright blue letters on a wooden board indicated the way to the bathrooms at the back of the restaurant. Hunter pointed at the sign. "I'll be right back."

Ella nodded. Hunter stood and looked down at her. She would hate him for what he was about to do. But it was for the best. Definitely for the best. And he could just add one more hater to his list. This would be the last time he lied. It had to be. If he stayed any longer, he would have to lie some more and he needed to be finished.

Before he opened the back door of the restaurant, before he stepped into the alley to leave, he stared at Ella. He wanted to remember her looking the way she did now, before she discovered he was a fraud and an asshole. Before she looked up and realized some sleazy, slick guy from L.A. had duped her. She smiled at the singer and took a sip of her sparkling water and then, as if she could feel him staring at her, she turned to look at him. Her eyebrows dropped in a look of confusion. Hunter opened the back door and she understood.

She didn't flinch. She didn't scowl or holler out. She sat with certitude and watched as if she knew that this was exactly what he would do, as if he'd told her that he was leaving. But he couldn't do it; he didn't want to do it. Their eyes locked in an unspoken language and Hunter smiled at her, closed the door, and wound his way through the tables to return to her side.

Blake flopped on the hotel bed fully clothed. He stared at the ceiling where a water stain looked like a VW bug. He wanted to write that down. He wanted to write everything down. The way he felt, the way this town enveloped him with something close to happiness. He wanted to write about the way Ella covered her face when she laughed, the

106

way her bangs fell across her forehead, the way he felt hearing her laugh.

It would be cowardly leaving town without telling her the truth. He knew that. He couldn't keep saying "just one more time." It was like the JD and the affairs and the lying. Just one more was never enough. This Ella. He didn't want to hurt her. He needed to get out while the getting out was good.

Already the scenes for the screenplay were running through his head. The courtship, the sailing lessons, the heartache and longing until they were finally together.

Blake started to dictate.

"What," he asked into the recorder, "is the death accomplishing? He saves her but what else?" He paused and then answered himself. "Finally proof of love. This character, this lovely woman, always doubted his love. She was never sure because he didn't know how to show his love, he didn't know how to say the words. Because he was always quiet and brooding, she never was sure. Now she is sure. Now she knows."

Blake stood up then and paced the room. He was missing something. He spoke again. "But where is my happy ending? The happy ending aside from the fact that now she knows he really did love her? We don't want to end in the dark valley."

And there were so many other blanks to fill in. Best friend? Mentor? Secrets? B plot? Blake needed to sketch these out, find out where to place each one.

The most important thing of all: What does his character (she) want? And why can't she get it? This was the crux of it all and he knew that better than anyone else. She wants her husband back—but he's dead so it's impossible. How would he work around this? That was the mystery and fun of it all—finding his way. The elements were there, and now it was time for the exhausting, dangerous, frustrating alchemy of screenwriting.

He sat on the stained couch. Weird how things become familiar. He was getting sentimental, which was a good sign. As for the story itself, he'd know more by the time he landed in L.A. Home. He just wanted to get home. He smiled and opened the mini-fridge, yanked out a tiny bottle of JD, and gulped it down before he was able to think what number it was or if he even gave a shit what number it was.

Home. Hell, what was it anyway?

Home used to be nowhere Florida, the place he grew up. It had been long enough now that he could call L.A. home. Twenty-five years longer than he'd ever lived in the cesspool of a town his parents had thought would bring them the dream—water and sun and fun as a family. What a joke.

Living with four brothers and two sisters in a three-bedroom house with two bathrooms wasn't the dream at all. It was a nightmare. Why it bothered only him was still a mystery. Smack in the middle of the sibling lineup, he always felt like he didn't belong—he wasn't in the older responsible group or the younger, fun-loving group. He was the outcast, the one they teased, "lovingly teasing, honey," his mother used to say. "Don't be so sensitive or you'll never survive in this family." And she was right. He didn't survive in the family. He, to this day, didn't speak to anyone of them on any kind of regular basis.

He'd been the one reading the book in the corner, the one hiding in the library until it closed. He was the president of the literary club. He was the kid who cried at a good ending or went to the movies alone because everyone else in his family played a sport or an instrument or was on a real date with a real boy or girl.

Blake read books and wrote stories. While everyone else was funneling beer after the football game, he hid in the movie theater watching the newest release. He helped bring home the Latin Award for his dilapidated school. He'd never attended a single football game and he'd never known the cheerleaders' names. In the end, he did go to the prom because he'd looked at it like an experiment, a story he could write. He went with Maureen Blaskovich, a girl in literary club with wide eyes and a high-pitched giggle. She wore the same dress to school almost every day: a *Little House on the Prairie* calico type with a lace collar. On Fridays she wore cut-off jeans and too-large T-shirts that looked as if she'd taken them from her father's closet. If you looked closely enough you'd see that she was very pretty. But no one looked. Even he barely looked.

When she asked him to go to the prom, he'd been unable to say no. If she was brave enough to ask then he was brave enough to go.

That prom had been the impetus for his first short-film script and it had won an award at SoCal. And the virgin groping that was part of his first sexual experience had become part of his first screenplay. He and Maureen had never talked again. He had heard that she was nanny to the children of a famous musician. And when he saw her on the cover of *US Today* under a headline that said "Home Wrecker," he realized she was much, much more than a nanny. He'd googled her. He called and she answered. They dated for a few months, the new and improved version of each of them unable to connect as the old and dorky versions had been able to do. They'd both remade themselves after South Florida, had become California dreamers and successful. And then they parted for some reason. He could never remember why.

The next screenplay he wrote was about two small-town dweeby kids who fell in love and then lost each other, only to find each other again years later, beautiful and successful and in love with each other still. His movies were much better than real life. It had always been true. He could write a great story, he just couldn't seem to live one.

He glanced at his cell phone and flicked through his contacts. He still had her number—Maureen, now going by Mauri. He pushed the call button and then quickly, before the first ring, the end button. No going backward.

The hotel room was spinning just the tiniest bit. He blamed fatigue. He set the alarm for 4:30 A.M., and also called the front desk for a wakeup call. He would get on that 6:00 A.M. flight and go home, write a great screenplay, and get on with his happy, happy life.

Every successful movie, every well-received script had been something mined from his own life, and he would do it again. He'd just needed to get out of California, find some new inspiration. He didn't need a new life, just a new idea.

He woke up before his alarm and dressed in the dark. It was time to get the hell out.

# *eight*

———————

Ella's apartment was quiet, only the creaking of a settling building and the whir of an air conditioner doing its best to fill the room with cold air. Far off a siren wailed and then quieted. Hunter would be on his way back to L.A. When she'd left him last night, she'd wanted to know something more about him, something about his life so far away. She'd googled "Hunter Adderman writer." Nothing. It was as if he didn't exist.

She'd slept well until only moments before when her cell rang with Amber's news that she was on her way over, that she was worried about Ella. Now Ella sat there in her pajama bottoms and tank top, wondering what she would say to her ex–best friend.

Amber knocked and Ella waited.

She wanted Amber to have to wait, too. No one, aside from Sims, had hurt Ella as Amber had. It was one damn thing to lose your husband, but to discover that your best friend was in on it? Or at least knew about it?

For a quick minute, Ella wanted Hunter there to see this, to hear it, to talk to him about it. Ridiculous.

Ella opened the door to Amber, who stood there in her adorable sundress, all blush pink and full of life as always. People often thought they were sisters. When they were at a bar or restaurant the guys would ask, "Are you two related?" and they'd laugh. Ella never saw the similarity, especially now as she looked at Amber, a vibrant, all-things-go-my-way girl. A woman who lived in her hometown with friends and family who had surrounded her for her entire life. Amber ran her parents' gift shop, and although it couldn't be true (it wasn't true of anyone), it seemed she was sprinkled with the best of luck all the time. Smooth sailing for the adorable one.

Amber flung herself into the room and hugged Ella. "I've missed you so much."

Ella couldn't make her arms surround her friend. Not yet.

"You hate me," Amber said, stepping back.

"No," Ella said. "I don't."

"It's not my fault, you know."

"I know." Ella walked into the kitchen, which only took a few steps "You want some tea?" she asked.

"No, thanks. But look, I brought you something."

Ella saw the box she knew contained homemade cookies—Amber's claim to fame in Watersend. She offered them whenever there was a death, a wedding, a graduation, a first date, making the cheerleading team, any monumental event (or what would be called a monumental event in Watersend). She decorated each cookie appropriately for the occasion: round sugar cookies with fluffed icing. She'd put smiley faces on them for kids' parties; wedding bells for a marriage; baby booties for the baby shower; a heart for funerals. (Yes, a heart.) Amber wouldn't share the recipe.

Ella looked at the open box. A single scripted word written in pale blue icing on top of the cookie: *Sorry*.

"Are you doing okay?" On the breakfast table, Amber pushed aside the lamp and Ella's sketches to make room for her cookie box.

"I'm fine." Ella took a large bite of a cookie and looked to Amber. "I'm fine."

"Do you accept my apology?" Amber's eyes filled with tears. She could do this on cue—both cry and sing.

"Why are you sorry?" Ella asked, taking a second bite.

"I should have told you as soon as I knew about it. I thought it would stop. I thought they'd get it out of their system and just get on with life. I thought it was terrible, I really did. But I also thought it would end quickly and we could all just go on like normal. I didn't know they thought . . . they were really in love."

"In love," Ella said, and cringed. "Really?"

"That came out the wrong way. They believe they are in love. I don't think they are. Sims has loved you forever. That doesn't just go away. And I thought, well . . . I don't know what I thought. I'm an idiot." She paused to wipe at her eyes. She smeared mascara across her face like any good actress would. "I'm sorry this has happened to you. I've tried to intervene. I've tried to tell my sister and Sims that you deserve better than this." She waved her hand around the apartment and then spotted Ella's list, the "how to get over your ex" list. "What's this?" she asked and picked it up.

Ella rushed to Amber and grabbed the sheet. "It's nothing."

"No, seriously. This is fantastic. You could blog this or write about it or whatever. You aren't just sitting here crying; you're trying to *do* something."

"Trying to do something?" Ella's voice rose as she crumpled the list and tossed it across the room. "I'm trying to survive. I think about how much I hate your sister, and I wonder how anyone could do what she's done. What was she thinking when she took off his clothes? When she snuck into his office at the marina and asked him to sail on top of her . . . ?"

"Ella, stop. You can't picture them like that. You can't go there."

"Really? Your sister is sleeping with my husband and *I* can't go there?"

"You're mad at her. You hate her. I get it. But I think Sims might have been a little complicit in this, Ella."

"I know that. So you know the best thing on that list so far?" Ella pointed at the crumpled paper resting in the corner of the room. "*Renounce hope. Give up. Let it go.* That's what I'm doing, Amber. And it seems that includes you since you just disappeared. My best friend. And in all this hell I've been living through, where have you been?"

"I'm sorry. I'm sorrier than I know how to be. How many more times can I say it?" Amber held out her hands. "You can't live here, Ella. You have to come live with me or your dad or—"

"No way."

Amber's eyes were dry now. Her voice strong. "I didn't sleep with Sims, Ella. It is not my fault. You can't blame me. We are best friends, always have been."

"The time I needed you the most, you disappeared."

"Because I didn't know what to say or do. You know that when I don't know what to do, I . . . I go into a cave. That's what I did. It's not like this hasn't also broken my heart."

Ella fought the desire to hug her friend, to tell her everything about the past weeks, the pain and longing, even about Hunter. Instead she asked, "This has broken *your* heart?"

"Yes. Of course it has. I love you. I loved Sims. I love my sister. What the hell was I supposed to do? I cried. I pleaded with Betsy. I baked cookies, ate them, and slept. I've missed parties . . ."

"Oh, parties?" Ella asked. "You went and missed parties?"

"Stop." Amber said, "You can't be mean to me. I know you're hurting, but—"

Ella sat on the edge of the coffee table, and motioned to the single chair, the one she'd picked up at the thrift store. "Sit," she said.

"Do you have anything to drink?" Amber asked.

"Like drink-drink or water?"

"A real drink."

"I have some cheap chardonnay."

Amber brushed her hand through the air. "Forget it."

"It's nine A.M.," Ella said.

"I know. Just forget it. I wasn't thinking straight."

"Are *you* okay?" Ella asked.

"No, didn't you hear me? I'm miserable. I don't know what to do. I mean . . . she's my sister. But you're like a sister. And there's Sims—I always believed he was the perfect one for you and now Betsy tells me he's perfect for her. And I don't believe in love anymore and I hate my sister for hurting you, but I hate Sims worse. But it's family and—"

"Stop." Ella raised her palm and dropped her elbows onto her knees. Here she sat looking up at Amber sitting in the chair and wanting to console her. This was crazy. "I know it's hard for you, Amber. But I'm miserable here. I have to wait on paperwork and all kinds of crazy just to get in my house. *My* house."

"Well, just go!"

"I can't. I tried. He changed the passcodes and the alarm system is always set, probably by your sister. If I get arrested, I lose . . . even more."

"He will calm down," she said. "He's reasonable."

"No man getting laid a few times a day is reasonable," Ella said.

"Why are you making jokes about this?" Amber's tears started again.

"Because I don't know what else to do."

"Go get him back?" Amber said this with hesitation, her voice rising at the end like a question.

"Really? You think I should just make a fool of myself and beg him when he has made it clear, abundantly clear, that he does *not* want me."

Amber groaned. "I know."

"You want to lecture me about what I did, don't you? You want to say that if I hadn't thrown his baseball card collection into the Dumpster, I would have a chance. Go ahead, say it."

"No. I won't."

"Amber, it's not like I was thinking straight. My husband came to tell me that he was in love with my best friend's sister, that they'd been sleeping together, that he wanted to leave me. I guess I just wanted to ruin something valuable, something that meant something to him. I couldn't really throw your sister in the Dumpster now, could I?"

"God, it's like I don't even know you."

"It's like I don't even know me, either."

Amber stared at Ella as if she expected the meeker version to show back up, her best friend, who did everything she wanted her to do, who didn't complain, who was adorable and sweet—almost too sweet. But Ella just sat there, without apology.

"I don't know what to say now," Amber said. " 'I'm sorry' doesn't seem to be enough for you and it's all I have."

"I forgive you, Amber." Ella stood up and looked down at her. "Is that what you want to hear?"

"Only if you mean it."

"I forgive you," Ella said again. "I do. This isn't your fault. I can't imagine being stuck in the middle like you are. Just sitting there not knowing what to do."

Amber nodded.

"Would you help me?" Ella asked.

"Of course. What do you need?"

"The code to the alarm system. I know he changed it." Shame brought with it a slight nausea. Ella didn't want to ask for these things. She didn't like to ask for anything. She didn't like much of anything lately, so what the hell. "I won't take anything of his or destroy anything. I just want a few things of my own. It's like he's holding our house hostage."

"He sort of is." Amber stood up to face her best friend. "I will get that code for you. Not sure how but I will." She then lowered her voice, as if Sims and Betsy were outside the door or hiding under the couch. "They just left for Napa for two days. They aren't even here."

"Are you kidding me?" Ella exhaled the anger. "He promised to take me to Napa so many times. . . ."

"I know. I'm sorry."

"Are they . . . happy?" Ella asked.

"You don't want me to answer that, do you?"

"No, I don't."

"I miss you, Ella. Do you think we can find a way to get back to normal?"

Ella shook her head. "No."

"Don't say that." Amber took both of Ella's hands.

"It's true, though," Ella said. "We can't go back to normal. Maybe later we can fix this. Begin again. Maybe we can find a new normal. But if you are hanging out with my husband and your sister, I can't see you. You know that, right?"

"Why not? I'm not dating Sims."

Ella looked at Amber, at her round, almost-purple eyes and short bob that curled into the air like it was reaching for something unseen, at the freckles that spread unevenly across her cheeks. Amber. Her best friend. Her selfish friend. Her do-it-my-way-all-the-time friend. Ella saw her for the first time with a clarity that only living in a crap apartment seemed to give her. "Let's give this some time," she said, and pulled her hands away. "Okay?"

"Okay," Amber said, and reached to hug Ella.

This time, Ella gave a little bit of a hug in return.


In Sole Mates at Swept Away, and in complete boredom, Ella spent her time rearranging the displays. She rearranged shoes, made pyramids, restacked them, and lined up the toes in a wave pattern. Margo hadn't been to work in two days. At least not when Ella was there. "Designing," everyone told her. "She's in one of those phases where she stays up all night sketching and drawing." Nadine whispered this as if Margo's designs were sacred somehow.

Ella calculated where Hunter would be: over the Midwest, heading into California, landing in L.A. It was then, as she estimated his landing, that his text came through. She smiled as she read his note.

*You at home or work?*

She told him she was at work, busy, busy she said. He replied that he was stuck in Savannah, nowhere near L.A.

*I'll cook you dinner if you stay.*

Ella stared at her phone. Had she really just asked him to dinner? His text took a few seconds, an interminable time in which she imagined him fashioning his response, typing and erasing and typing again to find a way to tell her "No, thank you, but no."
Instead she read:

*I might cancel the flight myself just for that. I'll keep you updated. Don't let the seagulls get you down.*

*How can I not? They are so sad all the damn time.*

*Ignore them.*

*Good luck. Let me know how it goes.*

*I will! xo*

He'd typed *xo.* Was that something he always did? A twitch of the thumbs, a good-bye that meant the same to everyone? Ella typed *xo* and then deleted and then typed it again, but didn't hit send. She left it there, unsent and dangling on her phone screen.

# *nine*

———————

Amber texted the four numbers without explanation. And thank God, because there was no way she was going to cook for Hunter at the Crumbling Chateau.

Evening arrived and the white ibis gathered above, extended against the sky, white on blue. Ella sat on the concrete bench in the courtyard at the back of the apartment. Weeds filled the garden areas once bloated with flowers. A dried-out concrete fountain held two beer cans, an empty bottle of vodka, and a pack of cigarettes. Ella noted each detail as if distraction was her best coping mechanism. Which it was, in a way. Thinking about the almost Gothic surroundings of her apartment building, about what to cook for Hunter, and how to sustain the facade just one evening longer, kept her from thinking about Sims.

A door slammed and Ella startled to see Mimi exit the building with Bruiser straining forward, his leash taut in her outstretched arm.

"Mimi!"

"Oh, darling, hello there." Mimi waved, and in doing so, released Bruiser to the freedom he obviously craved.

The fluff of white bolted toward the parking lot. Ella ran after him while Mimi hollered: "Bruiser. Stop, Bruiser!"

Ella never did understand why so many owners thought that yelling at their dogs was a good idea. No dog she'd ever seen had ever responded to the frantic screaming commands of their owners. Ella caught up to Bruiser just as he ran to the middle of the road, scurrying toward the oak tree on the other side. She stepped on his leash and his tiny head jerked back with a high-pitched yelp. A squeal of tires and a holler from Mimi combined in a grating jangle. Ella glanced up to see the hood of a white SUV van, one of those windowless utility vans she always associated with scary movies and kidnappers.

A greasy-haired man poked his head out of the window and yelled, "What the hell are you doing?"

"Catching this dog," Ella said, lifting Bruiser to her chest. He barked. Of course he barked.

"I almost killed the both of you. Get the hell out of the road before I run you over."

Ella stepped aside and joined Mimi. "Here you go," she said, and handed Bruiser to her.

The van drove off, a plume of toxic smoke blooming from its tail-pipe in a final insult. Together, Ella and Mimi walked across the street to the tree Bruiser seemed determined to find.

"Sorry about that," Mimi said.

"No problem," Ella said. "I'm so glad to see you."

Bruiser finished his business, and then circled around the oak tree until he found a soft patch of grass and clover blossoms gathered in a crochet pattern. Quiet. Ella exhaled and sat in the grass, Mimi on a bench. Ella drew her knees up to her chest. "What a gorgeous afternoon."

"Isn't it, though," Mimi said.

"Sure is," a deep voice answered.

Ella knew the voice. How quickly she'd come to feel comfortable hearing it. "Well, hey, you," she said to Hunter.

"I return to town just so I can see you almost get killed?" Hunter reached his hand down to pull Ella to her feet.

"Idiot driver," Mimi said from the bench.

Hunter turned to her. "Hi, there."

"This is my friend Mimi," Ella said. She searched quickly for lies to back up the truth. "She lives . . . next door. This is her dog, Bruiser." She pointed to the miraculously quiet dog.

"Well, you must be Hunter. The guy from California," Mimi said.

"The very one." Hunter offered his hand.

"Nice to meet you," Mimi said.

Bruiser lifted his head at the sound of Mimi's voice, sniffed the air with his padded black nose, and decided it was time to start barking.

Mimi shook her head. "Sorry."

Hunter bent down and ran his hand along Bruiser's back, once, twice. Bruiser stopped mid-bark and lifted his head to the sun. "He's awful cute," Hunter said.

"Sometimes, yes," Mimi said. "Most of the time, he's just annoying, but I love him anyhow."

"What are you doing here?" Ella asked. The Crumbling Chateau stood accusingly behind her. She averted her gaze as if that would be the one thing to expose her lies.

"I was just driving to the hotel when I saw you two in the street. Aren't you like a mile from home? That's quite the walk."

Mimi glanced at Ella and in Mimi's eyes, Ella saw the complicit acknowledgment: *I'm with you here. I've got this.*

"Yes, it would be a long walk," Mimi said, "if we'd walked it, but Ella drove here so Bruiser could sit by his favorite tree."

"So thoughtful," Hunter said.

"Yes, she's quite the girl," Mimi agreed.

"Well." Hunter stood. "I need to hit the shower. I guess I'd better be getting back to the hotel I thought I'd left for good. See you in a couple hours?" He looked to Ella.

The wind carried a scent of the river, a taste of water. Hunter's hair blew into his eyes. "Yes," she said. "See you soon."

"Would you like to join us?" Hunter turned to Mimi.

"No, but thank you so much," Mimi said. "I've got quite a schedule tonight and couldn't possibly make it."

Laughter caught itself under Ella's chest. Mimi there, joining in the liars club.

"Well, next time then," Hunter said.

He left awkwardly, not knowing if he should hug Ella or Mimi or neither or both. In the end, he just waved over his shoulder and walked toward the ugly turquoise car at the edge of the curb.

They waited until the car was well out of sight and then, as if on cue, Mimi and Ella busted out laughing, the kind of laughter reserved for the best moments between best friends. Who knew, Ella thought, who ever knew where a friend would be found?

"He came back to town?" Mimi asked.

"Sort of," Ella said, sitting next to Mimi now. "His flight was canceled."

"I'm sure it was," Mimi said.

"Really, it was. So I told him I'd cook him dinner. I think I might have taken this one step too far."

"Where are you going to do this dinner?"

"My house. Sims is on a little vacation with the love of his life."

"Well, this is just getting better and better." Mimi patted Ella's leg. "Way better than pound cake, and that is saying so very much."

Ella took Mimi's hand and held it in her own. "I am so glad you ended up being my neighbor."

"Me, too, dear. Me, too."

The gate to enter her garden and house was locked. Ella pushed against it just in case Sims had been his Sims-self and not locked it. The gate rattled against the lock. Ella kicked at its base. Even before she stuck the key in the lock, she knew it wouldn't work. She'd have to climb over. Or cancel.

She formed the words in her mind. *I'm sorry, Hunter, I didn't mean to invite you over. It was foolish to think I could have someone in my dead husband's house.* Then she thought of Sims and Betsy, tasting wine, making love in a vineyard, eating at French Laundry and getting drunk. Disgusting.

Change of plans: she would cook Hunter dinner, allow him into the house, get rid of him quickly, and pack up what she wanted to take.

She'd have to climb over the fence. She'd done it before after locking herself out, so no problem. Really. It wasn't some elaborate fence; just an ornamental enclosure. With two quick steps in the loops of the iron gate, she was at the top. She poised herself to take a little jump and land softly, but her T-shirt caught on the spike. Instead of the soft landing she had hoped for, she tumbled sideways, a sharp pull under her arm. Her right ankle took the brunt of it, twisting underneath her at an angle she was fairly sure her ankle had never bent before.

On the ground, she assessed her body. Slowly she sat and then bent over to pull her foot onto her lap as if she was in lotus position, ready to meditate. Her ankle was swollen. She yanked off her sneaker. She pushed on the anklebone with one finger and yelped out loud. A bird flew in haste from the feeder, seeds scattering wildly.

The cobblestones had always been quaint, an intimate part of the path in the entryway, but as she dragged herself across the garden, she cursed each ragged edge. The moss between the stones, soft lichen she had purposefully planted, was staining her pants. When she reached the bench she pulled herself up and hopped on one foot to the front door.

She would have to cancel. What the hell was she thinking? Her ankle was throbbing like it had a heartbeat, her clothes were ruined, and like most things lately, she hadn't thought through what to do next.

Folding onto the iron bench, Ella reached into her back pocket for the phone. She'd call Hunter with a quick *sorry, I'm sick*. Her hand, sliding into her back pocket, recoiled from a quick stab, a bite of some sort. "God, enough already," she hollered to the garden.

She stuck her finger in her mouth, the metal taste of blood on her tongue. Lifting herself up she looked for what could have bit her. Please don't let it be a brown recluse. But the bench was empty of anything but the small white petals of the azalea blooms, extravagant waste on the ground and seat. Slowly, she reached again and realized what had bit her: the shattered iPhone screen and its glass shards. The only way she was going to cancel with Hunter was to get in the house, and soon.

She rehearsed her speech as she hopped to the front door. *I'm sorry; I've been lying. I am a made-up person in a made-up world. Please go. Hurry. Don't look at me . . . .*

The key slid into the front door and Ella pushed it open. This was her house. Yes, her house. Damn you, Sims. Everything in here, from the way it smelled, to the paint colors, to the framed photos, and even the scatter rugs, were her doing.

Sims hadn't moved or changed a thing. Photos hung on the wall leading to the kitchen—a montage in white acrylic frames, which Ella had spent days arranging. She couldn't calculate the hours of her life embedded in this house. Did those add up to make it more hers? Did the time and love make the house an integral piece of her or was it really, as she was told many times, just an object, a possession? But she loved this house. It was hers. The end. Feelings didn't know right from wrong. She'd been exiled, and tonight she would stick her Ella Flynn flag in the ground or her plates in the sink, whatever metaphor worked.

Their married life slammed into her chest with such blunt sadness that she closed her eyes to catch her breath.

Loss pressed down on her with a stifling pressure. All she wanted, God, all she wanted, was to have all of this back. To come home and throw her coat over the chair, toss her keys in the bowl on the table. To pour a glass of chardonnay and light a candle, always the mimosa candle, and start dinner. She'd shuffle through the mail and separate the recycling from the bills. She wanted it all just the way it was before he came home and decided to tell her *the truth*.

The truth was overrated. If Sims hadn't told her about Betsy, she wouldn't know, and he'd be just as happy ambling through the door. Sims would be carrying on and she'd think he was busy at work while she waited at home. She would go to work, hang out with her friends, and ignorance would be bliss. At least for as long as it lasted.

With the code Amber gave her, Ella turned off the alarm system. She would follow through with the night. It would be the last time. One more time she would pretend to be *that girl* and then say goodbye to Hunter for good. But for now, this was her house and she would do exactly as she pleased.

She hobbled down the hallway to the bedroom. The bed was askew, sheets and pillows twisted. Nausea kicked in. She made her way to the closet and saw that her clothes were still there. They hadn't been replaced by Betsy's gauzy—and gaudy—outfits. That had to be a good sign.

In the kitchen, she picked up the house phone to order Chinese food. Whatever groceries she had in the backseat, she wasn't going out to get. She was putting her foot up on a cushion with a bag of ice.

She rummaged through the hall closet and found a pair of old crutches from the time Sims had twisted his knee in a "friendly" softball game. With the weight off her foot, she wandered around to the bedroom closet where she changed into a pair of white jeans and a loose silk top. Then she hopped through the house, touching things, fluffing pillows, and finding small items missing. The tray where she dropped the mail. The vase she kept on the coffee table even when there weren't any flowers (which was rare). Her favorite cashmere throw blanket with the fringe on the edges.

She wanted Hunter to be late so she could wallow in the misery, which was ridiculous. She made a mental list in her head of all the things she must find and put back right, or take, when Hunter left.

While looking at a photo of Sims and herself, framed and on the side table, she was overcome with exhaustion. She plopped down on the brown suede chaise longue and closed her eyes. She could sleep for days, maybe weeks. The grief, the pretending, the sleepless nights—what the hell was it all for?

Her body was heavy, holding her down on the chaise. Her ankle throbbed. She wanted out of her body. No, she didn't want to die. Not that. Quite the opposite: she wanted to live fully and creatively, but here she was trapped in a body pinned down with grief, and exhausted from wanting, wanting, wanting. If she could just escape it for a few minutes. Let go of it all.

*Let go.* Who the hell came up with that good advice? She closed her eyes. Colors danced behind her eyelids, the familiar evening light and the way it danced into the living room at this time on a spring evening. Familiar. Tenderly familiar. And then she was asleep, dreaming.

A brick wall enclosed the garden, ivy covering the wall in crisscross patterns. The iron gate, obviously ancient, was locked and withholding. The house itself—gray cedar shake, weathered to what looked like suede—stood strong, built to withstand any flood.

What a perfect set. Literally perfect.

The thought embarrassed him. It wasn't a movie set. It was the house where Ella lived. He needed to take some photos and notes. This house was meant to hold a love story. A good, Southern, dripping-with-charm love story to save his career. (And his life.)

He cocked his ear to listen for Ella, but it was the sound of crickets that persisted, a kind of white noise that made this place seem so *right*. Why right? He didn't know, since everything he was doing—lying and stealing stories—was wrong. He walked toward the house and saw that the gate was closed but the front door was wide open.

"Ella," he called her name softly, almost hoping she wouldn't answer so he could snap a few photos.

There came a burping, or croaking, he didn't know which. A frog? He aimed his phone at the house and took almost twenty photos in quick succession: the wide front porch, painted white but with a pale blue ceiling; the iron gate; the climbing roses on the banister; the cedar shake in pale gray with louvered shutters painted one shade darker.

What he couldn't catch in the photo was the sweet scent, one he couldn't label, not thick like gardenia and not sweet like honeysuckle, but something in between. He quickly hit the record button on his phone and said, "The fragrance surrounding the house is something otherworldly, something made of sea and flowers."

That was enough for now.

"Ella." This time he called louder.

He tapped her name on his cell phone contacts. It rang once and went straight to voice mail. His hands wound through the thick curls of the gate. He hollered her name louder this time. Once. Twice.

She appeared at the front door, disheveled as if he'd caught her in the middle of sex.

His thoughts embarrassed him.

"Hi, Hunter." She hobbled toward him on crutches. "I'm so sorry. I fell asleep. And my phone is broken and the groceries are still in the car and . . ."

Her hair was squashed up on one side, pushed backward and, frankly, it was adorable. She'd been asleep; he could tell. She unlocked the gate and he opened it as she stumbled backward, caught the edge of her crutch in a cobblestone and landed, hard, on her bottom, with a *thumph*.

"Oh, I'm sorry. God, are you okay?" Hunter bent down and picked up her crutches, which had scattered sideways. "Let me help you."

He held out his hand and she took it. "Thanks," she said. "I'm a klutz. I know."

"What happened? You were fine an hour ago."

"I fell, twisted my ankle."

"When?"

"Right after seeing you. I just flat out tripped walking to the front door. That's why the groceries are still in the car. I'm sorry." Her voice faded with each sentence, disappearing ink.

"It's okay," he said. "More important, are *you* okay?"

"I think it's just twisted."

Blake looked down now, at her foot, which was blue and swollen. "I think that might be more than twisted."

"It hurts."

He looked at her closely now. She was pale and she was almost crying.

"Let's get you inside. Get some ice on it. I have some pain pills in my briefcase."

"You carry pain pills with you?"

His laugh, the stilted one that came out, sounded false.

"I have a bad leg from an old break and when it flares up . . ."

She smiled halfway. "Sims has an old injury that does that, especially when it rains. His knee." She paused and looked toward the house. "*Had* an old injury."

Sims. It was a nice, solid name for a husband.

A high-pitched squeal broke the conversation and they both turned to see a beat-up Toyota, faded red with rust stains like amoebas on the passenger's-side door.

"Our food," Ella said.

A young boy, looking almost too young to drive, jumped out of the car. "Hi, Mrs. Flynn."

"Hi, there JoJo, how are you?"

"I'm good. Just totally wow, I didn't know you moved back into the house. Totes great."

"Hunter, will you grab the food and take it inside while I pay?" Her voice was sure and steady this time, like she was directing a stage crew.

"Got it," he told her, and took the paper bag.

Ella's voice followed him as he entered the house. "Just put it on the bill. And tell your mom hello from me."

Small towns. Blake could order Chinese food a hundred times and never know the name of the kid who brought it. The front door led into an open hallway flanked to the left by a dining room and to the right by a living room—two wings of equal proportion and depth. The floors, wide planked hardwood, were nicked and battered, but smooth.

Sure, he had imagined her house. It was the way his mind worked— placing people in their environments. But he'd been completely wrong. He'd imagined something more shabby chic, white large-cushioned couches and chairs, pale cream and maybe pink. An image from the movie *Something's Gotta Give.*

He waited in the hall as she came toward him on crutches. She focused on every step, as if this was the first time she'd ever used crutches. He wanted to hug her, draw her close, and carry her into the kitchen.

"Straight ahead," she said. "The kitchen is at the end of the hallway."

They worked their way into a room so filled with light and white and beauty, it was as if someone had purposed each and every thing in the room to make him feel welcome, peaceful. Gray and white, paired with dark wood and thick whitewashed beams overhead made him feel as if the room enfolded him.

"This," he said quietly, "is the most amazing kitchen."

"Oh, thank you." Ella sat on the long banquette that had been built against the back wall. The padded backboard was made of cream linen with a pattern in brass nail heads. She pulled a chair toward her and plopped her hurt foot up onto it. "It took almost two years to get it just right. I think I went a little crazy but . . . voilà." She spread her hands out.

"First things first," he said, and put the Chinese food on the island.

"Where are your Ziploc bags? I am going to get some ice on your foot. Do we need to get you to a doctor?"

"Not now." She ran her finger along the edge of the table. "Let's eat and then we can see if the swelling goes down. I really don't think it's broken or anything. I just landed sideways." She pointed across the room. "Second drawer down on the right for the Ziplocs."

Blake opened the drawer. "Nothing here . . ." He turned back to Ella but she didn't look like Ella, her face was blanched. Her lips were sucked in as if they'd disappeared into her mouth. "You okay?"

"Um, yes. Just open the drawer one down. Or up. Hell . . ."

To make her laugh, because he suddenly felt like that was exactly the thing to do, he opened all the drawers in the kitchen in a wild flurry. It worked, and she laughed out loud, slamming her hand over her mouth. He found them—the baggies and Saran wrap and tin foil—in a drawer on the other side of the kitchen. Blake filled up a large bag with ice, and wrapped it in a towel, which he gently placed on her ankle. He reached into his briefcase and took out one small Percocet and handed it to her. "Let me get you a glass of water," he said, rising again.

She swallowed the pill and then looked up at him. "That's the first real pain pill I've ever taken, except Advil. If I pass out or start babbling, just tuck me in bed. Don't tell a soul."

"Maybe you should have started with half."

She held up a crescent moon of the pill, the other half. "You read my mind. I bit it in half."

"I'd hate to have to remember CPR from my junior high class."

"Don't save people much?"

"Not even myself."

They sat in silence for a few minutes looking at each other, their eyes connected but wavering, looking away and then back, shy.

"I'm already feeling better. The ice and all . . ." She leaned back in the chair and closed her eyes. "Would you mind turning on the music? I have a house system on the back wall right there. Just push it on and pick a playlist. And the wine refrigerator is next to the sink. Please feel free to pour whatever you want."

He ambled across the kitchen to the lighted console built into the wall and pushed the on button. Names of various playlists popped up. "What a variety," he said, scrolling through them with his forefinger on the screen. "Rihanna. Sinatra. Daft Punk."

"Daft Punk?" she said. "What the hell is that?"

"My daughter listens to them, but I'm not entirely sure. This playlist looks like a multiple personality test."

"My sister-in-law has young kids. They must have been playing with it. . . ."

"Well, I'd like to think I could guess which one you want me to pick, but I'd hate to get it wrong."

"You choose," she said. "Go ahead. Your call."

For the first time in as long as he could possibly remember, he hesitated about his choice of music. Not because he didn't know what he liked, but because he cared, he actually cared, what she thought about him. What would she have chosen? What was the best next move for him?

"How about this Elvis Costello list?" he asked.

"Love," she said. "Just love."

"Hey." He looked over his shoulder at her. "Did you move out for a while after his—"

"Yes, I did. Why?"

"Just wondering because the delivery boy sounded surprised you were back in the house."

"It was just a couple of days."

Blake touched the playlist and music blared, reverberating, from the speakers. "Damn."

"Oh, my God," Ella shouted. "The volume is on the right. Turn it down."

Blake punched at the console, not able to turn the volume down fast enough. Elvis Costello sang "Waiting for the End of the World" so loudly that the words were mangled. When it was down to a tolerable level he turned to Ella with laughter. She wasn't laughing.

"I don't know what happened," she said. "The housekeeper must have been messing with it."

"She probably added the Daft Punk playlist," he said. She smiled and he loved it. He would never grow tired of that smile.

The world, or at least the one surrounding her at the moment, had a slight fuzziness to it as if she were covered in bubble wrap. She bounced up against that world, her voice soft and her mind softer. This was nice. Really nice. Except for the fact that Betsy had moved things around in her kitchen. The thought of Betsy touching anything in the house would have made Ella's skin crawl, if it weren't for the painkiller. What would have been a sharp pain under her ribs was more like an annoyance, like a far-off siren.

Elvis Costello sang about "Alison." "Doesn't it always sound like he's singing about Alison? In all his songs, he sings about her," Ella said with her eyes closed and her head back.

"It does. You're right," Hunter said. "You're funny."

He puttered around the kitchen, pulling out plates and distributing the Chinese food in little piles. He drank wine and hummed along to the songs. Once every minute or two, he'd turn to her and say something like "I met him once." Or "Oh, good, you got kung pao, my favorite." Or "Do you eat with chopsticks?" (Yes, she did.)

This was so nice. Ella sat there without a need to say or do anything, to fix anything, to know anything, to impress anything. Hunter moved around the kitchen as if he'd been there before. This gave her a slight thrill to know that Sims would never know they touched the dishes and ate and drank and listened to music. With great relief, she didn't even miss Sims. Missing him had become an ever-present companion like a swarm of bees around her body all the time. For now the bees had gone to the hive.

Hunter came to the table and placed the plates down and then crouched low and looked at her. "Thank goodness you didn't take the whole pill."

"Huh?" She looked to him.

He sat down and then pointed at her plate. "Eat."

She took a bite and then leaned back. "Tell me about your family, Hunter. Something good. Or bad. Or interesting. Or boring."

"It's a big family," he said. "I grew up in a place where the swamp met the land. That sweet aroma that's outside your house? It would never have reached my door."

"That's wisteria," Ella said.

"Wisteria," he said. "Nice."

"Your family," she repeated. "Tell me something about you and how you came to live in California."

He stared off toward the backyard and fence. She saw his eyes close and then open. Everything in slow motion, dragging, lackadaisical. He started talking, but it was as if he was on the phone to someone else, just reciting facts. "I have four brothers and two sisters. I grew up in nowhere Florida. Not near the beach, but out in the Everglades where the heat and the snakes and the alligators are closer than any beach you imagine when you hear 'Florida.' We were cramped in a three-bedroom house with only two bathrooms. I left the day I graduated from the asbestos-filled high school where I was tortured for giving a shit about my grades and the books I read. Movie theaters were my sanctuary, and I snuck away to them as much as I could. Eventually, I went to California to be a writer, for the big dream." He stopped and now looked to Ella, his face awake with his words.

"You always wanted to write historical . . . stuff?" she asked.

"No," he said. "Not always. It's just what I write now. I've tried other things."

"Like?"

"Plays. Novels. Short stories. Stuff like that."

"Did you decide this was what you were best at, so you stuck with it?"

"No. It's just what pays the bills."

"Yup. We do what we do to pay the bills, don't we?" She paused. "So tell me more about your family."

"Well, my dad passed away a couple of years ago. Mom is still in Florida. My siblings are scattered all over the United States and I don't really see them, either. Let's see—there's Gary in Indiana, Charlotte in North Carolina, Savannah in Georgia . . ."

"Ha-ha, real funny. I get it. You don't want to talk about your family."

"They're all still close and they try to get me to join them, but sometimes it feels like I'm not really related to them, you know? That someone made a mistake and put me with the wrong family." He stopped. "Anyway, that's all said and done. I'm fine with it."

"No, who could be fine about not talking to their family that much?" she asked.

"I just am." He leaned forward and rearranged the ice bag on her ankle. "There must be something wrong with me, I know that. I just don't know what it is."

"Don't you love anyone?" she asked as if the words were coming from somewhere else.

He laughed. "God, what a question."

Ella closed her eyes. "Sorry. That came out wrong."

"No, it's okay," he said. "I love my daughter. Endlessly. Otherwise, I'm not sure I really believe in romantic love. I believe in desire, but that always fades."

"Wow," she said. "You're quite the romantic."

"If you only knew," he said.

"Why don't you talk to your mom?" she asked. "I'd give anything to have my mom back."

"It's complicated," he said. "It's not that I don't call her or she me. Some things just can't be unbroken."

"But some things can be mended. I was reading this article the other day about repairing cracked bowls," Ella said, and searched for the name of them, nudging through the clouds inside her mind. "You know, the kind where they mend it with gold. The kitties?" She dropped her face in her hands. "What is the word?"

"Kintsugi," he said.

"Yes!" She clapped her hands together. "How'd you know?"

"Reader," he said, and pointed to himself with a smile.

"Then you know, sometimes when things are mended they are even prettier than what they were before."

"But, what if you've lost entire pieces of that bowl?" he asked.

Ella knew what that was like—losing pieces. "Right," she said. "I get it."

Hunter thrust his glasses up on his nose with a nervous gesture. Before she knew what she'd done, Ella reached forward and took them off his face and put them on her own.

Expecting a change of view, something warped or too close or too far away, she squinted when everything looked the same: his face, the kitchen, the food. "These don't work," she said. She knew it sounded stupid; it wasn't what she meant.

Hunter stood up and took the glasses off her face. "Just for reading, but I keep them on because I'm always reading." He ambled, taking his time, to the sink, where he rinsed his plate and refilled his wineglass.

They chatted a little more, about nothing really, about how the world was too fast, or was it too slow? How he was worried about finishing his book on time, how hot it was here because of, well . . . what they always say when they are from out of town, the humidity.

The music switched and Sinatra sang about the moon. The air felt yielding and silken, like Ella could sink into it. She thought about how quickly her world had changed, like she'd stepped into an underground well she didn't know was right there in her backyard. She glanced at Hunter. "Do you think the world has a hole in it?"

"You mean in the universe, like a black hole?"

"No," she said. "Right under our feet. Like the earth has a hole, and it's always there looming right below the surface of everything we do. We could step into it without knowing it was ever there."

"I don't know, Ella," he said in a soft voice. "Maybe there is?"

"Maybe? Well there is. I didn't know this about the world because no one told me and if they had, would I have listened? Probably not. We don't know until we know. We can be walking along, singing our song, doing our dance and the earth gives way and there we are, falling . . . and there's nothing to grab on to. After that happens once, even once, you will walk carefully, always looking before you take a step, always wanting a sure-footed way to avoid the gaping black hole. I want to tell everyone in the world, 'Be prepared. Grab on to something now.'"

"Wow," Hunter said. "You've given this some thought. So, maybe that's what we're always doing—grabbing on to things in case the ground gives way?"

"You can say 'maybe' because it's never happened to you. You wouldn't say that if it had. If your life had caved in, you would know that anything you grab on to doesn't stop the fall. Life is like this thin bubble. It looks for all the world like something real and round and full. But it's not."

"Your husband's death," Hunter said, taking a breath. "It changed the way you see the world."

"I didn't know before that it was so fragile, so casually meaning-less, so indifferent."

Hunter didn't say a word. What could he say?

"What about love?" he asked. "Don't you want to grab on to that when it comes again?"

"No. If it ever comes again, which I can't imagine, I want it to walk next to me, hold me. I don't want to grab it like a life preserver, like it's the one thing that will keep the ground from giving way. Love can't stop bad things from happening."

"No, it can't. It can't stop the tragedies, but surely it can help."

"And this from a man who doesn't believe in love?"

"In theory I believe it can save you. Sometimes . . ."

"In theory," Ella said, and smiled at him. "Yes, in theory everything is true."

"I love talking to you, Ella. I love the way you see things, like you're looking out a different window than the rest of us schmucks."

"Right now I think I am, and so I should probably shut up."

Hunter stood, but before he went to clean away the dishes, he kissed her on the forehead. "You going to be okay alone?" he asked. "Should I call one of your friends?"

That was it—one innocuous comment and she burst into tears. There was nothing to be done about it really. She just started and couldn't stop, like grief was running amok, as her mom used to say.

One time when Ella was in high school, she'd gone to the huge dictionary in the middle of the library, the one on a podium, and looked up "amok." "A murderous frenzy," she'd read. She'd gone home and told her mom to stop using that word, but she'd never stopped and what Ella would give to hear her say it now.

Hunter leaned over and draped both arms over her shoulders, pulled her toward him. She knocked his glasses off as she put her head on his chest, her arm swimming through the air, weighing too much, to bang into his face. "I'm sorry," she said.

"That's okay," he mumbled into her hair. "They don't work anyway."

Contentment, a feeling so foreign that she had to search for the word, came over her and the tears stopped. Just like they'd been turned off. Quit. And she was laughing, looking up to him and laughing.

She was never sure, even later, who kissed whom. Did she lean forward or did he? Or did they both? She liked to think they both did, simultaneously with the same intent. It was such a long, delicate kiss that in the middle of it she thought of the word "cashmere."

The kissing, it went on so long it moved into the category of making out, something she hadn't done in years. Even when she and Sims made love, he kissed her gently and moved on. Hunter was so warm, moving closer, kissing her but making sure her foot stayed put, that he didn't jostle her around. Then he picked her up, just like she was the pillow off the banquette, so easily. She didn't object or speak, just kept doing exactly what she wanted to do: kiss him.

He carried her to the living room and set her down on the chaise longue, the same one she'd fallen asleep on only a few hours ago. She pulled him toward her, wanting more of what they'd started, whatever that was. She closed her eyes and waited for the weight of him. It didn't happen. Her eyes popped open, a spring-loaded shock to see him standing above her looking down.

"You need to get some sleep." He smiled in that way people do when they are about to disappoint you. "I need to go," he said.

"Go?"

"Yes. I'm not going to take advantage of a Percocet." He tried to laugh, but it came out like a cough.

"Oh . . ."

He walked away, talking over his shoulder. "I'll get your ice, a glass of water, and the other half of the pill." Then he halted in his steps and turned. Ella saw their reflection in the hallway mirror: his back and her looking at him. God, she looked so pitiful and needy. Her hair was a mess, and that mascara she'd put on hours ago formed two raccoon eyes. No wonder he was leaving. Hell, she'd leave herself if she could.

"Do you have anyone to take care of you tomorrow? Get you to the doctor or whatever?" he asked.

"Of course I do. Just leave," she said and sounded . . . again, pitiful.

"Okay." He turned away and she closed her eyes. His footsteps were muffled as he headed down the hallway and into the kitchen. The freezer opened and shut with that hiss she knew. Hunter's sounds were quieter in the house than Sims's, not that he took up less space, but that he was gentler with the space he did fill.

Hunter returned to her side, and she feigned the soft sounds of slow breathing and the slight twitch of early sleep. He fell for it; she knew he did because he just stood there at her side. He placed the ice on her ankle with a dry towel and if she opened her eyes she knew she'd see the pill and a glass of water on the end table.

"Bye, Ella," he whispered. "It was great meeting you. And I'm so sorry."

He might be a scumbag lately, not giving his ex what she wanted, stealing love stories under pretense, sleeping with his assistant, but he would not, could not take advantage of Ella. No way.

The hotel room was stifling. Housekeeping had turned off the air conditioner, probably in some revolt to his sixty-four-degree thermostat, where he'd kept it for days now. He punched the numbers down, pushing harder than was necessary and thought of the console at Ella's house, the Elvis Costello blaring from the speakers. No. He would stop thinking about her now; only the story mattered. He'd obtained everything he needed from her, from her house, from her town.

The computer was open on the bed and he plugged in his cell phone to download the photos onto his computer for safekeeping. Then he started to write on a pad, something he hadn't done in years, and it felt good.

*Notes*: While the two lovers are fighting their love for each other, he is living in a house surrounded by a cloud of wisteria. She is working and living in a terrible tenement house, fending off her feelings for a man she can't have. Often, she wanders past his house, wondering what he is doing inside. And he does the same thing—driving by hers, hoping she will walk out. *Split screen showing them pining for each other and walking past each other's homes.*

Blake put his head back on the pillow and found himself remembering her kiss, still warm on his lips. Then he grabbed the pad and began to write again, furiously.

*Notes*: Their first kiss was when he offered to teach her to sail. She didn't know how, and yet she worked at the marina for him. This will foreshadow how he sacrifices himself for her. He is teaching her to do the one thing that will take his life.

*Added characters*: The quirky mother who says things like "Don't let the truth get in the way of a good story" and constantly mixed up her words to say things like "Let's stay in a shore-far hotel" instead of a four-star hotel. Who uttered clichés that were never meant to be clichés, who wore mascara to bed and wouldn't be seen without it.

*WHAT IS HER HAPPY ENDING?* Does she discover she is pregnant? That he isn't dead? (They never found his body?) Both? No, that was stupid.

*Can't let a little truth get in the way of a good story*, someone once said to him.

Well, this was a good story and he would write it. He already saw it unspooling in his head. Reese Witherspoon would be perfect for the lead.

For the rest of the night, Blake wrote notes, sent e-mails, and packed. By 5:00 A.M. he was out the door and on the way to the airport, exhausted and thrilled. This trip had been successful. It had worked—the harebrained scheme. No damage done.

# *ten*

---

Blake jolted awake as the plane skidded into LAX. Sunlight flared through the streaked window. He squinted to look out at the tarmac. Home.

He pulled out his cell, turned it on, and looked at the rolls of texts and missed calls. *Ashlee. Ashlee.* He closed his eyes because he stupidly realized that the only reason he looked so quickly was because he had hoped that one name would pop on the screen: *Ella.* But she would only text his second, Hunter Adderman phone. And really, why would she text him at all? He made sure, in his own self-destructive way, that she would never speak to him again.

He does this. He breaks things into so many irretrievable pieces that what he wants, what he really wants, he will never get. If he really wanted Ella to call or text or even just say good-bye, he wouldn't have done what he did.

He was the first to stand when the jet bridge bumped into the side of the plane and the cabin door opened with that airtight swoosh. The baggage claim was packed and people were hugging and grabbing bags and "going to get the car." He stood alone and rubbed at his face. He was exhausted but he had something he needed to do before he went home to shower and shake off the weirdness of the last few days.

L.A. traffic wasn't any better on a Sunday and after the freedom of wide open roads, these clogged highways seemed interminable. When he finally arrived at his old house, Marilee's house, his throat was tight and his eyes itched for sleep.

The gate was closed to the driveway of the Tudor-style house where his ex-wife lived. Blake lowered the driver's-side window and pushed the code to get in. Waited. Nothing. He tried again. Nothing.

He pushed the button on the lower left side and a voice came over the speaker. "May I help you?" A male voice, smooth and cultured like he'd been taught how to answer in some intercom-answering class.

"Yes, it's Blake. Open the gate."

"Let me check with Marilee." His voice distant as he hollered into the well-padded house. "Honey?"

Her voice echoed back. "What?" Blake knew that voice, that irritated what-the-hell-are-you-bothering-me-for-when-I'm-working-out voice.

"Blake is at the gate. Can I let him in?"

"Shit. Why not."

A long screeching sound and then the gates swung open. Blake drove around the circular drive to park directly in front of the house. His lawyer and his ex-wife had both warned him not to act as if he owned the house, although he did own the house. So, he'd told them, if he wanted to act like he owned it, he would.

The front door opened and Marilee stood in the doorframe as if she were posing for a photo, which is what she'd done most of her life. "What are you doing here?" she asked in her spandex outfit.

Blake put on his best face, a smiley one. "I'm here to see my daughter."

"You look like hell," Marilee said.

"Thank you, darling. You look radiant yourself." He'd been warned about this—the sarcasm. The petty meanness, which displayed his lesser self (according to his overly therapied ex-wife).

She rolled her eyes, a habit she'd passed on to their daughter. "She's still asleep."

"It's eleven in the morning. Could you please get her up? I want to see her."

"You know I let her sleep in during the weekend. She works so hard during the . . ." Marilee's voice trailed off because Blake walked toward her, and then around her and into the house. His house. The one he'd lived in when he'd believed in love and family. Before he turned into the villain in one of his own movies—the bad guy instead of the love interest.

*One mistake*, that's what he kept telling all his friends (the ones that remained), and his lawyer, and anyone who would listen. All it takes is one mistake. Granted, a big one.

"Amelia," he called up the staircase. Marilee stood behind him and he turned to her. "So, how are you?"

"I was great until you walked in."

"Sounds like a country song."

"God." She rolled her eyes again. "You make everything into a song or a story or some shit. Can't you just see life as life?"

"You know, darling, you've asked me that before. Sorry, I can't answer it yet. I'll still keep trying, though."

"As long as you don't try here."

"Who had the smooth voice on the intercom?" Blake waved his hand toward the kitchen, where he assumed the body that went with the voice resided.

"None of your business."

"Fair enough." He nodded toward the top of the stairs. "Will you please go wake our daughter?"

"Why don't you?"

"Okay. Will do." He took two steps up before Marilee stopped him with her voice, that tight voice of anger.

"And Blake?"

"Yes?"

"She likes to be called Amelie now. You know, like the French movie. She wants you to pronounce her name that way."

"Her name is Amelia."

"I'm just telling you what she wants."

Blake turned away from his ex and walked upstairs. Some of the art had been changed, and he wondered, only briefly, where the old photos had gone: the ones of their wedding and the family reunion, the ones at the fundraiser—he in a tux, she in a gown. These framed photos might be piled up in the attic, spiders crawling over them and wrapping their photo faces in webs, dust, and dead bugs.

"Amelie," he called out as he knocked on her door. He would do anything to repair this brokenness with his daughter. What had Ella said? Just be with her.

*Ella.*

Blake closed his eyes. She needed to be *just* a character in a screenplay.

He knocked again. "Sweetie," he called. "It's Dad. Can I come in?"

"No. I'm sleeping. Go far, far away."

He laughed, and opened the door. Her room was pitch-black, not a hint of light to let her know that she was missing out on the day. The blackout shades were pulled tight and Blake snapped the strings, one by one, letting the California sunlight pour into the room, spill onto her bed, and across her cheeks. Amelia buried her face into the pillow. "Dad!" she said. "Stop. It's Sunday. I can sleep all day."

"Why would you want to miss a day like this?" he asked. "It's almost perfect out. The beach. The pool. Your friends."

"My friends?" she mumbled into her pillow. "They're all asleep and I hate them anyway."

Blake sat on the edge of her bed and touched the back of her head,

144

her soft bleached hair. He loved her natural auburn color, but she insisted on the platinum. "Want to go to Egg-Land for breakfast? You can get a stack of pancakes with whipped cream."

She groaned. "God, I'm not five years old anymore."

"No," he said. "You're not. But that doesn't mean pancakes aren't the bomb-dot-com."

She lifted her face and looked at him through squinty eyes. "Oh, God, Dad. Don't say that ever again. Please. At least not in public."

"Okay, I promise I won't say it if you get up and go out to breakfast with me. Otherwise I will walk around mumbling 'the bomb-dot-com.'"

He swore she laughed but he couldn't be certain.

# eleven

Amber's name sat on Ella's phone screen, a text Ella ignored while she stacked the shoes on the shelves. A bride had tried on every shoe, every single one, to decide *for* her bridesmaids. Ella finished her job, popped another Advil for her throbbing ankle, and looked at the texts—Amber needing, oh, so desperately needing Ella to call her. A two-line string of question marks had ended the last text.

*Spend time with girlfriends.* It was on the list of things to do to get over the ex. But what if that friend disappeared or if that friend's sister slept with the ex? Amber had been her go-to friend since their sophomore year in college. Hardly a day had gone by that they hadn't talked. It really didn't matter about what. It was Amber who talked Ella into moving to Watersend. It was Amber who introduced her to Sims. It was Amber who had been her maid of honor.

How many times had she picked up the phone to call Amber and tell her how she felt? How happy she was. How sad. How the world had caved in. How there was a great hole inside, so great that she felt the wind blow right through her. But that was then and this was now. And now Ella didn't want to answer Amber's texts. She wanted peace.

This melancholy mood—Ella blamed it on her work situation. But she also knew it was because Hunter had returned to California. It wasn't that she missed him. It was more that she missed who she was with him. She liked Ella, the confident woman, even if it was a false self. The new pretend Ella had laughed easily and hadn't worried about how she looked. She spoke her mind, strong and sure, even offering advice. She was a wedding dress designer. She was a widow.

When she was with Hunter, it was almost as if Sims was really dead. She rarely thought of him and his rejection. She basked in Hunter's questions, in his creative way of looking at the world. She found herself almost free, looking at everything with new eyes. Curious. Maybe even hopeful.

Now there was no escape from her bleak life, just this, these shoes, a purple ankle, and divorce proceedings. And the damn sketch—she wanted it back right now.

The boxes were stacked neatly and by category. Ella hobbled, favoring her right foot, to the back of the store and knocked on her boss's door. "Margo," she called out.

Margo came to the door and opened it in her white sundress and white headband. "Hello, Ella. Great job today with the bride. She bought seven pairs of the Princess Grace shoe."

"Thanks. It always feels good to make a strong sale. But I'm here about something else actually. I'd like to have my sketch back. I'd like it for my portfolio." As if she had a portfolio.

"What sketch?"

"The wedding dress. My design. The one you were going to copy."

"Oh, darling. I gave that back to you."

"No, you didn't. When?"

"I put it in your paycheck envelope."

Ella shook her head, dread washing over her like smoke slipping under the door. "No."

"I did."

"Well, please make a copy of the copy."

"Oh, I didn't make a copy after all. I decided it looked too much like one of *my* designs."

"Huh?" A buzzing began in Ella's ears and then moved further, deeper into her skull. It was the same sensation she'd had right before she ran out of the house with the box of baseball cards. If she didn't leave right this second she would do something just as irreversible. As unforgivable. As irrevocable.

"Are you okay?" Margo asked, pursing her too-red lips.

"Do you mind looking on your desk?"

"I know it's not there."

Ella turned away, walking slowly to the exit. The store as unfamiliar as if she'd walked through it for the first time: the white wooden-planked walls with photos of cakes and flowers. Mirrors, lots of mirrors because brides liked to look at themselves. There were pink linen benches and round oak tables full of wedding paraphernalia (garters, bridesmaid T-shirts, cake toppers)—these things were blurring in Ella's sight. The buzzing in her ears grew louder until she burst out the front door and sat on a bench with her hands over her ears. She was such a fool. She gave away her drawing. She gave away her heart. All to people who didn't give a damn about the value of what she offered. The tears wanted to come; she felt them threatening like small pins stuck into the back of her throat.

No more.

She stood up. She would not give away one more piece of herself to undeserving people. Speaking of undeserving, what did Amber want so badly?

She dialed Amber's number.

"Hey!" Amber's happy voice filled the air. Ella pulled the phone away.

"What's up?" Ella asked.

"Well, I think it's what you want to tell me," Amber said.

"Huh?"

"I'm so glad you stopped by. Come in. Come in." Mimi opened the door wide and brushed her hand into the room. "Oh, dear, are you here to complain about Bruiser's bark getting worse? I'm getting all excited about your visit and you might just be here to . . ."

"No. I'm here to say hello. Check in. Take you up on your offer. You know"—she leaned closer to Mimi—"the bourbon *and* pound cake."

"I was hoping so." Mimi shuffled to the kitchen. She never fully lifted her feet off the ground and her slippers were worn thin. Her white hair stuck out on the right side, flattened and then puffy as if she'd slept on it and not moved at all. Maybe she got halfway through doing her hair and forgot to finish.

Ella dropped her purse on the kitchen table. "What can I do to help?" she asked.

"Not a thing. Just sit right there in the big chair and let me serve you. I bet you've been on your feet all day."

Ella obeyed, and dropped into the chair. She flipped off her shoes and wiggled her toes. Her ankle looked better and she twisted it to stretch. Last night, she'd painted her toes a seashell pink and today already they were chipped and ragged. But what else was there to do? Watch *E! TV* and see the "reality" that was not reality at all?

Mimi sang in the kitchen, a song about stars and heavens.

"Sinatra," Ella called out.

"My favorite," Mimi said.

Bruiser rested on a doggie bed so large that it looked like a hand-me-down from a taller brother to a smaller one. Ella felt she needed to whisper so she wouldn't wake Bruiser.

Mimi shuffled to Ella, her feet almost murmuring, and put a piece of cake on the side table. The plate was the same as last time, bone-thin china with a smattering of pink roses in a woven pattern around the edges. "I'm afraid to eat off that gorgeous plate," Ella said as Mimi placed a small silver fork next to it.

"Always use the good stuff," Mimi said. "Why else have it?"

"You acted so sad and broken up about Sims, but I heard that you were with some guy the other night at Sunset. That you were . . ."

"Drunk," Ella filled in the blank.

"Yes," Amber said. "So tell me, who was the guy? Our favorite cabbie, Billy, said he was cute. That he seemed really into you."

"As if he could tell from inside the car at night?" Ella said. "Please."

"Well, I also heard it from a couple of people who were on the roof that night."

"Seriously?"

"Yep. So . . . spill the beans, my friend. What is going on?"

"Nothing really. It was a writer in town gathering information. I drank too much. End of story. Nothing interesting here, Amber. Sorry to disappoint you."

"Well, Sims asked me questions. He heard about it, too. And he said it sounds like the same guy he saw you with at the Patio."

Ella could practically hear the exclamation point on the end of Amber's sentence. "His name is Hunter Adderman and he had a million questions about the town and the history and all that."

"Questions he couldn't go to the historical society for?"

"I asked the same thing. He said he went there."

"Well, Sims wants to know if you have some new guy."

"Sims? What does he care?" The buzzing in Ella's ears stopped then and a hope rose, or something close to hope. Anticipation?

"Well, he must care because he asked me about him."

"Well, you can tell him that what's good for the goose is good for the gander. Or whatever, because that was dumb."

Amber laughed and for a minute it felt like they were friends again. Why was Amber calling about Hunter now? That had happened days ago. But if Sims had just heard about it . . .

"Wait," Ella said. "I thought they were still in Napa."

"They got home yesterday."

Ella calculated. God, she'd missed him by only hours. Had she cleaned the house well enough so he wouldn't notice she'd been there, eating Chinese food? Kissing a man? Sleeping there until her ankle felt better? He must have noticed she took some clothes and dishes.

"Listen, I have to go." Ella looked back toward Swept Away. Her heart still beat erratically with Margo's lie. Of course Margo had the drawing. This, for the first time in a long time, was something that mattered more to Ella than Sims.

"Don't hang up," Amber said.

"I need to work," Ella said. "I'll call you later."

"You're still mad at me."

"No. I'm not." Ella paused as she watched Margo exit the front of the store. This was the time Margo went to get her afternoon coffee: double shot of espresso.

"Please don't be mad," Amber begged again.

"Gotta go, Amber. I promise I'll call you later." Ella hung up and bolted back to the store.

The tiny wedding bell tinkled as she entered the store and ran straight back to Margo's office. Ella yanked on the doorknob but it was locked. She looked frantically around and found Nadine, the assistant. She hollered. "Nadine, where's the key?"

Nadine walked to Ella and held it out. "What do you need?"

"I left my paycheck in there."

"Well, she'll be back in a second. She's just . . ."

"Getting her coffee. I know. But I'm running to the bank now."

Nadine unlocked the office and then looked to Ella. "Are you sure?"

"What a weird question." Ella smiled at Nadine and entered the office under Nadine's watchful eye. She glanced around Margo's workspace, also done in all white and beige. God, did the woman ever get tired of white? If Ella ever married again, she'd get married in red, or maybe black.

"Where is it?" Nadine asked.

"I thought I left it right here on the desk." Ella leafed through a pile of invoices. *Think quick. Where would she put sketches?*

A scrap of paper poked out of a file folder labeled TO DO. There was the water stain on the lower right corner. Silently she thanked herself for the clumsy spill at the café. With a quick move, she grabbed the paper from the file and stuck it into her back pocket. "Got it," she said, and turned to smile at Nadine, although her lips shook with the effort.

"Oh, good."

Nadine locked the door to the office and Ella returned to Sole Mates, slowly, slowly. . . .

It must be a good design if Margo wanted it, lied about it. Ella reached for her phone and before she knew what she'd done, she dialed Hunter's number. By the second ring, she'd hung up. What was she thinking? If she ever called him or talked to him again, she was going to have to tell him the truth. All it would take is one quick Google search to find out she was a liar. Maybe he'd already found out, which was why she hadn't heard a word from him since he left two days ago.

She wanted to tell someone about the design. Not Amber. Not Sims. Not her dad, who was on a trip.

Ella smiled as she thought of Mimi. Yes. Just knock on the door and tell her that she stole back the sketch from her boss, that she'd stood up for herself in a way that she'd never done before.

Small shuffles and a "shush" to the dog came from behind the door. Mimi's left eye and her nose appeared from the crack of the door. The chain, latched from the inside, ran across the space. "Oh, Ella, what a lovely surprise." She shut the door and there was the sound of chain dropping before the door flung open.

"Hi, Mimi." Embarrassment overcame Ella. In her impetuous need to tell someone about her petty crime she hadn't weighed the situation, she hadn't really thought it all through. The thrill of it was already gone.

"Life by Mimi," Ella said.

"If only I'd ever taken my own advice." Mimi's laughter was deep, as if she'd earned it through her years. She returned to the kitchen and then brought back a small antique glass with a pale pink hue to it, a splash of bourbon resting on the bottom.

"Thanks," Ella said, and took it from Mimi's hands. "More Mimi life rules for me, please?" Ella smiled and lifted her shoulders in a pleading expression.

"How about this?" Mimi shuffled toward her seat. "After watching you be someone new with Hunter. Here's one: *Be the person you want to be.*"

"I'm trying; I really am."

"And this isn't my rule, because I really don't have any rules, but please try to remember that we teach people how to treat us. We really do."

"God, I'm a terrible teacher then," Ella said.

Mimi laughed. "Begin again. Always begin again." She sat across from Ella and lifted her own glass. "Well, here's to the end of another day. A good one, I hope."

Ella lifted her glass and took a sip. Warmth spread across her chest and she remembered standing on the rooftop bar with Hunter, slugging back his drink and listening to the story about his invitation to a dead man. She remembered how for a second she almost touched him. "Yes," she said to Mimi. "Here's to a good finish to a good day."

Ella took a bite of the pound cake and groaned out loud. "What is in this? This is the best cake I've ever tasted. It's better than Amber's cookies."

Mimi laughed. "Oh, yes. I've heard of Amber's cookies."

"You have? She's my best friend."

"Really?"

"Well, not really. Not right now. She was, though."

"What happened?"

"The girlfriend, the one sleeping with my husband, that one."

"Your best friend? God, I'm getting you more bourbon."

"No. Not Amber. Her sister, Betsy, a girl I've known for years. The younger sister who grew up and out and then slept with my husband."

"Oh—so, this part I didn't know. Your husband's affair is with your best friend's sister."

"Yes."

"Please run away with that gorgeous Hunter. Please."

Ella tried to smile, but it was useless. "He's already gone, Mimi. He's back home to his life and his work. I was a quick intermission, and—"

"You could never be an intermission."

"Anyway, this cake is amazing. Secret ingredient?"

"I'll never tell." Mimi winked.

"You don't have to tell me. As long as I can eat it, I don't have to make it." Ella took another bite. "So, I have a little story to tell you."

"Please do." Mimi settled back into her chair and took another sip of her bourbon, so Ella did the same.

Her tongue loosened, her breath deeper and warmer. "I stole something."

"Stole?"

"Took it back."

"I'm confused," Mimi said.

"You see, a few days ago my boss, Margo, saw one of my wedding dress design sketches, and she told me she wanted to make a copy of it and then she'd give me back my original. But when I asked for the original back today, she said she gave it to me, that she'd put it into my paycheck envelope, but she hadn't. Then"—Ella leaned forward, placed her hands on her knees in urgency—"and get this, she said she never made a copy because it was so much like one she'd already designed."

"Oh, she's evil," Mimi said with a little hiss behind her words.

Some internal cue brought Bruiser back into the world, and he went off and started barking, still in his sleep almost, only one eye open and a whimpering noise in the back of his throat, and then he was off to sleep again.

Ella exhaled in relief. "Anyway, when she went for her coffee, I had Nadine open the office and I stole it out of a file."

"Good," Mimi said with authority. "Very good. Not that I have any right to be, but I am proud of you."

"Thank you," Ella said. "So am I. And further, it seems Sims is now jealous. He is asking about the guy who was with me the other night when he saw me. Maybe he's having . . . second thoughts."

"Do you want him back?" Mimi asked. "Really?"

Ella answered so quickly that she surprised herself. "Of course I do. He's my husband." Then she paused. "And I love him."

"Yes. Love." Mimi looked off toward the window like the word was etched in the grime on the glass.

"Love," Ella repeated.

"It's one of those things we put in the gap." Mimi stood and shuffled over to Bruiser, leaned down, and scratched between his ears. "A gap filler."

"What?" A soft warm haze settled over Ella: the cake, the bourbon, the stolen sketch. "Love is a gap filler."

"The hole inside. You know, that place we talked about before— the hole in the soul. The place we are *always* trying to fill."

"I don't know what you mean. I just miss my husband. I miss Sims. It's like he has his very own empty space inside me. His. Like it belongs to him." Ella had that feeling again, the helium inside her skull, the heaviness of tears behind her face.

"Well, it's not *just* his space. It's yours. You just put him in there."

"I didn't put him anywhere."

"Listen, Ella, I don't know a lot, but I know this, everything changes and you can't stop it. There is nothing, not one thing in the world, you can do to stop turning another day older every day. But there is a bonus, and it's this: I've learned to live with my gap. I wouldn't trade all those years of looking prettier for what I know how to do now."

"The gap?"

"The hole. You know. The thing no one talks about. The missing piece inside. The spot inside you're always trying to fill. It has its purpose. It makes us search for love, for meaning, for something larger than ourselves. But the emptiness also makes us stuff silly things inside."

Mimi waved her hand through the air. "I know it sounds nutty. I bet a smarter person could explain it better. A psychology book perhaps. I just call it a gap. Every time you try to put something in there, it just falls out the other open side. You can't keep anything. Nothing stays. It's all temporary. And when you realize that"—she took a breath as if she had been running while talking—"it's all just a little bit better. You can enjoy everything in a different way."

"Stop with this, Mimi. Seriously. I didn't put Sims anywhere. I fell in love with him. I do love him. It's not an empty space. Or a gap. Or anything of the sort. Stop. Don't you believe in love at all? Falling in love?" Ella's frustration, the pent-up bird inside her chest, fluttered.

"Of course I do. I'm sorry, dear. I'm not trying to be flippant."

"Well, you don't know him or me really. I shouldn't have even told you so much. I don't know why I did." Ella dropped her face into her hands. "He's not a gap filler." Tears filled her eyes and she looked up. "He's my husband."

"Well, it's not something to be taken biblically or anything. It's just my idea of how we work and how I can be happy and still have this gaping hole inside. It's always been there. It always will be."

"Really? Always? That's ridiculous."

"Yes. Always. It's an ache where you want more and more. Nothing is ever enough."

"Oh." Ella wanted to stay mad, but something in what Mimi said made sense. She couldn't find truth's edges, the shape of it all yet.

"Well, I'm not trying to fill some hole with Sims. I just miss him terribly. Or the Sims that he used to be. That's all."

"I know." Mimi stared off. "Love is always the exception."

Ella smiled now. "Maybe it's just an idea anyway. That's what Hunter said, too. A theory. An idea. Not much more."

"No," Mimi said. "It's real. A real thing that changes everything."

Ella leaned back in her chair and looked up at the water stain on Mimi's ceiling. It looked like a butterfly. "I bet that's from my sink," she said. "It won't stop dripping. I've called the landlord at least ten times."

Mimi looked up now also. "Oh, I didn't even see that. Funny."

"What?"

"It looks like a butterfly."

This hit Ella with such relevance, how they both saw the same thing in a stupid water stain. She was awash with the feeling she labeled love and she went to Mimi. She bent over the small woman in the slipper chair and hugged her so hard that Mimi laughed and said, "Ow. You're gonna crush these old bones."

Bruiser barked louder now, maybe afraid Ella was hurting his master. So Mimi rose with a sigh of resignation and popped a doggie Xanax in his mouth, hidden inside a treat.

"If only I had one of those every time I felt like coming undone," Ella said.

"Oh, you don't want to start that, honey. Been there, done that, as the young ones say."

"Really?" Ella sat back down, lifted her bourbon, and took another chest-warming sip.

"Yes. But that was a long, long time ago." Mimi sat down in her chair and closed her eyes, and just like that there was the slight sound of her snoring, a breathing in and out that signaled sleep.

Ella was envious of the way Mimi fell asleep so quickly. Since the breakup, it took Ella hours to find sleep, even when she was exhausted. Her mind, it wouldn't stop, it wouldn't be quiet. She'd never, until recently, thought of her brain as something separate, but now she did.

She tried the mantras, the mindfulness of focusing on her breathing, the counting, all of it. But still she never found sleep the way that Mimi just had.

Ella rose quietly and picked up the dishes, gently placing them in the sink. She wrapped the extra cake slices in tin foil and when she placed them in the tiny refrigerator she saw it: Sara Lee All Butter Pound Cake in the aluminum container, the saw-toothed tin-foil edges folded down to keep the cake fresh. Ella held in her laughter and glanced over at Mimi. She was flooded with love and a very particular kind of happiness that felt like home.

During the one-floor climb to her apartment, it hit Ella how glad she was that Hunter hadn't answered the phone. She wanted to tell him about the sketch, but he thought she *was* the designer. He believed it was what she did all the time. Why would she need to steal a sketch back? Lying was confusing. She didn't know how Sims did it for so damn long. It got tangled with the truth, and then you stumbled over every word.

Her apartment seemed dingier than normal. Even with the extra clothes and towels, the dishes and bakeware she'd taken from home, the space seemed just as empty. But she was happy she'd stopped at Mimi's. Happy she ate pound cake for dinner, and happy that Sims was jealous. She dug her sketch out of the satchel and put it on the table with the rest of her drawings.

That's when she saw four missed calls from "hubby." She picked up the phone and took a long breath before listening to the voice mails.

"I see you've been to the house and you took a few things."

Next one: "Did you take the Le Creuset? Low blow, Ella. You know my mom gave that to me."

Next one: "Please call me."

Next one: "Are you okay?"

Ella turned the window air conditioner fan to high, hoping for some cool air to wash into the room. Even these messages couldn't dampen her mood. Call the cops, Sims. Go ahead. And when you do, tell them I stole from my boss also.

She spread her dress designs across the coffee table. She'd drawn at least twenty dresses by now, a *collection* it would be called if she were a real designer. What could she do with the collection, if anything? She flipped on the TV and walked the four or five steps to her bed. There was no bedroom here; it was all one room.

She slipped on her cotton tank and pajama bottoms, fresh ones she'd taken from the house. God, she was so glad to have them back. Little things. Then she returned Sims's call while *E! TV* muttered something about the latest celebrity sightings, about the Kardashians and their new season. Ella stared at the screen, punching the channel button on the remote, which wasn't working. The phone rang five times and Ella decided she wouldn't leave a message. She reached for the end button when Sims answered.

"Hey, Ella," he said.

"Hi, Sims." Her voice was cold, flat.

"What's up?" he asked as if she had called from work on a regular day and he wanted to know what she needed, if they'd eat in or go out.

"Nothing is up. I'm calling you back. You called four times."

"Well, first, I wanted to let you know that I know you were in the house, that you took some things. And I'm not going to report it."

"How generous of you," Ella said.

"You know I could."

"Yes, I do."

"But I'm curious. How did you get in?"

"The alarm wasn't on."

"Shit," he said.

Ella closed her eyes, fighting her need to ask for something from him, something he couldn't give: a promise, a word of encouragement, some love.

Ambient noise filled the line, birds maybe, clattering of dishes, she couldn't tell. He spoke again. "Did you bring that guy into my house?"

"What guy?"

"The guy I saw you with . . . the guy . . ."

"I don't know who you're talking about."

"Come on, Ella. I even know his name. Hunter Addison."

"Adderman," she said.

"Okay. I get it. It's none of my business what you do. But if you brought him into my house—" He dropped the end of the sentence, left it unknown.

A shift occurred, a little bit of his need came across, and she didn't appease it. At that moment, he could say, "Come back to me now. I've made a mistake. I love only you." And she would, but he didn't need to know this. Not even for a minute.

"You hate me," he said.

Why did everyone keep asking her this? She placed her hand over her belly and closed her eyes. He needed something and he wanted something and she fought not to give it to him: assurance that she still loved him and would be there to accept him the way it was. No.

"I don't hate," she answered.

"I know," he said. "It's one of the things I love the most about you."

"I have to go," she said. "I'm really busy."

"Okay."

"You were right before, Sims. It's time to get this over with. I can't live this way, in this apartment . . . let's just get it over with."

"Over with?"

"Yes," she said. "Over with. It's obvious this is what you want, so why wait? Okay?"

"Okay," he said. "I'll call my lawyer first thing in the morning."

Ella hung up without saying another word. With full force, she lifted her hand and swiped across the table, scattering her sketches through the room, watching them flutter and then fall to the floor.

Sims had gone and ruined one of the first good nights she'd had in a long, long time. She'd been happy, hadn't she?

Blake was back to work and it felt good. His office was in perfect order. He had Ashlee to thank for that. His computer open, hot coffee on the desk, the notes he'd dictated to her through the past few weeks sitting in a pile, labeled. He'd printed his own notes and within days he would have a story. It felt good. No, better than good. It felt like a victory in a war he'd been losing.

Ashlee was waiting for him when he came home, in his bedroom, in his bed. He'd just finished eating that pancake breakfast with his daughter and after the long flight, he just wanted some sleep. But when he saw Ashlee waiting for him like that, he wanted something else altogether. Afterward, tangled in bed almost asleep, she said, "I missed you so much and you seemed so happy over there. I'm glad you're home."

"Me, too," he lied.

Ashlee was gone when he awoke, but his desk and papers were ready for work. She left a note. *Went for breakfast, back soon. Xoxoxo.*

Coffee was enough for him. Work was satisfying enough. Finally. He filled in the blanks. *Setting. Off-screen sounds. Names. Characters. Plot.* He had it all, all except the ending, but that always came with the writing. He'd find it before he hit the last page.

He never questioned the creative process. As long as he was willing to go through the times of abandonment and loneliness, as long as he pushed through . . . God, it felt good. He longed to call Ella and tell her. "It's back."

He stopped, his fingers poised over the keyboard. Hell. He couldn't tell her. She had no idea what he really did or why. He was such an ass. Why hadn't he just told her? This want for her would pass. He'd stop thinking about her soon. Except he was writing about her. That didn't help.

Ashlee had downloaded the pictures onto the computer. He went through them slowly, typing notes about the setting into the blank spots of the screenplay. Wisteria. Iron gate. Steps with moss. An antique bench and bird feeder. He clicked again and there was a picture of Ella, standing at the end of the dock. She held up her hand to wave and he'd captured her smile, her hair in the wind. He'd caught her in the net of this photo and he stared at it for too long, an ache in his chest he'd once known as the feeling of missing someone.

He couldn't miss her. He didn't even know her. And she definitely didn't know him. Not one other woman on his months-long journey had a name. They were faces and stories, nothing more. Not Ella. She was a name, a face, and a life. He picked up his phone and glanced at it as if she might be there, ready to talk, and that's when he saw it: Ella's missed call on his extra phone.

Should he call her back? It was too late there. Or was it? In a quick flash, he pushed the call back button and the phone rang. He imagined her in the bed in that cottage, asleep. Or maybe watching TV in the chaise longue where he'd left her without saying good-bye.

Blake sat the phone on the desk and put the phone on speaker. He'd leave a message. "Hello?" her voice came over the line, full of fog and distance.

"Ella?" he asked.

"Yes."

"It's Hunter. I just thought . . . I saw you called. Are you okay?"

"Yes. Of course. Yes."

"Did I wake you?"

"It's okay. How was your trip home?" she asked.

"Good. I saw my daughter. Took her to breakfast and didn't try to talk about anything serious. Just hung out with her." He felt like a teenager, a kid who'd never called a girl on the phone.

"Good move."

"Thanks for that advice," he said.

"Mmm . . ."

"I'm sorry. I'll let you go back to sleep," he said.

"Do you think we all have a gap?" she asked.

"I have no idea what you mean."

"I didn't think so."

"What do you mean?" Then she was quiet so long he thought she might have fallen back asleep. "Ella?" he asked.

"Do you think everyone all the time feels like they're missing something?"

"Maybe. I don't know."

"Me neither," she said.

"Like Leonard Cohen sings, 'There is a crack in everything,'" he said.

"I know, I know. . . . 'That's how the light gets in.' Nice. Anyway . . . I was just talking to Mimi and . . . forget it."

"Well, I just wanted to say hello and that I'm home safely."

"Good night then," she said, and she was gone. Her name disappeared from the screen.

Blake started to type again, moving quickly, a runaway train of words and dialogue.


EMILY

Do you think there's a crack in everything?


HUSBAND

(struggling to keep his feet in storm)

There's going to be a crack in this boat soon if I can't keep
her steady! And yes! There is a crack in everything and
everyone. How else can love find its way in?


He was almost finished with the section when Ashlee returned with food. "Hi, sweetie bug," she said, and kissed the back of his neck.

"Sweetie bug? It sounds like you're talking to a two-year-old."

She turned his swivel chair around and then placed the food on the side of the desk. Her pout was ridiculous, meant for a child. "Well, what do you want me to call you?" she asked.

"Hunter," he said.

"Huh?"

"I'm kidding. No nicknames, okay? Just saying my name will do nicely."

"Blake," she said, and leaned down, kissing his forehead and then his eyelids. She moved closer and straddled him before she sat down and kissed his mouth. "Blake," she said again. "I missed you."

"I missed you, too, Ashlee." He returned her kiss but felt nothing. A mouth. Lips. A tongue. His mind was on the work behind him. He placed his hands on her hips, which were moving in small circles on his lap, and lifted her up. "Not now."

A whine came from her, like the squirrel that had once been caught under his living room couch. "Whyyyy not?" She stood above him and looked down, ran her fingers through his hair.

"Work, baby, work. I'm on a roll," he said.

"Okay. I get it. When the muse shows up, you have to dance."

"Something like that." He took her hand and kissed the inside of her palm. "Thank you so much for getting everything organized for me. It's the reason I'm able to work so quickly. Thank you. Thank you. Thank you."

"Okay, I'll let you work, but later, you're all mine."

"You acted so sad and broken up about Sims, but I heard that you were with some guy the other night at Sunset. That you were . . ."

"Drunk," Ella filled in the blank.

"Yes," Amber said. "So tell me, who was the guy? Our favorite cabbie, Billy, said he was cute. That he seemed really into you."

"As if he could tell from inside the car at night?" Ella said. "Please."

"Well, I also heard it from a couple of people who were on the roof that night."

"Seriously?"

"Yep. So . . . spill the beans, my friend. What is going on?"

"Nothing really. It was a writer in town gathering information. I drank too much. End of story. Nothing interesting here, Amber. Sorry to disappoint you."

"Well, Sims asked me questions. He heard about it, too. And he said it sounds like the same guy he saw you with at the Patio."

Ella could practically hear the exclamation point on the end of Amber's sentence. "His name is Hunter Adderman and he had a million questions about the town and the history and all that."

"Questions he couldn't go to the historical society for?"

"I asked the same thing. He said he went there."

"Well, Sims wants to know if you have some new guy."

"Sims? What does he care?" The buzzing in Ella's ears stopped then and a hope rose, or something close to hope. Anticipation?

"Well, he must care because he asked me about him."

"Well, you can tell him that what's good for the goose is good for the gander. Or whatever, because that was dumb."

Amber laughed and for a minute it felt like they were friends again. Why was Amber calling about Hunter now? That had happened days ago. But if Sims had just heard about it . . .

"Wait," Ella said. "I thought they were still in Napa."

"They got home yesterday."

Ella calculated. God, she'd missed him by only hours. Had she cleaned the house well enough so he wouldn't notice she'd been there, eating Chinese food? Kissing a man? Sleeping there until her ankle felt better? He must have noticed she took some clothes and dishes.

"Listen, I have to go." Ella looked back toward Swept Away. Her heart still beat erratically with Margo's lie. Of course Margo had the drawing. This, for the first time in a long time, was something that mattered more to Ella than Sims.

"Don't hang up," Amber said.

"I need to work," Ella said. "I'll call you later."

"You're still mad at me."

"No. I'm not." Ella paused as she watched Margo exit the front of the store. This was the time Margo went to get her afternoon coffee: double shot of espresso.

"Please don't be mad," Amber begged again.

"Gotta go, Amber. I promise I'll call you later." Ella hung up and bolted back to the store.

The tiny wedding bell tinkled as she entered the store and ran straight back to Margo's office. Ella yanked on the doorknob but it was locked. She looked frantically around and found Nadine, the assistant. She hollered. "Nadine, where's the key?"

Nadine walked to Ella and held it out. "What do you need?"

"I left my paycheck in there."

"Well, she'll be back in a second. She's just . . ."

"Getting her coffee. I know. But I'm running to the bank now."

Nadine unlocked the office and then looked to Ella. "Are you sure?"

"What a weird question." Ella smiled at Nadine and entered the office under Nadine's watchful eye. She glanced around Margo's workspace, also done in all white and beige. God, did the woman ever get tired of white? If Ella ever married again, she'd get married in red, or maybe black.

"Where is it?" Nadine asked.

"I thought I left it right here on the desk." Ella leafed through a pile of invoices. *Think quick. Where would she put sketches?*

A scrap of paper poked out of a file folder labeled TO DO. There was the water stain on the lower right corner. Silently she thanked herself for the clumsy spill at the café. With a quick move, she grabbed the paper from the file and stuck it into her back pocket. "Got it," she said, and turned to smile at Nadine, although her lips shook with the effort.

"Oh, good."

Nadine locked the door to the office and Ella returned to Sole Mates, slowly, slowly. . . .

It must be a good design if Margo wanted it, lied about it. Ella reached for her phone and before she knew what she'd done, she dialed Hunter's number. By the second ring, she'd hung up. What was she thinking? If she ever called him or talked to him again, she was going to have to tell him the truth. All it would take is one quick Google search to find out she was a liar. Maybe he'd already found out, which was why she hadn't heard a word from him since he left two days ago.

She wanted to tell someone about the design. Not Amber. Not Sims. Not her dad, who was on a trip.

Ella smiled as she thought of Mimi. Yes. Just knock on the door and tell her that she stole back the sketch from her boss, that she'd stood up for herself in a way that she'd never done before.

Small shuffles and a "shush" to the dog came from behind the door. Mimi's left eye and her nose appeared from the crack of the door. The chain, latched from the inside, ran across the space. "Oh, Ella, what a lovely surprise." She shut the door and there was the sound of chain dropping before the door flung open.

"Hi, Mimi." Embarrassment overcame Ella. In her impetuous need to tell someone about her petty crime she hadn't weighed the situation, she hadn't really thought it all through. The thrill of it was already gone.

"I'm so glad you stopped by. Come in. Come in." Mimi opened the door wide and brushed her hand into the room. "Oh, dear, are you here to complain about Bruiser's bark getting worse? I'm getting all excited about your visit and you might just be here to . . ."

"No. I'm here to say hello. Check in. Take you up on your offer. You know"—she leaned closer to Mimi—"the bourbon *and* pound cake."

"I was hoping so." Mimi shuffled to the kitchen. She never fully lifted her feet off the ground and her slippers were worn thin. Her white hair stuck out on the right side, flattened and then puffy as if she'd slept on it and not moved at all. Maybe she got halfway through doing her hair and forgot to finish.

Ella dropped her purse on the kitchen table. "What can I do to help?" she asked.

"Not a thing. Just sit right there in the big chair and let me serve you. I bet you've been on your feet all day."

Ella obeyed, and dropped into the chair. She flipped off her shoes and wiggled her toes. Her ankle looked better and she twisted it to stretch. Last night, she'd painted her toes a seashell pink and today already they were chipped and ragged. But what else was there to do? Watch *E! TV* and see the "reality" that was not reality at all?

Mimi sang in the kitchen, a song about stars and heavens.

"Sinatra," Ella called out.

"My favorite," Mimi said.

Bruiser rested on a doggie bed so large that it looked like a hand-me-down from a taller brother to a smaller one. Ella felt she needed to whisper so she wouldn't wake Bruiser.

Mimi shuffled to Ella, her feet almost murmuring, and put a piece of cake on the side table. The plate was the same as last time, bone-thin china with a smattering of pink roses in a woven pattern around the edges. "I'm afraid to eat off that gorgeous plate," Ella said as Mimi placed a small silver fork next to it.

"Always use the good stuff," Mimi said. "Why else have it?"

"Life by Mimi," Ella said.

"If only I'd ever taken my own advice." Mimi's laughter was deep, as if she'd earned it through her years. She returned to the kitchen and then brought back a small antique glass with a pale pink hue to it, a splash of bourbon resting on the bottom.

"Thanks," Ella said, and took it from Mimi's hands. "More Mimi life rules for me, please?" Ella smiled and lifted her shoulders in a pleading expression.

"How about this?" Mimi shuffled toward her seat. "After watching you be someone new with Hunter. Here's one: *Be the person you want to be.*"

"I'm trying; I really am."

"And this isn't my rule, because I really don't have any rules, but please try to remember that we teach people how to treat us. We really do."

"God, I'm a terrible teacher then," Ella said.

Mimi laughed. "Begin again. Always begin again." She sat across from Ella and lifted her own glass. "Well, here's to the end of another day. A good one, I hope."

Ella lifted her glass and took a sip. Warmth spread across her chest and she remembered standing on the rooftop bar with Hunter, slugging back his drink and listening to the story about his invitation to a dead man. She remembered how for a second she almost touched him. "Yes," she said to Mimi. "Here's to a good finish to a good day."

Ella took a bite of the pound cake and groaned out loud. "What is in this? This is the best cake I've ever tasted. It's better than Amber's cookies."

Mimi laughed. "Oh, yes. I've heard of Amber's cookies."

"You have? She's my best friend."

"Really?"

"Well, not really. Not right now. She was, though."

"What happened?"

"The girlfriend, the one sleeping with my husband, that one."

"Your best friend? God, I'm getting you more bourbon."

"No. Not Amber. Her sister, Betsy, a girl I've known for years. The younger sister who grew up and out and then slept with my husband."

"Oh—so, this part I didn't know. Your husband's affair is with your best friend's sister."

"Yes."

"Please run away with that gorgeous Hunter. Please."

Ella tried to smile, but it was useless. "He's already gone, Mimi. He's back home to his life and his work. I was a quick intermission, and—"

"You could never be an intermission."

"Anyway, this cake is amazing. Secret ingredient?"

"I'll never tell." Mimi winked.

"You don't have to tell me. As long as I can eat it, I don't have to make it." Ella took another bite. "So, I have a little story to tell you."

"Please do." Mimi settled back into her chair and took another sip of her bourbon, so Ella did the same.

Her tongue loosened, her breath deeper and warmer. "I stole something."

"Stole?"

"Took it back."

"I'm confused," Mimi said.

"You see, a few days ago my boss, Margo, saw one of my wedding dress design sketches, and she told me she wanted to make a copy of it and then she'd give me back my original. But when I asked for the original back today, she said she gave it to me, that she'd put it into my paycheck envelope, but she hadn't. Then"—Ella leaned forward, placed her hands on her knees in urgency—"and get this, she said she never made a copy because it was so much like one she'd already designed."

"Oh, she's evil," Mimi said with a little hiss behind her words.

Some internal cue brought Bruiser back into the world, and he went off and started barking, still in his sleep almost, only one eye open and a whimpering noise in the back of his throat, and then he was off to sleep again.

Ella exhaled in relief. "Anyway, when she went for her coffee, I had Nadine open the office and I stole it out of a file."

"Good," Mimi said with authority. "Very good. Not that I have any right to be, but I am proud of you."

"Thank you," Ella said. "So am I. And further, it seems Sims is now jealous. He is asking about the guy who was with me the other night when he saw me. Maybe he's having . . . second thoughts."

"Do you want him back?" Mimi asked. "Really?"

Ella answered so quickly that she surprised herself. "Of course I do. He's my husband." Then she paused. "And I love him."

"Yes. Love." Mimi looked off toward the window like the word was etched in the grime on the glass.

"Love," Ella repeated.

"It's one of those things we put in the gap." Mimi stood and shuffled over to Bruiser, leaned down, and scratched between his ears. "A gap filler."

"What?" A soft warm haze settled over Ella: the cake, the bourbon, the stolen sketch. "Love is a gap filler."

"The hole inside. You know, that place we talked about before— the hole in the soul. The place we are *always* trying to fill."

"I don't know what you mean. I just miss my husband. I miss Sims. It's like he has his very own empty space inside me. His. Like it belongs to him." Ella had that feeling again, the helium inside her skull, the heaviness of tears behind her face.

"Well, it's not *just* his space. It's yours. You just put him in there."

"I didn't put him anywhere."

"Listen, Ella, I don't know a lot, but I know this, everything changes and you can't stop it. There is nothing, not one thing in the world, you can do to stop turning another day older every day. But there is a bonus, and it's this: I've learned to live with my gap. I wouldn't trade all those years of looking prettier for what I know how to do now."

"The gap?"

"The hole. You know. The thing no one talks about. The missing piece inside. The spot inside you're always trying to fill. It has its purpose. It makes us search for love, for meaning, for something larger than ourselves. But the emptiness also makes us stuff silly things inside."

Mimi waved her hand through the air. "I know it sounds nutty. I bet a smarter person could explain it better. A psychology book perhaps. I just call it a gap. Every time you try to put something in there, it just falls out the other open side. You can't keep anything. Nothing stays. It's all temporary. And when you realize that"—she took a breath as if she had been running while talking—"it's all just a little bit better. You can enjoy everything in a different way."

"Stop with this, Mimi. Seriously. I didn't put Sims anywhere. I fell in love with him. I do love him. It's not an empty space. Or a gap. Or anything of the sort. Stop. Don't you believe in love at all? Falling in love?" Ella's frustration, the pent-up bird inside her chest, fluttered.

"Of course I do. I'm sorry, dear. I'm not trying to be flippant."

"Well, you don't know him or me really. I shouldn't have even told you so much. I don't know why I did." Ella dropped her face into her hands. "He's not a gap filler." Tears filled her eyes and she looked up. "He's my husband."

"Well, it's not something to be taken biblically or anything. It's just my idea of how we work and how I can be happy and still have this gaping hole inside. It's always been there. It always will be."

"Really? Always? That's ridiculous."

"Yes. Always. It's an ache where you want more and more. Nothing is ever enough."

"Oh." Ella wanted to stay mad, but something in what Mimi said made sense. She couldn't find truth's edges, the shape of it all yet.

"Well, I'm not trying to fill some hole with Sims. I just miss him terribly. Or the Sims that he used to be. That's all."

"I know." Mimi stared off. "Love is always the exception."

Ella smiled now. "Maybe it's just an idea anyway. That's what Hunter said, too. A theory. An idea. Not much more."

"No," Mimi said. "It's real. A real thing that changes everything."

Ella leaned back in her chair and looked up at the water stain on Mimi's ceiling. It looked like a butterfly. "I bet that's from my sink," she said. "It won't stop dripping. I've called the landlord at least ten times."

Mimi looked up now also. "Oh, I didn't even see that. Funny."

"What?"

"It looks like a butterfly."

This hit Ella with such relevance, how they both saw the same thing in a stupid water stain. She was awash with the feeling she labeled love and she went to Mimi. She bent over the small woman in the slipper chair and hugged her so hard that Mimi laughed and said, "Ow. You're gonna crush these old bones."

Bruiser barked louder now, maybe afraid Ella was hurting his master. So Mimi rose with a sigh of resignation and popped a doggie Xanax in his mouth, hidden inside a treat.

"If only I had one of those every time I felt like coming undone," Ella said.

"Oh, you don't want to start that, honey. Been there, done that, as the young ones say."

"Really?" Ella sat back down, lifted her bourbon, and took another chest-warming sip.

"Yes. But that was a long, long time ago." Mimi sat down in her chair and closed her eyes, and just like that there was the slight sound of her snoring, a breathing in and out that signaled sleep.

Ella was envious of the way Mimi fell asleep so quickly. Since the breakup, it took Ella hours to find sleep, even when she was exhausted. Her mind, it wouldn't stop, it wouldn't be quiet. She'd never, until recently, thought of her brain as something separate, but now she did.

She tried the mantras, the mindfulness of focusing on her breathing, the counting, all of it. But still she never found sleep the way that Mimi just had.

Ella rose quietly and picked up the dishes, gently placing them in the sink. She wrapped the extra cake slices in tin foil and when she placed them in the tiny refrigerator she saw it: Sara Lee All Butter Pound Cake in the aluminum container, the saw-toothed tin-foil edges folded down to keep the cake fresh. Ella held in her laughter and glanced over at Mimi. She was flooded with love and a very particular kind of happiness that felt like home.

During the one-floor climb to her apartment, it hit Ella how glad she was that Hunter hadn't answered the phone. She wanted to tell him about the sketch, but he thought she *was* the designer. He believed it was what she did all the time. Why would she need to steal a sketch back? Lying was confusing. She didn't know how Sims did it for so damn long. It got tangled with the truth, and then you stumbled over every word.

Her apartment seemed dingier than normal. Even with the extra clothes and towels, the dishes and bakeware she'd taken from home, the space seemed just as empty. But she was happy she'd stopped at Mimi's. Happy she ate pound cake for dinner, and happy that Sims was jealous. She dug her sketch out of the satchel and put it on the table with the rest of her drawings.

That's when she saw four missed calls from "hubby." She picked up the phone and took a long breath before listening to the voice mails.

"I see you've been to the house and you took a few things."

Next one: "Did you take the Le Creuset? Low blow, Ella. You know my mom gave that to me."

Next one: "Please call me."

Next one: "Are you okay?"

Ella turned the window air conditioner fan to high, hoping for some cool air to wash into the room. Even these messages couldn't dampen her mood. Call the cops, Sims. Go ahead. And when you do, tell them I stole from my boss also.

She spread her dress designs across the coffee table. She'd drawn at least twenty dresses by now, a *collection* it would be called if she were a real designer. What could she do with the collection, if anything? She flipped on the TV and walked the four or five steps to her bed. There was no bedroom here; it was all one room.

She slipped on her cotton tank and pajama bottoms, fresh ones she'd taken from the house. God, she was so glad to have them back. Little things. Then she returned Sims's call while *E! TV* muttered something about the latest celebrity sightings, about the Kardashians and their new season. Ella stared at the screen, punching the channel button on the remote, which wasn't working. The phone rang five times and Ella decided she wouldn't leave a message. She reached for the end button when Sims answered.

"Hey, Ella," he said.

"Hi, Sims." Her voice was cold, flat.

"What's up?" he asked as if she had called from work on a regular day and he wanted to know what she needed, if they'd eat in or go out.

"Nothing is up. I'm calling you back. You called four times."

"Well, first, I wanted to let you know that I know you were in the house, that you took some things. And I'm not going to report it."

"How generous of you," Ella said.

"You know I could."

"Yes, I do."

"But I'm curious. How did you get in?"

"The alarm wasn't on."

"Shit," he said.

Ella closed her eyes, fighting her need to ask for something from him, something he couldn't give: a promise, a word of encouragement, some love.

Ambient noise filled the line, birds maybe, clattering of dishes, she couldn't tell. He spoke again. "Did you bring that guy into my house?"

"What guy?"

"The guy I saw you with . . . the guy . . ."

"I don't know who you're talking about."

"Come on, Ella. I even know his name. Hunter Addison."

"Adderman," she said.

"Okay. I get it. It's none of my business what you do. But if you brought him into my house—" He dropped the end of the sentence, left it unknown.

A shift occurred, a little bit of his need came across, and she didn't appease it. At that moment, he could say, "Come back to me now. I've made a mistake. I love only you." And she would, but he didn't need to know this. Not even for a minute.

"You hate me," he said.

Why did everyone keep asking her this? She placed her hand over her belly and closed her eyes. He needed something and he wanted something and she fought not to give it to him: assurance that she still loved him and would be there to accept him the way it was. No.

"I don't hate," she answered.

"I know," he said. "It's one of the things I love the most about you."

"I have to go," she said. "I'm really busy."

"Okay."

"You were right before, Sims. It's time to get this over with. I can't live this way, in this apartment . . . let's just get it over with."

"Over with?"

"Yes," she said. "Over with. It's obvious this is what you want, so why wait? Okay?"

"Okay," he said. "I'll call my lawyer first thing in the morning."

Ella hung up without saying another word. With full force, she lifted her hand and swiped across the table, scattering her sketches through the room, watching them flutter and then fall to the floor.

Sims had gone and ruined one of the first good nights she'd had in a long, long time. She'd been happy, hadn't she?

Blake was back to work and it felt good. His office was in perfect order. He had Ashlee to thank for that. His computer open, hot coffee on the desk, the notes he'd dictated to her through the past few weeks sitting in a pile, labeled. He'd printed his own notes and within days he would have a story. It felt good. No, better than good. It felt like a victory in a war he'd been losing.

Ashlee was waiting for him when he came home, in his bedroom, in his bed. He'd just finished eating that pancake breakfast with his daughter and after the long flight, he just wanted some sleep. But when he saw Ashlee waiting for him like that, he wanted something else altogether. Afterward, tangled in bed almost asleep, she said, "I missed you so much and you seemed so happy over there. I'm glad you're home."

"Me, too," he lied.

Ashlee was gone when he awoke, but his desk and papers were ready for work. She left a note. *Went for breakfast, back soon. Xoxoxo.*

Coffee was enough for him. Work was satisfying enough. Finally. He filled in the blanks. *Setting. Off-screen sounds. Names. Characters. Plot.* He had it all, all except the ending, but that always came with the writing. He'd find it before he hit the last page.

He never questioned the creative process. As long as he was willing to go through the times of abandonment and loneliness, as long as he pushed through . . . God, it felt good. He longed to call Ella and tell her. "It's back."

He stopped, his fingers poised over the keyboard. Hell. He couldn't tell her. She had no idea what he really did or why. He was such an ass. Why hadn't he just told her? This want for her would pass. He'd stop thinking about her soon. Except he was writing about her. That didn't help.

Ashlee had downloaded the pictures onto the computer. He went through them slowly, typing notes about the setting into the blank spots of the screenplay. Wisteria. Iron gate. Steps with moss. An antique bench and bird feeder. He clicked again and there was a picture of Ella, standing at the end of the dock. She held up her hand to wave and he'd captured her smile, her hair in the wind. He'd caught her in the net of this photo and he stared at it for too long, an ache in his chest he'd once known as the feeling of missing someone.

He couldn't miss her. He didn't even know her. And she definitely didn't know him. Not one other woman on his months-long journey had a name. They were faces and stories, nothing more. Not Ella. She was a name, a face, and a life. He picked up his phone and glanced at it as if she might be there, ready to talk, and that's when he saw it: Ella's missed call on his extra phone.

Should he call her back? It was too late there. Or was it? In a quick flash, he pushed the call back button and the phone rang. He imagined her in the bed in that cottage, asleep. Or maybe watching TV in the chaise longue where he'd left her without saying good-bye.

Blake sat the phone on the desk and put the phone on speaker. He'd leave a message. "Hello?" her voice came over the line, full of fog and distance.

"Ella?" he asked.

"Yes."

"It's Hunter. I just thought . . . I saw you called. Are you okay?"

"Yes. Of course. Yes."

"Did I wake you?"

"It's okay. How was your trip home?" she asked.

"Good. I saw my daughter. Took her to breakfast and didn't try to talk about anything serious. Just hung out with her." He felt like a teenager, a kid who'd never called a girl on the phone.

"Good move."

"Thanks for that advice," he said.

# twelve

Coffee. That was the only place to start. Ella would figure out the rest later. Today was her day off and she would clean up the mess of her apartment and then go find her own lawyer. She would go get a hell-cat lawyer, and maybe even move into the house. Or . . . she flopped back into bed . . . or "take to the bed" as her mom used to say.

Downstairs a door slammed and Bruiser began his frenzied bark-ing. It faded slowly as, Ella knew, Mimi was trying to take him out-side, seeing if a walk would calm him down. Ella did nothing but stare at her surroundings as if taking them into account, solidifying her place in the world. Outside her window, ivy crawled and tangled its way across the bottom of the window frame, as if trying to peek into her apartment. A crack, thin as hair, maneuvered its way from the top of her wall down to the floorboards, spawning new cracks before mov-ing on.

Even coffee seemed too big an effort, but she rose and went to the sink. Nothing would change if she didn't change. She'd read that in one of the many books stacked on the side of her bed. She needed to return them to the library before she got a late fine. When she'd checked them out, a pyramid of self-help I've-been-ditched books, the librarian had given her that look, the one Ella hated: *I'm so sorry. Poor, poor you.*

The coffee was too hot and it singed the roof of her mouth, a scorched feeling that didn't improve her mood. All her good intentions for the day faded into gray. She lifted the remote from the chair and sank into the cushions, clicked on for the TV and off for her mind.

The TV droned on, and beautiful people flashed on and off the screen, a montage of life so perfect that it seemed like science fiction. Get up, she told herself. *Do something.*

Now *E! News* was on and her cell phone was buzzing across the room and finally, with her coffee cold and only half drunk, she rose from the chair to answer it: Amber.

She pushed decline and looked at the missed messages. Sims had called twice. Her eyes opened wider, like someone had pulled up on her eyelids, quivering. All those times she'd frantically checked her phone every five minutes and here he was calling and she'd been ignoring him for the TV. Well, good, let him worry why she wasn't answering.

He answered on the first ring. "Are you okay?" he asked.

"I'm fine. Why?"

"Amber and I have both been trying to call you and you're never without your phone and . . ."

"I'm super busy," she said. "What do you need?"

"I . . . want to talk. Can you talk?"

"Talk?"

"Yes. Like see you and talk. Try to have a real conversation about all of this mess."

"I'm pretty sure you've told me everything I need to know. You're in love. You want a divorce. What else is there to talk about?"

"Ella. Please."

"Please what?"

"Can I come over?"

"Here? You sure you want to lower yourself to my level?" She wanted him back. She loved him, so she took a long moment and then said, "Sims, I'm sorry. It's coming out wrong. If you want to come here to talk, that's fine."

"Well, I'm outside so I'll be up in a minute."

"You're outside?"

"Yes," he said. "Outside."

"Give me ten," she said. "I've been . . . Stuff is everywhere."

"I don't care about that."

Ella saw herself through Sims's eyes. Messy hair. Dark circles under her eyes. Yesterday's clothes. Hell, yesterday's makeup. There wasn't time for the whole routine—cleanse, tone, moisturize, and tint. A quick swipe of mascara and a brush through her hair would have to do.

He stood there in the hallway, her husband of seven years. He held his hands behind his back and waited to be invited in. She didn't say a word.

"Oh, Ella," he said.

She stepped aside to let him in. Her throat held the tears she wanted to cry.

"Yes?" she asked, hiding her need.

"I can't believe you're living here. Why—"

"Because you've locked me out."

"I just thought you'd go to your dad's while we worked things out. Why didn't you?"

"I can't. I can't go there."

Below their feet the barking started. "What the hell?"

"That's Bruiser. He's my neighbor's dog. He's kind of cute."

"That is not cute." He pointed to the floor. "That is hell."

"Sometimes," she said as a smile moved across her face. "But if you knew Mimi you would have some sympathy."

He laughed. God, how she missed that laugh. "Figures you'd make friends," he said.

167

"Actually I went there to tell her what a nuisance the dog was and then . . ."

"And then you were friends. That's so you."

"Is it?" she asked.

"Yes," Sims said with affection. "You're the kindest person I know." He smiled at her and motioned to the kitchen. "Do you have any coffee?"

"Sure." She stopped. "Wait." She spun around. "Why are you here?"

"I miss you," he said.

"You miss me?" she repeated. He might as well have been talking in another language.

"I know. It's confusing. I've spent the past weeks so mad at you. I mean, what you did—"

"What I did?"

"The baseball cards. It was like you turned into a crazy person."

"Can we go back to why I did that? From what I remember, you told me that you were in love with my best friend's sister and you wanted—"

"I wanted to talk about it. I wanted to find a way to get through it. But you went crazy."

"Yes. Crazy." Ella rolled her eyes. "Sims, you broke my heart. I didn't know what to do. I came undone. Who wouldn't? But you can't say we aren't together because I threw a few baseball cards in the Dumpster."

"A few baseball cards?"

"I know. I know. John Smoltz. I get it."

"I don't think you do."

"I don't think you get it," Ella said, and took two steps away from the kitchen, away from getting him the coffee he asked for. "I don't think you get it at all."

Sims's eyes welled up. Was he crying?

"Are you okay?" she asked.

"I messed up, Ella. I don't know how to fix this. I hurt you. I am so sorry. And now it's like you aren't even you. You hate me. I've never seen you like this." He reached to hug her. She let him.

His arms were strong around her. She closed her eyes and allowed his warmth to soak into all the lonely places. Finally she stepped back. "Tell me, Sims. What is it? What do you need?"

"I don't know. I'm confused, Ella."

"Confused about what?"

"I think I made a mistake."

"A mistake? In like you don't really love Betsy? That she isn't the love of your life?"

"Don't say it like that."

"That's how I heard it, Sims. Love of your life. I'm only repeating."

"I'm sorry," he said. "It's not like that. She's not. I do love her, or it feels like it. But you—"

"Me?"

"I still love you, Ella. I do. I'm such a mess. We're a family. You've always been my home."

"Listen, Sims. Why don't you go get your head together and then tell me what you want? I can't be with you if you're in love with Betsy. I can't."

"I know. But can we slow down on the divorce proceedings though? Don't go to the lawyer today."

"No. I'm going today." Why didn't she agree to the one thing *she* wanted—to slow it all down? She had no idea.

"I'll pay for a nicer apartment if you want one. I can't stand to think of you living here."

"No." She felt outside her body now, watching all of this unfold. "I want to move back home. That's all I want."

"I guess we could do something like week on, week off while we try to figure out what we're . . . what we're doing."

"You mean, whether we are getting divorced or not?"

"I hate that word. I can't stand to think of us as that."

"Sims, you are acting like I left you. Like I was the one who ran away. And you're telling me that *you're* confused."

"I know." He sat in the sole chair and dropped his head into his hands. "Who is the guy I saw you with at the Patio? Same guy Billy saw you with at Sunset?"

"Seriously?"

"Amber said his name was Hunter Adderman and that he was from California, writing a history book or some shit like that. But I looked him up, Ella. There is no such person or such writer."

"That's what this is about? Hunter?"

He looked up and in the dim light she saw how tired he was, the way his eyes were half-lidded, the stubble on his chin, the dry lips. "No, it's not just about that. It's about how I've ruined everything."

Suddenly she was exhausted. She didn't want to placate him. How on earth could he expect her to make him feel better when she didn't even know how to make herself feel better? How could he think that he even deserved to feel better? "Sims, it's probably best if you leave now. I have so much work to do."

"I thought today was your day off."

"It is, but I'm doing other . . . things."

He stood and looked at the pile of sketches on the warped table. "These are really good, Ella. But I've always told you that."

Now she wanted to tell him everything. All there was to know about her life and how she'd missed him, how she'd fantasized about his return, how she needed him back. But she didn't. She had to bide her time, make him want it. Don't give in too early or too easily.

He looked up at her. "So, you won't go see a lawyer today?"

She saw the gap in time, the slim moment she had. "No, but I want to move back in today."

He stared at her and she trembled inside with the need to fill the silence, to drop words and explanations in the space where he decided what to do. "Is tomorrow okay? Starting tomorrow we will do week on, week off while we try to figure out what to do."

"Okay," she said. "But what does 'figure out what to do' mean?"

"I don't know. But I know I'm not ready to start dividing things and signing forms. Are you?"

"No," she said quietly. "No, I'm not."

"Okay . . ."

"Wait!" She looked up. "Are you still with Betsy? I mean, are you still together? Like when I'm not at the house, will she be there?"

"I don't know."

"How can you *not* know?"

"I just don't. I'm confused and I'm trying to work it out so we can find a way to fix this."

Ella held up her hand. "Stop. You're serious, aren't you? You want me to stand here and wait while you try to decide whom you love best? Do you have a scale you're using to weigh us?"

"It's nothing like that, Ella."

"It's not?"

"No."

"What do you want, Sims?"

"That's what I'm trying to figure out, Ella. Can't you see that?"

She stepped toward the door. "This is absurd. You come here to tell me you love me and miss me but you're going back to Betsy also? You're not just confused, you're ridiculous."

"You are twisting my words. I'm here to say I love you, and I'm sorry."

"And you're confused. I heard that part loud and clear, too, Sims. I'm learning, slowly, I guess, that I can't just hear the parts I want to hear."

"I guess I should go." He glanced toward the bed and she knew what he wanted. She knew what she wanted. But she would deny them both for the long run. For the good, for later. For the real reconciliation.

"Yes," she said, "you should go." She opened the front door.

He walked toward it and then turned to her. "I never got that coffee."

"No, I guess you didn't."

She shut the door quickly, before she made him that cup of coffee, before she took him to the bed and reminded him of all they were together.

If she'd known all it would take was seeing her with another man, she would have hired someone a month ago. Her heart picked up its pace. She stood to the side of her window and looked out to watch him walk away. He pulled out his cell phone to call someone. Probably Betsy. Would she ever, even if she could reconcile, would she ever not think about every phone call he made? Every moment he couldn't account for his whereabouts? Was trust destroyed for good?

Sims stood there outside her window, alone. It took everything in her not to run down and beg him back, tell him she loved him and only him and to please leave Betsy. Hope, it was a powerful thing.

# *thirteen*

---

The week went by like a single day. Blake slept when he couldn't keep his eyes open any longer, ate when Ashlee brought him food, and made love when he needed to clear his mind. The story obsessed him. He finished it faster than anything he'd ever written. The only time he'd even come close was when he wrote with the producer who shot *The Mess of Love*. They'd written that in six weeks.

His office was a mess—a beautiful mess full of Post-it notes, charts, and graphs. Plot points were written in red marker on large white sheets. Scene notes scribbled on scrap paper and then pinned to the bulletin board. Discarded scenes clustered together in an origami-like pile next to the trash can. The pictures he'd taken of the house, of Ella, of the water, the bay, and even the slave relic museum were attached to the wall with double-sided tape. He looked at everything now. He'd been living inside this story until this very moment, when reality seeped back into his world, little by little, cracks of light.

He ran his hand across his face. He needed a shave and a long run on the beach. Fresh air. Real food. Sun. And a change of underwear, too. The thought made him laugh as he stood and walked to the wall where the pictures hung. He would save the photos for the director lucky enough to get this screenplay. He wanted it to look exactly like this. And the main character to look . . . He touched Ella's photo. Her hand was up, trying to prevent him from taking the picture. Her eyes, those blue eyes with the long lashes, red tipped and flirty. He'd described them in the script without even having to look at the photo.

Returning to his computer, he typed "Fade out" and leaned back in his chair, stretched. He knew it was good. Not in a conceited, too-big-for-his-britches kind of way, but with the innate understanding about how a story worked and when it didn't. His last two flops . . . he'd known they weren't working, he'd just hoped that the audience would be fooled. But this? It worked. It only needed a title, and then he would send it off and get things moving. It would go quickly now. This was what they'd all been waiting for: a great love story. Everybody—producers, studios, agents—would be telling him how much they loved his work . . . as soon as he'd scored another hit. And this was it.

Ashlee walked in the room. Her yoga pants stretched over her ass like a second skin. Her tank top a scrap of material. She was sweaty from her workout. "You're done, aren't you?"

"I am," he said.

"Let's celebrate." She ran toward him and jumped into his lap. "I've missed you. You were here and not here at the same time. Now I can have my man back."

Blake kissed her, tasted the salty sweat of her workout. "I couldn't have done it without you. The notes. The organization. The food . . . the . . ."

"Really great sex," she said. "I know you couldn't have done it without that." She kissed him again.

"Yes, that, too. Absolutely," he said, and shifted her to move off his lap. "I still need a title and then I hit the send button."

"Don't you want me to read it before you send it off?" she asked.

"No." He twisted a coffee cup in circles on the desk. "You don't have to do that. I know it works."

"Oh," she said, and shrugged. "Just thought you might want a second eye before you hit send."

"I'm not going to ask you to do one more thing," he said.

"I want to," she said. "I want you to ask me to do one more thing."

"All right then." He turned back to the screen and keyed in a few letters. "I just e-mailed it to you."

She jumped up. "I'm on it." Ashlee was gone, running to her computer in the bedroom while Blake tapped his fingers on the keys. A title. A title.

He closed his eyes. This was the first story he'd ever written without the touchstone of a title hanging on a note above his computer. Behind his eyelids, like an inlaid mosaic, he saw Ella walking, her skirt swinging around her knees and her bangs swept sideways by the wind. The story wasn't about her, he told himself over and over, but it wouldn't exist without her. In the end of his story, her lover returned, unharmed and safe, willing to sacrifice himself but not needing to. Her lover spared, washed ashore safely when everyone had thought him gone, swept to sea.

What had Ella said about him? Something about never loving again. "He's the only one."

His eyes popped open and the smile he felt move across and then up his face was both authentic and relieved.

*The Only One.*

He typed the words on the title page and then underneath that, his name and the date. He attached the screenplay to an e-mail and typed his agent's name in the recipient line. In the subject line he wrote, "This Is It."

He wanted to call Ella, tell her how she'd inspired his breakthrough, how she'd changed him. But that action came with a cost. Calling Ella would require admitting his lies.

He'd imagined, a few times, how he would go to her and tell her the truth, that he'd mined her story for his own good. For his career. What stopped him was the pain he knew he would see in her eyes, how she would look at him with disgust. That pain wasn't any worse than thinking he'd never talk to her again, but he knew from experience that his desire to talk to her would fade. Desire *always* dissolved. He'd even told her that. Her look of disgust would never fade, so he chose the lesser of two evils: never telling her in trade for never seeing her again.

"Blake," Ashlee called from the bedroom. "Get in here."

He entered his bedroom, lit by the late-afternoon sun, a warm glow across the bedspread where Ashlee sat in lotus position with her computer open. She looked at him with a curious expression, her eyes drawn downward, her lips pursed out. "Blake?"

"Yes?"

"Did you fall for this girl? The one you wrote this story about?"

"What?"

"Did you . . . fall for her? Sleep with her?"

"God, no. What are you talking about?"

"The way you describe the main character, this 'Emily.' It's like she's a goddess. You have her photos all over the bulletin board out there. You describe her hair and eyes like you . . . really know her."

"It's called fiction, Ashlee. Writing. Making it up. She's just . . . a girl who lost her husband and designs wedding dresses."

"Okay, then." Ashlee continued reading. "This is brilliant, Blake. Really amazing. You're right. You nailed it."

"Thanks so much. I'm going for a run. I'll be back in a bit."

"Uh-huh," Ashlee mumbled and scrolled through his script. He could see over her shoulder. She was at the part where the boat's rudder was found.

Blake slipped on his running clothes and when he bent over to tie his shoes, he was dizzy. The room spun like he'd been drinking JD for days. He was so deeply tired that he changed his mind and walked into the living room, flopped down on the couch, and fell into a sleep so deep that he didn't even notice when Ashlee came in, dropped a note on the desk, and left.

Nesting. That was the divorce term for their week-on-week-off arrangement, although usually it applied to families who were taking turns living in the house and taking care of the kids, not to a man staying put while two women rotated in and out of his life. Being there, in her house, with her things, obliterated almost all other concerns.

Amber was there the last morning of Ella's "week." They sat across from each other at the kitchen table where they cradled their coffee mugs in their hands.

"Either he's in or out," Amber said. "He can't have it both ways like this."

"You want him to end up with your sister, don't you?" Ella didn't feel any heat in the words; it just seemed a fact. "Can't you just be happy that we are trying to work things out?"

"I am happy for you. If you want Sims back and he's coming back, I'm happy for you. But I'm not happy that he's jerking you both around. Keeping you both on a string while he figures out what is best for him."

"That's not what he's doing. He's been with me every day. We've never talked so honestly. We are talking about why it might have happened. Where we went wrong. How we can fix it. We've talked about forgiveness and reconciliation and how to prevent growing apart again."

"Prevent what he did? Like you can get a shot for it? Or wear protective gear?"

"No." Ella exhaled. "I don't know what to say to you, Amber. I love him. He's my husband. We're talking it through. I haven't even let him spend the night yet."

"Well, then where do you think he's spending the night?"

"At the apartment he rented."

"Sure thing."

"What are you saying?"

"I'm not saying anything. I just don't want you to get hurt again."

"Listen, there are two parts to every marriage and I know that I wasn't perfect, either. Relationships are complicated and . . ."

"Have you considered therapy or anything like that?"

"Maybe . . . not yet."

Amber reached across the table and took Ella's hand. "I know. And I also know that I'm not a relationship expert. Hell, I can't make one last more than six months. But please don't take blame where there isn't any."

"Can we talk about something else, please?"

"Absolutely. Like me?"

"Like you," Ella agreed. "Tell me what is going on in Amber World."

"Well—" Amber leaned back in the chair and smiled. "Now that you ask. Let's see. Best Day Bakery wants to sell my cookies but I really don't want to get into that—you know, becoming a full-time baker or whatever. I love just making them for special occasions. What would my parents do? I mean, I'm here to run the family gift shop. It would collapse without me."

"But you could be the Sister Schubert of sugar cookies," Ella said.

"Great, so I get famous for making everyone fat, and my parents lose their store."

"So dramatic," Ella said. "But you know what this town really needs?"

"Good men?"

"That, and a movie theater and a bookstore."

As they talked through the options, life appeared as it always had: something manageable that could be solved over a cup of coffee. They talked about friends Ella hadn't seen or had been avoiding, about Amber's parents' need for her to work for them and not go out on her own. They debated the pros and cons of the town's wedding business and whether Amber would ever want to marry after seeing all the heartbreak of her best friend and sister.

When Amber finally left, Ella returned to her preoccupation with the house. She was so immersed in reunion with Sims, with her soft bed and familiar kitchen, that she called in sick to work. She filled the refrigerator, cooked Sims a few good meals, and caught up on some sleep without Bruiser barking below.

Tomorrow she'd return to Crumbling Chateau and Swept Away. The honeymoon was over, so to speak, but it had been a remarkable high even without Sims spending the night. Some semblance of normalcy was starting to take hold. He'd rented a loft apartment in the new building downtown: fresh and clean, with a view of the square. Ella wasn't even jealous. She was just content to be in her house for a full week spending time with Sims, talking, and trying to find their way again. She felt hopeful. No, more than hopeful. He'd tried to spend the night every night, but she'd refused. "Not until you come home for good," she told him. Hope, it was a light and breezy thing.

Her walk to work the next afternoon was glorious, the kind of day when the wind was gentle and the sun held its full blaze behind the clouds. The sidewalk, cracked and uneven, seemed right. Almost everything seemed right. Except when she thought of Hunter.

Ella approached the front door of Swept Away just as Margo walked out. She moved aside to let Ella in. On instinct, Ella glanced toward the shoe section and made sure it was all in order. Far from it. Boxes were stranded in the middle of the floor, shoes were unmatched and discarded on the couch and chair. "God, who had the shoe section yesterday?" Ella asked.

"No one because you called in sick," Margo answered.

"Why didn't Nadine or Jackie do it?"

"Because they were busy with their jobs while you weren't doing yours."

Ella didn't give Margo the satisfaction of a reply. She just walked to her section and began to put everything back in place. Dead flowers drooped over the white vase like they'd fainted. Ella threw the rotting stems in the trash. It might be a crap job, selling shoes to bratty brides, but she took pride in it.

Margo entered the section and stepped over a box. "I have a big announcement, so there's a staff meeting in fifteen minutes in the backroom."

"Okay," Ella said.

"You don't look sick," Margo said. "That was a quick recovery."

"It must have been food poisoning," Ella said.

"Sure thing," Margo said.

In the fifteen minutes before the meeting, Ella had her section looking exactly as it should. She ran next door, grabbed peonies from the flower shop, and then entered the backroom where the staff waited. Margo entered the room in her white suit, one she only wore for important occasions or interviews with new clients, and clapped her hands. "I have the most fabulous news," she said. "One that's not only career changing for me, but will affect the store in the most positive way."

No one said a word. The four staff members waited while Margo just beamed at them. She stood in front of a desk and leaned back on its edges, her hands behind her back.

"Well, what is it?" Nadine finally asked.

Margo flung her hands out and held up a drawing, a wedding dress in full color on cotton paper. Ella took in a breath; God, she wished she could sketch something that beautiful: the way the bodice held at the waist and then blossomed out like a flower, the lace and threading pattern in expanding echoes through the skirt and to the hemline. The tiny pearls that lined the sleeves and neckline were exquisite.

"This design, my White Diamond, which is named after my favorite hydrangea bush, has been chosen as a finalist in the Vogue Bridal Design Contest. I'll fly to New York in two weeks to attend a ceremony where they'll announce the winner." Margo took a deep breath and placed the sketch back on the desk. "Even if I don't win, the design will be featured in *Vogue*. This can only be good news for all of us."

Nadine was the first to respond. She jumped up and ran to hug Margo. "This is so fantastic."

Margo clasped her hands in a prayer position and said, "Prayers for all of it."

Ella couldn't move. Something was wrong. The wistful need to have drawn something that beautiful turned upside down, inside out: she *had* drawn that dress. That was her dress. Yes, it was gussied up, as her mom used to say. It had been colored in and brought to life, but it was still hers, the one she'd drawn at the café table with Hunter.

Jackie and Trey had joined in the congratulations, but Ella couldn't move. She was stuck to her seat, a weight like concrete on top of her.

"Ella?" Jackie called back. "Are you okay?"

For Ella, this was a familiar feeling, one she wished she didn't know, the same one she'd had when Sims had said, "I'm in love." A fearful loneliness without a way out. An almost claustrophobic panic.

"She's been out sick," Trey said, and then walked to Ella. "Baby, you need water or something?"

Ella shook her head and then stood. She would do this differently. She walked to Margo. "You know that's my design. We both know that."

"Wait"—Nadine touched Ella's elbow—"What are you talking about?"

"That design. It's mine. You took it, Margo. You know that."

"No." Margo's voice was so calm, like Sims's, as if the facts were indisputable. "I gave you back your design. I told you—it was too much like mine so I didn't keep it."

Ella shook her head. "No."

"Oh, please," Margo said. "You're not a designer. I saw a little drawing you did and then gave it back to you."

"I have it," Ella said, and turned to Nadine and Trey and Jackie. "I can show you."

"Oh, Ella," Margo said.

Ella felt the crazy coming on, the need to tear apart Margo's sketch, or throw all the shoes in the river. That wouldn't get her anywhere. She needed solid ground to stand on, some self-respect. She took in a long breath and walked out of the room, through the dress shop, past the dressing rooms, through the flower pavilion, and veils. She grabbed her bag, put one shoe box back in its place so it lined up perfectly with the others, and then walked out the front door, hollering over her shoulder, "Bye, bye."

Ella paced through Watersend, back and forth, landmarks familiar and not seen as her mind scrolled through the options. Even if she showed everyone the sketch, they would say she drew it right there, right then. She could call *Vogue* and tell them, but she'd sound like a jealous employee, a wannabe who sold shoes in a small town.

"Enough," she said out loud to the sidewalk, to the air, and to the world. "Enough."

She was exhausted. She was finished with things happening *to* her. Sims. Margo. Amber. The landlord. It was time to *make* things happen.

Mimi's apartment was so quiet that Ella didn't want to knock. She placed her ear on the door and listened. Nothing. She reentered the stairwell and went back up to her apartment, where the musty smell washed over her. She lit a candle and put on some music—her mom's favorite—Ella Fitzgerald. She turned the volume to high and put the kettle on to boil. Her sketches were still on the table, and there it was: the dress. She ran her finger over the edges of the sketch, the pearls on the sleeves and neckline. This was hers, even if Margo claimed it as her own. This design was Ella's alone.

With a hot cup of tea, she sat down and organized her portfolio. Lost in the anatomy of dresses, she divided them by style. She named each dress and sorted them according to waistlines, sleeves, and embellishments. Hours passed. Her mind quieted, the heartache of the day became a dull throb.

When she'd finished, she looked down and saw what had been there all along in the art of her designs: collections. She had three distinct collections. She was, without anyone labeling her as such, a wedding dress designer.

In a long stretch, she surveyed her apartment. She wouldn't stay. She was going home and staying home. Sims could make his own decisions. It didn't take long to pack her suitcase, put her few dishes and kitchen appliances in a box. The bedspread and sheets were folded and in a plastic bag when she called Sims and left a message. "I'm moving back into the house for good. You can join me if you'd like or you can stay in your apartment."


Blake sat on the metal bleachers at the lacrosse fields, watching his daughter play midfield. Her plaid skirt and navy T-shirt made her indistinguishable from any of the other girls. But Blake knew the way she ran, the twist of her arm when she threw, the holler of joy when something went right. What he didn't know was how she felt about anything. He'd tried to spend time with her—every day, in fact. They'd had nice times, but still she was quiet. She spoke only when spoken to. He fought hard not to ask too many questions. How are you? What do you feel? What do you need? Do you still hate me?

While the game went into overtime and Amelia sat on the bench (he could not and would not call her Amelie), Blake let his mind wander to the screenplay. The meetings were going well. Reese Witherspoon and Anne Hathaway were both "interested." A director was circling and as soon as an actor or director the studio loved actually committed to the project, others would fall into place and they'd be off and running. Blake was telling anyone who would listen that he knew the perfect small town to shoot it in.

"Blake." He looked up to see his ex-wife walking toward him.

"Hi, Marilee," he said, ignoring the coiffed boyfriend, whose name he really did keep forgetting.

They sat next to Blake and tried to chat. Nice day. Good game. Wicked coach. Blake nodded when appropriate and stared at the field until his cell phone buzzed. His agent. He excused himself and walked toward the tree line at the edge of the field. Marilee's voice followed him. "Just typical," she said.

But he was in too good a mood to let it bother him.

"Blake, man, got the call. Reese is in. The studio is putting out the press release this afternoon. You ready for the buzz?"

"Nothing has ever happened this fast." Blake stared out at the field, at his little girl running the length of it.

"Nothing you've written has been this good."

Hollywood moves so slowly, except when it doesn't, so let the chaos begin. The casting and the budget. The funding and the fighting. But it had started and that's what mattered. It had started.

He returned to the bench and watched the end of the game. Everything was brightly lit, outlined in a way it hadn't been before. He even smiled at his ex-wife. She looked at him, a crusty smile and asked, "What?"

"Nothing," he said. "I'm just happy."

"A little Jack Daniel's maybe?"

"No, sweetie. Sober as a judge."

"Even your judge isn't sober," she said, turning away.

He was weary of her anger. He leaned down and spoke. "I prom-ise you've made me as miserable as you can. We've hit our limit, I'm sure. Can we stop fighting now? The day is gorgeous. Our daughter is kicking butt out there. And you look beautiful, just like the day we met in the Palisades. Maybe even better."

She looked like she was going to cry. "Why do you have to be so charming? Can't you just let me hate you for a while?"

"I've let you hate me long enough. Can't you just let me be done now?"

"I don't know." She turned around and he saw her wipe at her eyes and then leave to join her boyfriend, the nameless guy, at the edge of the field.

In-N-Out Burger had a line out the door, but it was where Amelia wanted to go for her postgame burger. If they won, it was a celebration burger but if they lost, it was a consolation burger, which is what it was that afternoon. The customers were such an eclectic mix: a hip-hop guy in sagging jeans; two young girls so blond they looked like mannequins; a family with two small red-haired boys, obviously twins, pushing at each other in fun.

Amelia leaned down to the boys, laughing. "It's all fun and games until someone loses an eye," she said.

They looked up at her, all wide-eyed with small little noses that looked like clay globs on their freckled faces. "What?" one of them asked. He looked six or maybe seven, Blake could never tell ages.

Amelia pointed to Blake. "That's what my dad always used to say to me and my friends when we were goofing off. It's all fun and games until someone loses an eye."

"Did anyone ever lose an eye?" one of the boys asked.

"Never." Amelia wrapped her arm around her father's waist and gave him a little squeeze.

The boys looked at each other with the silent language of twins, then started in again. "Boys," their mother said, "please stop pushing!"

"Did I really used to say that?"

"All the time."

"How do you remember things like that?"

Amelia shrugged. "There's a lot I don't remember, but my friends and I still say it sometimes for fun, you know, when someone's doing something stupid."

"It's a great line. Wish I remember saying it." He tried to recall those long ago days when she was small enough to wrestle with her friends or pop her thumb in her mouth. It was yesterday and yet it never happened. He should have been more present. He should have been more attentive. He should have been . . .

They grabbed their food and sat at an outside table. Regret. It sucked. He took a long swallow of his chocolate milk shake to wash out the bad taste. How many things he would have done differently. He tried Ella's advice. He sat quietly, watching his daughter eating French fries. "You're awful quiet," she said.

"Yes, I guess I am. What a great game you had today. I'm so proud of you."

"Well, thanks, Dad. I think you'd say you were proud of me if I shot the ball into my own team's goal." She punched the side of his arm.

He'd described Amelia to Ella one time, but now that he sat with his daughter, looking at her across the sticky picnic table at In-N-Out Burger, the table where a thousand other people drank their milk shakes and dripped ketchup and rubbed the greasy side of the burger wrapper onto the metal, he saw what he didn't describe. The way her eyes changed color in the sunlight, becoming almost green. How her hair formed a widow's peak in the middle of her forehead. He hadn't told Ella how his daughter's nose was the slightest bit crooked to the left after getting hit in a kickball game in second grade, how she'd never wanted a nose job to fix it because "everyone will think I just wanted a better nose, and I don't." Her cheeks, they were fuller than her mom's but the same rounded shape, like two tiny plums sitting on top of the bones.

"You know you're beautiful," Blake said.

"Wow, Dad. You sure are sappy lately. What's gotten into you? Are you in love or something?"

He didn't laugh. It was a legitimate question, he guessed. He smiled at his daughter. "I am," he said.

"Oh, you are?"

He knew she didn't want that answer, not really, because who wants their dad in love with anyone but their mom? "With my new script."

"Ah!" She lifted her milk shake to him and tapped the edges of his paper cup. "A new script?"

"Yup. Reese Witherspoon wants the lead."

"Oh, Dad. You've gotta introduce me. She's like totally one of my favorites."

"It's not a done deal, sweetie."

"Gross, don't call me 'sweetie.' That's what Jake calls Mom. It makes me feel scaly."

"Deal."

The sunlight filtered through the awning above them, fell in stripes along the table. Amelia twirled her straw for a minute. "Monica is in rehab," she said.

"Your friend from ballet?"

"Yes."

"I'm sorry. What happened?"

His daughter started talking to him as if she'd never stopped. She told him about the guy she was dating, and the school play she'd tried out for. She told him about her friends who were in trouble and those who weren't. And at the end, when dusk had approached and they were still at the picnic table, she told him that she missed him. It might not be everything in the world, but it sure was everything to Blake.

Ella stood in the kitchen, cooking spaghetti with homemade tomato sauce. A salad with fresh local vegetables sat on the side of the counter and she sipped on a chilled glass of rosé. Mimi sat at the kitchen table, sipping bourbon.

"You sure about this, dear?" Mimi asked again, glancing around the room.

"Yes," Ella said, and lifted her glass to Mimi. "I'm staying. If he wants to leave, he can, but I'm here."

"What if he calls the cops?" she asked.

Ella had told Mimi everything, as though she were a living journal. "If he does, well, I guess that answers how he really feels. If he's only pretending to want to get back together, then let's get the show on the road," Ella said.

Mimi laughed. "Who is this new girl, all strong and ready to fight?"

Ella turned the sauce to low and sat at the table with Mimi. "Hunter told me that he had a dog that barked like Bruiser and couldn't stop, and they found out that he was allergic to his medicine. Have you thought of that?"

Mimi shook her head. "No, that hasn't once been mentioned. I wonder."

"I wonder, too. I can take you to the vet tomorrow if you want."

"Oh, no, I can't make you do that."

"Let me," Ella said. "I'd like to."

"That would be great," Mimi said. "I sure am glad you came into my life."

"Me, too, you." Ella hugged Mimi before standing up to stir the sauce.

Music rested between them until they both turned to the sound of the front door opening. "Well, now you get to meet Sims," Ella said.

"God, something smells great," a voice said, a female voice—a loud, grating female voice.

"Shit," Sims said as he and Betsy appeared in the kitchen.

What is there to say in moments like this? Surely there was something perfect to say, a witty comment, a smart-ass retort. It was Betsy who opened her mouth first, but the noise that came out wasn't really a sentence, it was more of a whine that contained a few words like "why" and "her" and "ridiculous."

"Ella?" Sims said in a quiet voice. He was afraid, she knew, that the crazy would return.

"Yes, Sims?"

"Why are you here?"

"Didn't you get my message?" She stirred the sauce, sipped her wine. "Oh, and this is my friend Mimi. I wanted her to meet you."

"What is going on?" Betsy asked in that voice.

Sims pulled out his phone and looked at his messages and then at Ella. "But we agreed."

"Looks like I changed my mind." Ella heard her voice, strong and sure. But inside she was being thrashed around in a wave, an undertow.

"You can't change your mind," he said. His voice sounded tremulous, uncertain.

"Why not? You did." She pointed at Mimi. "Please don't be so rude."

"Hello, Mimi." Sims walked to the older woman and shook her hand. "Nice to meet you."

"Wowza," Mimi said with a sip of bourbon. "I wish I could say the same to you."

Betsy walked to Ella's side. "You need to leave. You know Sims can call the police."

"He won't," Ella said.

"Then I will," Betsy said, and she walked toward the phone on the wall, picked it up.

Sims was at her side before she'd dialed. "Don't," he said.

"What?" Betsy turned on him. She had tears in her eyes. "Are you telling me that you're going to let her stay here?"

"No, I'm not telling you that. But I'm not calling the police on my wife. Stop it."

"That bitch . . ." Betsy almost hissed the words.

Mimi tilted her head and stared at Betsy. "Maybe now is a good time for *you* to leave," she said.

"Me? No way." Betsy pointed at Ella. "She needs to leave. He loves *me*. He's told her it's over."

"Really?" Ella said.

"He didn't?" Betsy's voice started to slow like it was running out of gas, sputtering. She spun to Sims. "Tell me this is a bad dream. You haven't told her?"

"Told me what?" Ella asked.

"We're getting married." Betsy kept her gaze on Sims, who folded into the chair next to Mimi.

"That's not it," he said. "We were not planning to get married." He looked at Betsy. "I did not say that."

Ella felt her mouth go dry, a tingle at the edges of her tongue, a metallic taste in the back of her throat. God, please don't throw up here, she thought. "What happened to 'I'm so confused' and 'I love you so much' and 'Let's talk this through'?"

"He said that to you?" Betsy asked Ella. "You're serious?"

"Yes," Ella said.

"You son of a bitch," Betsy said, and ran to her purse, dumped it upside down on the table, and drew out an envelope. She waved the white rectangle in the air, back and forth like a flag. "This was your wedding present. This was your surprise. This was for you . . ."

Sims stood up and took one step and then dropped back into the chair, exhausted. He drank Mimi's bourbon.

Betsy drew near, her face twisting, a hot wax version of herself. "Do you want to see it?"

"No," Sims said. "I want to leave. We can talk about this outside."

"Talk?" she asked with a weird laugh behind her question.

"I guess not."

Betsy drew something out of the envelope and held it up to his face. "See this?"

Ella squinted to see it from the stove. *John Smoltz.* Betsy had John Smoltz. Hell, who would have thought it? Ella busted out laughing. "Are you kidding me?"

"Where did you find it?" Sims reached for the card, but his hand swiped at empty air as Betsy pulled back her hand.

"I went back to the Dumpster the next day and searched the street and curbs and the disgusting back alley. That's how much I love you. After we couldn't find it that night, I couldn't sleep thinking where it might be. I thought maybe one card might have missed the Dumpster."

"My God," Sims said, and stood, took a tentative step toward her. "Thank you so much, baby. So much."

"You're thanking me?" She held the card high in the air.

Sims looked toward Ella and together they knew what Betsy was about to do, so together they screamed.

"Stop."

"Don't."

But she did. She brought her hands together. Sims lunged for her and Ella closed her eyes as Betsy ripped John Smoltz in half and tossed him into the spaghetti sauce. He sunk into the red sauce, the tip of his bat poking up, his baseball cap submerged. The other half floated and then dipped lower as if Smoltz's feet pulled him down to the bottom of the pot. They watched him sink in silence. Death by red sauce.

Sims sank to the chair again. "What is with you women and base-ball cards? I don't get it."

Betsy picked up her purse, but everywhere there were pieces of its innards: lipstick, keys, a checkbook, scattered change, some of it stuck together with gum, a pack of Trojans, a grocery list scribbled in pink pen, a ribbon left over from something, crumpled and ruined. Betsy sobbed as she picked up each item and threw it back into her purse. Ella couldn't stand it anymore. She started to help.

The purse was full again, and Sims was at the table with his head in his hands. Mimi sat quietly with a closed-mouth smile. Ella looked around at the havoc and said, "You ruined my spaghetti sauce."

"Sorry," Betsy said, "you ruined my life."

And she was gone. The front door slammed so hard that they all jumped even as they knew it was coming. Ella Fitzgerald sang, and Mimi said, "That was the most fun I've had in a long time."

"Who *are* you?" Sims asked.

Mimi looked up at Ella and then the laughter came. It was tear-producing, hiccupping laughter that neither of them could stop. When they finally took a breath, Sims was staring at them as if they were mad.

"I'm sorry, Ella," Sims said. "I brought Betsy here tonight to break it off. I was going to tell her that we . . . me and you . . . were trying to mend our marriage."

"Really?" she asked.

"Yes."

"Well, that's odd because that's what I came here to tell you—to break it off."

"No you didn't, sweetie. Don't do that."

Ella picked up the spoon and fished out the two pieces of John Smotlz. She carried them over to Sims and dropped them in his lap.

"Hell, Ella." He jumped up, sauce spattering on his pressed khakis, the baseball card disintegrating slowly.

"It's probably best if you leave now," she said.

"No. It's my house. I'm staying. We are going to fix this. I promise. We will fix it."

Ella looked to Mimi, who still sat quietly with a grin on her face as if she was watching a movie or a show. "You ready to go?" Ella asked.

"Sure thing," Mimi said, and stood.

They walked toward the door. Sims didn't say a thing. Mimi, however, had the last word. "You should try a little grated Parmesan with that sauce."


Ella took Mimi home and flopped onto the chair. Mimi clicked on the TV. *E! News* flickered across the screen, silent and full of color.

"My nightly empty calories," Mimi said as she walked to the kitchen. "So let's find ourselves something to eat here since your spaghetti was fully ruined."

"More than ruined," Ella said. "What was that? Insanity?"

"Love makes us all do crazy things," Mimi said. "I mean, look at Romeo and Juliet. Tristan and Isolde. The Greek gods, all of them went crazy for love. It's just the thing to do."

Ella laughed, but the pit in her stomach didn't feel the humor. She punched at the volume button for the TV and the anchor, a blonde so skinny it didn't look like her body should be able to hold up her boobs and head combined, chatted in a high-pitched voice.

"I've got some frozen pizza," Mimi said from the kitchen. "How does that sound?"

"I'm not that hungry. Besides, I should be getting home," Ella said. "Wherever that is."

"No, stay here. Let's eat pizza, and watch mindless TV. It heals. Ancient healing ritual no one has told you about."

Ella smiled and it felt very real. "Good idea." She settled back and stared at the TV. It seemed that Angelina and Brad were having another child, although that didn't seem possible. Action movies topped the list of hits that season. When didn't they? Taylor Swift broke up with yet another boyfriend and wrote yet another song about it. Someone had plastic surgery and someone else was pregnant. The dull details in a regular life, but newsworthy in the famous.

Mimi handed Ella a glass of bourbon and Ella took a long swig, but drinking on an empty stomach was not a good idea because there, on the screen, was a man who looked like Hunter. Yes, Ella thought about him all the time, but this was ridiculous, like seeing Mother Mary in an oil stain on the pavement. She leaned closer, and if she had glasses (which she didn't), she would have put them on. His picture, this man, was in a square on the upper right side of the TV, and the blond anchor was talking about him with the co-anchor who had joined her, a dark-haired man Ella couldn't see because she was too preoccupied looking at the photo with the words "Blake Hunter" written underneath.

Then she tuned into the words they spoke, blurry, fuzzy, she didn't understand until she did.

"Yes," the blonde said. "We've all been waiting for this. After two flops—and let's be honest they were flops no matter how many people went to see them—we've all been holding our breath for the next Blake Hunter film."

The man spoke. "And to have Witherspoon agree so quickly after the last movie, it must be a spectacular script."

"I for one can't wait to hear about it. Adam, do you know anything about it?"

"Only what has been officially released today, which is that the movie is called *The Only One,* is set in the South, and Reese Witherspoon has agreed to play the lead."

"Thanks for the information. We'll wait and see what else we can learn and get back to you soon." Ella looked at her glass and it was empty. It had to be the bourbon. Must be.

*The Only One?* Isn't that what she'd called Sims when she'd described him to Hunter? Southern setting? The photo?

The photo. It was of a man who looked just like Hunter, but more . . . handsome. His hair was longer, almost shoulder length and wavy. He had a goatee and wore a button-down, something she'd never seen Hunter wear. A brother? A cousin? What the hell? *The Only One?*

Her mind spun around like those damn teacups at Disney World.

"Mimi," she hollered too loudly for the small space.

"What, dear?"

"Look. Hurry, look at the TV."

Mimi came to Ella's side and a smile spread across her face, a recognition. "Well, well," Mimi said. "Isn't life so much fun?"

"Fun?" Ella stood up and started pacing the room. "Oh, my God, it all makes sense now. Like anything does in hindsight. Like Sims cheating. Like this . . ."

"How?" Mimi asked.

"There was something wrong about it all. Like the way he couldn't sit through the movie. His eyeglasses that didn't work. He always stumbled over names. He never told me the names of any of his books. He—" Ella looked at Mimi. "He lied to me the entire time. God, Mimi." Ella poured some more bourbon. "I was so busy weaving my own lies, so engrossed in my story that I didn't even see Hunter's . . . well, Blake's lies. His made-up life. What kind of idiot am I?"

How could she be mad at him? But she was. She was furious. Mad as hell. Throw-the-bourbon-across-the-room mad. Watch it shatter, splinter, make-a-noise that-would-wake-the-building mad.

"Hunter lied to me," Ella said as if speaking it out loud would convince her heart of the truth.

"Now there's a twist." Mimi smiled.

"Here I was feeling all guilty and thinking I should tell him the truth, call him up and come clean, and all this time he was telling me some crazy story also. He was using me; stealing my love story."

"Your fake love story. Listen, Ella, not everyone is who they say they are. The world just isn't so clear. We all have our secrets and pasts, and so he told you he was a history writer and he was really a movie maker?" She shrugged. "I don't know that it matters so much."

"He was using me."

"Really?"

"He stole from me."

"He did?"

"You are infuriating," Ella said with a loud exhale. "Yes, he used me to get to a story and he stole the story to use to make money . . . to . . . I don't know."

"Are you sure it's Hunter you're mad at?"

"No. I'm not sure at all. And he goes by Blake." Ella pointed at the screen, which had already switched to another story. "So you see, everyone, I mean everyone, is taking advantage of me."

"Well, what are you going to do about it?" Mimi asked.

"Eat our pizza and then some pound cake?" Ella asked with a smile.

"That's a good start but there has to be something after that."

Mimi rose to go to the kitchen. Ella didn't interfere, and she didn't let Mimi know that she was aware about the Sara Lee masquerade. At least someone got to keep their secret.

"I don't know what's next, but—"

Impetuous, she lifted her phone and typed.

*Oh, hey there, Blake. Congratulations on your movie deal.*

Ashlee wasn't home that night, and he was glad. She'd left a note that said, *"Guess you forgot about the party tonight. Meet me there if you want."*

He wasn't meeting her anywhere. He was taking off his shoes, pouring a drink—just one—and watching *Entertainment News* for any mention of the press release.

His house finally felt a little bit like home. Slowly, his decorator had framed and hung some pictures. Rugs were scattered in random patterns, which he liked. Soft, plush pillows were everywhere and she'd done exactly as he asked—made sure it didn't look anything like his old house. The view was incredible. Even now he looked out over the water instead of at the TV, until he heard his name and turned to watch the hostess announce the movie, talk about the expectations.

There were so few moments of celebration in the entertainment world. That's what no one really knew. All the work, all the loneliness for just this thirty-second mention on TV. Then more work. Then the release and the holding of the breath for reviews and opening week financial statistics. The world saw the moments of celebration (and defeat) and so they believed that was all there was to it. The viewers didn't think of any of them as real people, humans with heartbreak and friends and lovers and children. They were tabloid fodder, outfits and hairdos, success and failure. And he knew this, because if viewers (and reviewers, which anyone could be on the Internet these days) saw them as real people in a broken world, they would never write the way they did.

Viewers never saw the tossed ideas, the dark nights, the fear of never creating again. But in this moment, Blake absorbed the goodness of it all and in a motion he gave very little thought to, he reached for his phone. He wanted to tell Ella. That's the one person he wanted to share all of this with.

He lifted the phone and saw text messages rolling in from everywhere: friends, enemies, all wanting to say "Oh, congrats, man, just saw the news."

But he grabbed the second phone and saw Ella's text:

*Oh, hey there, Blake. Congratulations on your movie deal.*

Right there, without Ashlee in the house, with his name and news still echoing in the well-decorated but empty room, he understood that he was falling in love with Ella Flynn and that Ella Flynn would hate him for the rest of her life, just like everyone else he'd messed over.

Why had he lied to her? For what? Kept the lie going? For this moment alone in an empty house to hear his name on TV? What a fool. He stared at his empty glass and felt the emptiness inside. What had Ella called it? A gap. A crack, he'd said, quoting Leonard Cohen, trying to sound smart and sophisticated. What an ass he was.

Ella woke on Mimi's couch, blurry-eyed with a dull bourbon headache. She sat up and slowly remembered everything.

She'd been had. Again.

But so had Hunter. This guy, whoever he was—Blake or Hunter— the man she thought was a friend, had stolen her fake love story for a film. And yet it wasn't her love story at all. He'd stolen some alternate life she'd imagined. How could you steal something that wasn't real to begin with? Like stealing air or dreams. What he'd taken didn't belong to anyone.

She couldn't make much sense of any of it. Margo took her design. Sims took her heart. And Hunter took her story and made it into a movie. A movie! He didn't even try to hide it. *The Only One.* Not only a thief, but also a brazen one. She had to give him credit—he had nerve for sure.

But what about their friendship?

What about the connection she'd felt?

God, what a fool she'd been.

The worst part was that the first person she wanted to talk to about the mess was Hunter, and there was no such thing as Hunter.

Her eyes were still dusky with sleep, but she could see that there weren't any messages on her phone. She deleted Hunter's name and number as if he'd never existed. As if a swipe of her finger on a delete button could erase him and all he'd become to her.

She gave too much of herself away. She did it too easily and too often. It would stop now. Ella snuck quietly out of Mimi's apartment. The stairwell was still dark. Of course it was. Why would the landlord do anything she asked? A single lightbulb dropped a circle of light onto the floor. Ella stepped over it like it was a puddle.


Fog spread across the landscape and softened the edges of her house. The wisteria was in full bloom now. Ella closed her eyes and smiled, inhaling the scent. Hunter was right. It was exactly between gardenia and rose, the idea of the smell, not too much and not so little that you had to get right into the bloom. Along the top of the brick wall, two cardinals—a male and a female—sat looking down at her, quiet and still. She glanced at the birdfeeder: empty. Ella opened the container at the end of the bench and filled the feeder. "Sorry," she said. "It won't happen again. I'm home now."

She entered the house with a few careful steps. Inside, a single light cast a warm glow over the living room where Sims lay asleep on the chaise, an empty glass beside him on a table. Ella didn't wake him. She walked into the kitchen and started a pot of coffee. She turned on some music—Elvis Costello just for fun—and scanned the refrigerator for food. Sims's bachelor fridge contained three eggs, a half-carton of milk, half a stick of butter, some wilted lettuce, and foil-covered leftovers that Ella couldn't identify. Condiments lined the door, along with expired salad dressings, sauces, and Coke bottles. She grabbed the eggs and placed them on a towel on the counter. After finding a loaf of bread in the pantry, she toasted two slices while she scrambled the eggs with butter. She snapped a sprig from a fragile rosemary plant growing on the windowsill, and chopped it up before tossing it on top of the eggs. A simple meal had never tasted so good.

"What are you doing?" Ella turned to see a groggy Sims enter the kitchen.

"Eating, drinking coffee . . . you know," Ella said.

"I mean, what are you doing *here*?"

"I live here," she said. "And *you*?"

He walked toward her, rubbing his face and stretching. "Well, then," he said, in that I-just-woke-up voice she knew so well. "I guess that means we live here together. And you know what that means . . ." He trailed off.

"I thought I did."

Sims responded with something like enthusiasm in his voice. "God, I'm so glad you're back. I didn't sleep all night and finally I just got up and went to your favorite chair. I thought, If I just stay here and wait, she'll come home."

He drew closer. Ella took two steps back.

"I'm so sorry, Ella. I am *so* sorry. You're all I've ever wanted. All

I've ever needed. I don't know what I can do to make up for this hell, for what I've done. Tell me what to do and I'll do it. Anything."

"I don't know, Sims. But I need more than words."

He reached for her then and drew her close, wrapping his arms around her. She fell into his chest and he held her there, running his hands through her hair, mumbling into her neck. "It was like I lost my mind."

At first she thought it was him, but then she understood that she was the one trembling. This, right here, was what she'd dreamed about. All those weeks in that apartment, slipping shoes onto bridesmaids' feet, eating food she cooked off a hot plate. This is what she'd wanted. Exactly this. Even the words he was saying. It was like she had scripted them.

Ella drew back and looked at her husband's familiar features, his blue eyes, his etched forehead. "I don't know how to do this, Sims. I don't know how to pretend nothing ever happened. Things happened. Terrible things. My heart is a mess."

"I know." His eyes were dry, but his voice held pain. "I'm a mess, too."

"What happened, Sims? Tell me what happened."

"That's what I need to figure out. And I will. I promise. But I love you and you alone."

"No." She backed up. "No, I don't think you do. If you had, you wouldn't have done what you did."

He shook his head. "That's not true. I loved you even while I was with . . ." He stopped short of Betsy's name. "I just got lost. That's all. You have to forgive me."

"Have to?"

"Yes. You'll kill me if you can't."

"I already killed you," Ella said quietly.

"What?"

"Nothing . . . it's just . . . nothing."

He held her close again. "Anything you say, I'll do. I just can't live without you. It's like it was all a terrible dream."

"No," she said. "It was all very real."

He backed away. "I am going to win you back. There's enough love here to save us. I know there is."

"But I don't want that kind of love—the kind with limits and secrets and love-by-half. I don't want that. I loved you completely and still you were able to go be with Betsy. As if what we had was cheap. As if our marriage wasn't enough."

"It's not that. It's everything. I will show you. I made a mistake." Her husband, the man she loved, took her by the shoulders and looked at her so intensely she needed to look away. He pulled her to him and kissed her. His hands ran up her back and nestled into her hair, pulling her even closer as if he needed to feel her body contact his on every surface. He clung to her as if he was a drowning man.

Hunter was wrong. Love was not just an idea. It was real. It was a man. A woman. A marriage.

After a while, Sims let go and pulled back. This time he had tears in his eyes. "I have to go to the marina, but then I'm coming home. We're going to start over."

Ella faltered. "How are we supposed to start over?" she asked.

"We'll find a way. We have to."

It wasn't until she heard the front door click shut that Ella realized that she wasn't doubting his love. She was doubting her own.


She spent the next days in a haze of organization. With the music on high, Ella weeded the garden, adjusted the kitchen, and the closets. She dusted and swept, vacuumed and polished. She scrubbed everything with Lysol. She washed every dish in the kitchen and soaked the pots and pans in lethally hot water. The slipcovers were sent to the dry cleaner. The pillows, too. She bought a smudge stick and walked through the house, trailing smoke behind her. Betsy was like a ghost that needed exorcising. A virus that had infected her home.

In between, in the hours when cleaning became too much, Ella sat down and worked on her portfolio. Spreading her sketches across the kitchen table, organizing them, she could see how they worked together, how they formed a collection. It was as if the designs had gathered themselves into groupings almost without her knowledge. Yes, she had intended that some garments appear flowing, others more structured, and others casual. But only now, looking at them collectively instead of focusing on one particular design or one particular detail—the stability of a shoulder, the hang of a skirt, the paneling of a bodice—could she see that the collections each had a distinct personality. Flirty. Sexy. Classic.

White Diamond. That's what Margo had named the hijacked design. Margo probably had no idea that she'd named her design perfectly, that hydrangeas represented "heartlessness, arrogance, and vanity." Yes, exactly.

Ella lifted the sketch and held it up to the light. It was obvious it was hers (her hand strokes were distinct), although she supposed that anyone could say she'd drawn it only after seeing Margo's entry. But would they say that if they saw the entire collection? If they saw all the designs that preceded this one?

After the weekend, Ella started her letter to *Vogue*.

She was in the kitchen. Sims was home, too. Monday morning had arrived with a thunderstorm so brutal he delayed the opening of the marina. The rain slammed hard against the windows, but Ella barely heard it. She had to act quickly. Only one more week until the contest was closed, until the winner was chosen. She would do the first draft by hand before she typed it up, found her way into the words. She didn't want to sound like a crazy person, but she did have a legitimate grievance. This was her design. Her creation. Her life.

Sims came into the kitchen, bleary-eyed and yawning. "Come back to bed. It's the first time in weeks that I don't have to get up at five A.M."

"I'm . . . trying to write a letter."

"To who?"

"I'm writing to . . . ." Ella stopped. Why hadn't she told her husband? "I guess I didn't tell you about Margo," she said.

"What about Margo?" he asked.

"What she did to me."

"What did she do?" Sims nuzzled the back of Ella's neck, ran his fingers across her collarbone, and then slipped his hand under her shirt. "Come back to bed."

"I want to finish this. I've been thinking about it all night. What to say, how to say it."

"Well, I've been thinking about this all night," he said, and slid his hand further down, running his finger along the waistline of her jeans. "I can't get enough of you."

Ella twisted in her chair to lift her face to his, but not to kiss him. "Not now, Sims. Let me finish this."

He made a small huffing noise and walked off to the coffeepot. She had to smile. It was true. He couldn't get enough of her. They'd made love every morning, every night. A starving man finding his way to food. Her, too. She'd needed to feel his body next to her, near her. But right this minute she needed his ear, which he seemed unable to offer. She tried again. "Margo stole my design," she said.

"Your what?" He came to her side, glanced at his cell phone, and scrolled through a list of messages.

"My dog. She stole my dog and gave it to a bridesmaid in the shop. And then she did a cartwheel through the store and ran off with one of the groomsmen."

Sims looked up from his phone "I'm sorry she did that. I'm sure you'll work it out." He walked off, still talking. "I'm headed out. Seems the workshop flooded. I have to get a crew in."

"Okay," Ella called after him. "Be safe."

If it were someone else, anyone really, she would have laughed. This was the man trying hard to win back her heart? Well, it didn't seem funny at all.

She would focus on her work.

*Editor-in-Chief*
Vogue *Magazine*
*Re: Wedding Design Contest*

*Dear Judges:*

*My name is Ella Flynn. I live in Watersend, South Carolina, and work for the premier wedding destination shop in the southeast: Swept Away. During the months that I worked there, I designed at least twenty dresses, not one of which I've shown to anyone but the store owner, Margo Sands. A few weeks ago, she saw one of my designs, the Wisteria, and asked if she could look at it, even make a copy of it. She then took this design and redrew it, renamed it the White Diamond and entered it into your Wedding Design Contest. I understand it is now a finalist.*

*I know this must seem a preposterous claim, but sadly, it's true. For the integrity of your esteemed magazine, and the validity of the contest, I urge you to look closely at my claim. I am enclosing some of my other sketches and designs to show you the similarity between my drawings and White Diamond. You will notice the drawings are too similar to be coincidental, and the embellishments are exactly the same.*

*You can contact me at any of the below numbers.*
*Sincerely,*

Ella read the letter four or five times before typing it up. She designed a logo, drawing a peony and writing "Ella" in script font across the flower. It looked official. Would it be enough?

She needed a second pair of eyes on the letter. Really, there was only one person to read it, and he was in L.A., out of her life now. So, Mimi, then. She'd have Mimi read it.

Ella visited Mimi every day. She liked looking in on her friend and her bedraggled little dog, especially now that he had stopped barking. *Almost* stopped barking, that is. It seemed that Hunter was right; Bruiser was allergic to his medicine. At least *that* wasn't a lie.

Mimi would have something to say about the letter. Something smart and practical. She could count on Mimi.

But the woman who answered the door was just a shadow of her friend. She looked paper thin and worn, like she would tear apart if she were touched. Her face, faded to pale, was wet with tears. Her hair, that white coif that usually puffed out from her head like a pom-pom, was flat, stuck to the side of her head. And her clothes—usually so carefully chosen—were just a pair of drawstring pants and a sweatshirt worn at the edges.

"Oh, Ella," Mimi said. "I don't know what to do."

"What's wrong?" Ella looked inside for clues.

"Bruiser."

"He's not barking," Ella said. "That's good, right?"

"No, it's not good. He's not barking because . . ." Mimi stepped back and pointed at the back of the room, where the oversized dog bed dominated the corner.

Ella understood before another word was spoken.

"Oh, Mimi," Ella said. "I'm so, so sorry. What can I do?"

"I don't know. I just don't know."

"Let me call the vet," Ella said. "Where's his number?"

Mimi shuffled to the refrigerator and took down a piece of paper. "Here."

Ella forgot about her letter, which she dropped on Mimi's coffee table. She forgot about everything but Mimi's grief, which seemed as large as she was small. Mimi crumpled into her chair, the one where she sat every time Ella visited, the one where she ate pound cake and drank bourbon, the one from which she offered advice and consolation and took in Ella's secrets like a vault.

After Ella called the vet they sent a tech, Floyd something or other. His dark hair curled around his ears. He wore pale blue scrubs and a nametag that hung crooked from the left pocket. He was past a teenager, but probably still in college. He had the look of sympathy, his eyes downcast and his hands clasped behind his back. "I'm so sorry, ma'am," he said. "I know this is so difficult. I'm here to help. I will wrap him up and take him and then . . ."

"Then what?" Mimi asked in a whisper. "My God, then what?"

"We can have him cremated and if you want . . . we can give you the ashes to keep forever."

"No!" Mimi said. "You can't cremate him. You can't."

"I know it's terrible to think about." Floyd touched Mimi's arm. "It's the good-bye that's the terrible part. I know."

"I want to bury him," Mimi said, and closed her eyes. "Somewhere beautiful."

"I'll find a place," Ella said. "I will."

"Well, let me take him for now." Floyd had kind eyes, soft and aware. He was perfect for his job.

"I'll come with you," Ella said, and then, leaning down to Mimi. "Stay here. I'll be right back. We'll honor Bruiser. We will."

Ella was awash in grief. Bruiser. Mimi. Her mom. Her marriage. Her job. Hunter's false friendship. It was a porous pain that acknowledged all the hurt that came from being alive, from trying to live a good life, from just being human. It was then that Ella realized all the energy she had put into keeping this precise knowledge at bay. That pain came no matter what. That life offered to everyone their own grief and despair. It was a part of living, a part of everything.

Floyd lifted Bruiser so gently, as if he were still alive. Ella held the tears until they were in the stairwell. When they reached the sidewalk, Floyd turned to Ella. "I'll take care of this. Okay?"

"Can I pick him up later? I'm going to find a nice place to bury him." Ella spoke through tears.

Ella knew this much: She owed it to Mimi to do the right thing for this ornery little guy, for all loss to be acknowledged. She touched his tiny little head, and all the warmth was gone. She lifted his little face and touched the tip of his black nose. "Rest well," she said. Whatever that means.

Floyd nodded and she saw his own tears, little ones, private ones, in the far corners of each eye. He gently placed Bruiser in the back of a van.

Floyd drove off. Ella let herself cry a little longer. She sat on a bench at the edge of the sidewalk until she felt almost empty. Far off, a seagull cried out.

If only she could call Hunter.

## fourteen

That next morning they gathered in Ella's front garden. Sims was there with Ella and Mimi, his hands behind his back, his face tight. "I had a dog once. It's why I never got another."

"Why?" Mimi looked up at him. She was so tiny next to Sims, a little doll.

"He was my best friend," Sims said simply. "And he got hit by a car. I realized then that I could never again have a best friend that could be lost so easily."

"Anyone can die that way," Mimi said.

"But people usually don't. Dogs do."

Mimi shrugged. "So you're the kind of man who guards his heart, who thinks he can outrun it. Good for you."

Sims didn't answer. What could he say that wasn't defensive and rude?

Ella wore her gardening gloves, the red ones with the big daisy on the back of the hands. She liked these best because it always looked like she was planting Red Gerbera, no matter what she was doing. She pulled at a dead hydrangea, the small petals of the now brown and dried flower blossoms crumbled, dust and dry twigs puffing out like smoke. She thought of how they'd looked when she planted them—a bright, vibrant blue. Now they were wasted.

The root ball broke loose with a final tug and Ella landed on her bottom without a sound. She looked up at Sims. "Here." She handed him the dead plant, then picked up the spade, which was crusted in rust and old dirt. The ground gave way easily and within three shovelfuls, Ella had made a hole big enough for the tiniest Bruiser.

Sims stood next to her and twice offered to dig, to take the spade from her. "I want to do this," she said. "Let me do this."

He was trying so hard to be a good husband. Ella took his hand and squeezed it in a silent thank-you. It was the least she could do.

Mimi sat on the bench Ella had pulled over and looked down into the hole. "I can't watch this."

"Okay," Ella said.

"I've already said good-bye to Bruiser. I'm going inside. Okay?"

Ella nodded. She looked at Sims. "Will you take Mimi inside?"

Mimi held up her hand as she stood, unsteady and strong at the same time. "No, thank you, though."

Sims looked at Ella and shrugged. She knew what he'd say later, when he could: whatamisupposedtodo? She'd heard that a lot this past week.

Ella covered Bruiser, topping off the plot with the rock Mimi had chosen from the jetty. "I'll plant flowers later," she said to Sims. She wiped her hands down her jeans, leaving a streak of dirt.

"She hates me," Sims said. "What did you tell her about me?"

Ella stopped. She'd already taken a few steps toward the door and she turned back to Sims. "What?"

"What did you tell her that makes her hate me? Did you hear what she said about my heart? She has no idea."

"I don't think that was about you." That was all it took to bring the conversation to a close.

Ella found Mimi at the table, twirling ice cubes in a glass with her finger.

"You two sure love your sailing," Mimi said, looking around.

Ella nodded and laughed. "Are you okay?" she asked her friend.

"I think so, yes." Mimi looked up. "This was very kind of you, Ella. You know that, right? I didn't have anywhere to . . ."

"I know."

"I was rude to your husband. I'm sorry. It's not polite. . . ."

"No worries, Mimi. It's okay. Today you get a free pass to say anything you want about anything you want."

"Thanks."

They sat quietly the way they would in Mimi's apartment, not needing to say anything or fill the space with chatter. A few minutes later, Sims entered the kitchen. "Can I do anything for you two before I go back to the marina?"

Mimi and Ella shook their heads and he was gone, the back door latching behind him with an assured click.

"I like Hunter better," Mimi said.

"There's no such person."

They shared a look and smiled. "I get you," it said.

"I should go home," Mimi said.

"Why?" Ella asked.

"Because I don't live here."

"Why don't you take a nap? Just stay for a little while? Eat dinner with us and when you're rested, I'll take you home. Okay?"

Ella showed Mimi to the back guest bedroom. Her head settled into the pillow, barely enough to dent it. She looked so small, so delicate. "Oh, by the way. I sent that letter you left at my apartment. I sent it overnight."

"What?"

But Mimi didn't answer. She was already asleep. Her small hands were folded at her throat, her feet were crossed, and her head lolled slightly to one side. Ella pulled up the blue-striped blanket and tucked it under her friend's chin before kissing her on the forehead. She returned to the kitchen and sighed. Ella imagined the envelope somewhere between her house and a chrome-covered desk at *Vogue*, where there wouldn't be a nautical knickknack in sight.

Ella called Sims immediately. "I need to go see Dad."

"Right now?" he asked.

"In the morning," she said. "First thing in the morning."

"Ten years you don't go there, and you need to go right now?"

"Yes," she said. "Yes, I do."

The drive to her hometown was only two hours, yet Ella felt like she was going back ten years. She kept the car windows down and the radio off. The whish and hum of coastal air slowly morphed into the denser breeze of the farms and inland plains. She drove past dormant cotton fields and crisp white houses with front porches. There were the gas stations with neon signs, where boiled peanuts were sold from mucky pots in the parking lot. She passed the misspelled signs for roadside stands selling peaches and shrimp (peeches and shimp). With every mile that passed, her heartbeat increased. When she was within ten miles of Greenboro, her palms were sweating and she forgot all the words to the long, lovely speech she had planned.

This was a different woman driving back to Greenboro, far different from the girl who'd run away. She hadn't returned since the week after her mother's funeral, when she'd hugged her dad good-bye and said, "I just can't stay here." Amber had secured a job for Ella at the marina. "I'll go for just a little while," Ella had thought. "Anything is better than staying here and seeing my mom on every corner, in every glance of sympathy."

She was returning now to see her dad, to make some peace where there hadn't been any for so, so long. Her dad moved to a smaller house only a mile from the one where she'd grown up, and Ella drove past the old house first. It was a single-level brick house, ranch-style it was called. In a cul-de-sac where she'd spent her entire childhood playing kick the can, ghost in the graveyard, and hide-and-seek, Ella parked and stared at the house. The new owners had painted the brick white. The shutters had been replaced with a farmhouse-style, painted pale blue with iron hardware. She hardly recognized it. But yes, this was her childhood home. This was where she'd grown up, where she'd lived when her mom died and the place she'd left in hopes of finding some peace. *But that's the problem*, she said to herself, *when you go you take yourself with you.* She'd left anyway.

After a few minutes of staring at her old house, Ella drove away and quickly found her dad's new home a few blocks away. It was a small Tudor with window boxes and a brick sidewalk that led to the front door. Ella got out of the car and looked at the house, trying to reconcile her dad's new life in a place she'd never seen. He appeared at the front door before she had a chance to even walk up the path. He waved and Ella smiled at him.

He looked so much older, so sunken into himself and yet still the handsome man who had dominated her childhood with laughter and a boisterous voice. "Ella," he hollered. Same voice, too.

"Hi, Dad," she said and walked toward him, slowly and then faster, until she realized that she was running into his arms.

He hugged her so close, so tight that Ella rested her head on his shoulder and exhaled. "I'm so sorry, Dad."

"For what?" His voice loud in her ear.

She lifted her head and looked at him. "For leaving you. For blaming you. For being a terrible daughter and believing that running away from you could solve anything."

He took her face in his hands. "My God, I've missed you."

Together they sat on the front steps and Ella leaned her head on his shoulder. "Dad, I've really messed things up. And I've realized that all this time I've been searching and searching for someone to cure this grief . . . to make me feel better."

"No one can do that, Ella."

"I know that now. I know." She lifted her head and took her dad's hand. "I blamed you. I'm sorry."

"You thought I should have saved her," he said.

"Yes," Ella said with a catch of leftover weeping in the back of her throat. "I did think that."

"So did I," he said. "I'm still tortured by it every day, Ella. What could I have done differently that day on the lake? She reached for that hat . . . she fell off . . . I jumped . . . I try to change the sequence in my mind. Maybe I shouldn't have taken the time to turn off the boat. Maybe I should have dove deeper or held my breath longer or . . . anything that could bring her back."

"But there wasn't anything to be done about it, Dad. I know that in my mind, but my heart wanted you to have saved her."

"Me, too, baby. Me, too."

"All these lost years . . . being mad at you, wishing for something to change, believing that Sims could save me. I've wasted time wanting things to be different instead of looking at the way things really are. Like I've been fighting the world, grabbing at something outside for something that can only be found inside."

"Well, at least you found love in all of this," he said and stroked the top of Ella's hand.

"Not so much." She tried to laugh.

"I'm sorry." That was all he said, and it was enough, perfectly enough.


Blake spent the next days thinking about Ella and avoiding Ashlee. He knew what he had to do. This wasn't a silence that could be broken by a text or an e-mail. This wasn't a wrong that could be put right with flowers or lyrics from a perfect love song. He had to stand before her and confess to everything, no matter the humiliation or what it meant or what she would do. He had to stand before her.

With two phone calls and a bag packed, he was on the way to LAX. He texted Ashlee from the limo:

*I have to go back to Watersend. We need to talk when I get back.*

*F.U.*

Her reply was short and sweet. Of course it was. Everyone knows what "we need to talk" means.

Mimi stayed at Ella's house; she'd settled in quietly, teaching Ella about the garden, digging in the dirt with her own hands, naming the birds that came to the feeder. Ella was a self-taught gardener. She planted and watered and hoped. If something lived, she did it right. If it died, she did it wrong. Kind of simple, really. But Mimi knew the seasons and the reasons for every plant, where it would grow best, where it would wither. She knew the birds and what kind of food they liked. In those few days, Mimi offered a glimpse into her past life, one that had been thriving and full. One that had nothing to do with Crumbling Chateau.

"Where did you used to live?" Ella asked as Mimi trimmed the buds off a rosebush.

"About three houses down from here," Mimi said.

"Are you kidding?"

"Why would I do that?" she asked.

"You've just never said anything. When did you move out?"

"Years ago, sweetie. Years ago. After my bookstore closed, I sold the house and moved."

"Why to those apartments?"

Mimi held out her hand for the shovel. "Oh, the apartment came later, after I ran out of money."

Ella searched for something to say. This moment needed a kind word or sympathy but Mimi didn't want that. If there was one thing Ella knew about Mimi, it was that she hated sympathy.

"So, where did you go to after—"

Her question was interrupted by a singsong voice.

"Ella." It was Amber.

Ella opened the gate. "Hey, there," she said.

"You've been avoiding me," Amber said with a pout.

"Yep, I have."

"Why?" Amber glanced toward Mimi and then back at Ella with a who-is-that? expression on her face.

"Just been busy," Ella said. "Come on in and meet my neighbor, Mimi."

"Neighbor? Oh, how nice," Amber said, and walked to Mimi. "Which house?"

Mimi sat on the ground, a blanket underneath as she leaned into the earth with the hand shovel. "Hello, there. Nice to finally meet you, Amber."

"Which house did you move into?"

"Oh," Ella said. "No. She's my neighbor from the apartments."

"Oh?" Amber said. "That's nice, I guess."

Mimi stood up, slowly as she always did, like any fast movement might break her in two. She walked to the bench. "So you're Amber," she said.

"You know me?"

"I've told her all about you," Ella said.

"Just great. We've been best friends for twenty years and you probably told her about the last horrible month instead of all the good stuff."

Ella shook her head. "No, that's not true." She shook dirt off her hands. "So, what's up?"

"I just came to say hello and see why you were ignoring me."

Ella approached her friend and hugged her, not caring if the dirt was transferred. "I'm not ignoring you. I'm trying to get my feet on the ground again. You know . . . find my way again."

"Well, I miss you."

"What about me?" The three women turned to see Sims standing on the opposite side of the fence. He peered over the top with a grin and then opened the gate and walked in. "You miss me, too?"

"Nope," Amber said. "I officially hate you for what you've put my best friend and my sister through. I don't miss you one bit." Her voice did not match her words, though. There was fun in her voice. Laughter.

Now it was Ella's turn to give Amber a look. But she didn't have a chance. Her phone rang. A 212 area code.

She turned away from Sims and Amber and their cute little exchange. "Hello?" she said tentatively.

"May I please speak with Ella Flynn?"

"Speaking," she said.

"This is *Vogue*. I'm calling about your letter."

Ella's lungs refused to take in air.

"Are you there?" the voice asked.

"Yes, I'm here," Ella exhaled

"I have to say, your letter took us by surprise. I have to be honest and say that at first we thought it was a hoax. But we reviewed your claim. We looked at your designs, looked at the lines and patterns. We asked Ms. Sands for her other designs."

"And—?"

"Well, we've determined that you are telling the truth and this dress is your design, upgraded and redrawn. We are giving you and Ms. Sands two choices. One: you can submit this design as a team, or two, you alone can submit one of your other designs."

"As a team?"

"She did add to the design, an embellished pattern of sequins at the hemline, pleats along the zipper line, and a larger bustle. So we can't technically put your name on it."

"But she committed . . . fraud."

"You can't prove that, I'm afraid. Besides, she says you knew. If you want to pursue a claim of fraud, well, that's up to you. But for the contest, which will be decided tomorrow, you must decide whether to submit as a team, withdraw the design, or enter on your own."

Ella closed her eyes and tried to find that calm place inside, the one that would tell her what to do. "Can I call you back in ten minutes?" she asked.

"Of course. But we need to know within the hour."

"Yes, I understand. And thank you for taking the time to review this. That design is one of my favorites."

"Listen, Ms. Flynn, what she did—your boss—wasn't right, but she did admit to your contribution. She didn't think it was wrong to submit under the store's name since you worked there. Obviously you should get credit."

"Here's the thing," Ella said. "She knew what she was doing. And I don't work there anymore. She stole the design."

"I understand. But from here, from this end, we only have a couple of options."

"Thank you." Ella looked to Sims and then Amber, and then Mimi, but the person she wanted to ask what to do—Hunter—wasn't there.

And then he was.

Ella hung up without saying good-bye, or maybe she didn't even hang up. She didn't know. When she saw Blake standing there, she did something that Sims and Amber and Mimi would bring up later. She rushed to the gate and opened it, ran to the sidewalk where he stood, and threw her arms around him without a word.

They saw all that. What they didn't see, what they didn't hear, were the simple words she whispered in his ear. "Oh, you're here."

Blake hugged her back, held her tight. "I'm so sorry," he said. "Ella." He took her face in his hands.

She felt everyone watching. Listening. The palmetto tree branches rattled in the wind and Ella knew that everyone else would hear what he said, but she didn't want to stop Blake from talking—she needed to know.

"Ella Flynn," he said, his hands on either cheek, holding her face. "I am so sorry I lied to you about who I am. I'd been doing it for so long that it just came naturally."

She didn't know what to say. She was mad as hell. She hated him. She wanted to throw something at him. She wanted to hurt him. And she was so glad he was there. "I'm still mad at you," she said.

"I know," he said. "But I'm here to tell you this, and even if you hate me, even if you can never forgive me, I want to say these things to you. Without you in L.A.—well, I wanted you near me. I wanted to tell you things. Every time something happened my first thought was 'I have to tell Ella . . .'" He trailed off.

"Me, too," she said.

"And then I got your text. I was devastated that you had found out who I really was. But underneath it I was relieved. It was as if—"

"Stop there. I have to tell you something . . ."

"Wait. Please." Blake kept on, his words coming out quickly, tumbling over hers. "I want to live a love story. I don't want to just write one; I want to live one. With you."

"Me?"

"I don't know when it happened or how, but I'm falling in love with you, Ella Flynn, and I want to see where this could go. I know you're still grieving your husband, and I'll give you time if you need it, but I wanted to tell you . . ." He leaned in for the kiss, the one she wanted.

"Who the hell is this?" Sims's voice interrupted.

Ella turned. The moment was surreal, like worlds colliding in a half sleep.

Sims was at their side. "Someone want to tell me what the hell is going on?"

Blake took Ella's hand. "I'm Blake Hunter. I'm here to see Ella."

"Hunter," Mimi's voice called from the bench. "So good to see you again."

Blake focused across the yard and went to Mimi, bent over to hug her. "Well, hello there. How's Bruiser? Still barking?"

Mimi pointed to the fresh mound of flowers and the stone.

"Oh, no." Blake took her hands and clasped them between his own. "I'm so sorry."

"Me, too." Mimi glanced furtively between Blake, Amber, Sims, and Ella.

"Can someone tell me what's going on?" Amber asked.

Ella walked to Mimi and Blake. "That was *Vogue* on the phone. They believe me. And my design is a finalist in the contest." She didn't know what else to do or say.

"Oh, honey, that's amazing," Mimi said.

Amber threw her hands in the air. "What is going on? I feel like I fell down some rabbit hole. What's *Vogue* got to do with anything?" she asked, and then turned to Blake, "Are you from *Vogue*?"

"*Vogue*? Me?"

"I don't understand anything right now." Amber held her hands up in surrender.

"Who believes what?" Sims asked. "And again, who are you?" He pointed to Blake.

"Blake Hunter . . ."

"I know your name, I mean, who are you to Ella? Why are you here?"

"*Vogue*," Ella said. "They believe that the design is mine. I have to decide whether to submit it as a team with Margo."

"That's it," Amber said. "You've gone crazy. I have no idea what you're talking about and who is this Blake?"

"Okay, I've obviously walked into a situation here," Blake said. "Ella?"

"Yes?" she said, a hive of bees beneath her chest.

"Wait!" Amber hollered out. "Blake Hunter. I know that name. You're the guy who does all the romance comedies. The one about messy love, and that one with the hurricane . . . and the one with the cop who falls in love with his prisoner. God, I loved that one. Drew Barrymore was in it." Amber rushed toward him. "You're him, aren't you?"

"Yes," he said, keeping his eyes on Ella.

"And you're here to profess your love to Ella? I'm so confused. Are you sure you didn't get her mixed up with someone else?"

"No," he said. "It's Ella."

"Are you sleeping with this guy?" Sims stepped between Blake and Ella.

"You do not get to ask me that," Ella said, and the garden silenced with her proclamation.


Blake had let his fantasies run away with him. He should have thought this through before jumping on a plane and proclaiming his love to a woman he hardly knew. He was prepared for her anger. But this? He should have waited until she was alone. Her garden, her friend Mimi. And the other couple, who were they?

"I'm Sims Flynn," the man said. "What the hell are you doing here with my wife?"

"Your wife?"

"My wife. My. Wife. Ella."

Blake looked to Ella. "You remarried already?"

"No," she said, and covered her face with her hands.

"Wait a minute. *Sims?*"

The man, Blake had seen him before. In the restaurant with the girl who'd proclaimed true love with the married man. He understood with a slow creep of embarrassment. This was the dead man. Sims Flynn, drowned in the bay, the husband who sacrificed his life for his wife. Seems the screenplay wasn't the only place where he rose from the dead.

"Oh, wow," Mimi said. "This might be the most entertaining afternoon I've had in ages."

"You look great for a dead man," Blake said.

"What?"

Ella stepped between them. "I can explain," she said to Blake.

"You can?" Blake said.

"Really?" Sims asked.

They spoke at the same time.

"Yes, I can." She touched Blake's arm and he took two steps back, not because he didn't want Ella to touch him, but because he saw Sims's fist ball up at his side.

"I'm going to leave now," Blake said. "This was a really bad idea."

"A bad idea," Ella said. "Don't say that."

Blake knew what she meant, the bad idea being the idea of love. He wanted to laugh. Her lies . . . God, it was all too much. It was all a fantasy, an acting job done without a script. An improvisation.

Blake opened the gate and walked out to his rental car. They'd given him the same damn one—the turquoise one—as if they'd saved it for him.

Ella ran to his side. "Please, let me explain."

"It's okay, Ella." God, she was so beautiful. She was flushed, her cheeks burning like she had a fever, dirt smeared across her forehead, her hands covered in those gloves. And that dress. She was wearing the little flowered dress he liked so much.

"Really, I understand," he said. "It wasn't really us. Make-believe people became make-believe friends."

"Yes, it was. It was really me," she said.

"Ella!" Sims's voice hollered from the garden gate.

"This all of a sudden seems really complicated," he said. "You better go."

"I'm sorry," she said. "I'm so sorry I said Sims was dead. I didn't mean to keep lying. It was a single moment that just got bigger. I kept thinking I'd stop but I didn't and—"

"I know," he said. "Me, too."

Sims moved toward them, quickly, taking large steps. Blake looked over Ella's shoulder. "You better go."

She walked toward her husband, her hands held out to keep him from advancing. *Her husband.* Blake shook his head as he started the car. Did he think he was the only one full of shit? The only one who told a lie to get what he wanted?

# *fifteen*

He needed to go home, back to L.A. At least there he expected people to lie to him. So why was he driving in circles listening to a radio station stuck to static like the sound of the waves? By the fifth time he'd passed the Sunset, he stopped and went in. It was the middle of the day and the rooftop bar was empty. He ordered what else but a JD, and settled into a chair overlooking the water. Two sips in and he realized that it wasn't a good idea getting sloshed in the middle of the day. He needed to think straight.

Ella loved her husband. They'd reconciled.

What a fool he was. He'd gotten so sappy during the writing of the screenplay that he'd believed he was falling in love with a woman who didn't even exist, a woman he wrote into being.

The JD sloshed at the bottom of his glass and he tossed it over the side of the railing.

Damn. Damn. Damn.

Back in his turquoise car, Blake drove through the town. He recalled each conversation with Ella. Every spoken word. Every single laugh. He saw her hair in the wind and the way it caught in the corner of her mouth. It was making sense now—the "hubby" on her phone; the way she ran out of the restaurant; the delivery guy asking if she'd moved back in; the stereo with the loud music. If he'd been paying attention to anything but his own desire to steal her story, he would have noticed something was off. But he was a self-absorbed ass; he'd only seen what he wanted to see, what was useful to him.

The sky was wiped clean as if all clouds had been erased. The endless blue was cheerful, and it irritated the hell out of him. He parked in front of the movie theater. They never had gone inside. He pulled on the doors just as he had before. Locked. He peered through the glass and saw the remnants of the theater. A long linoleum counter for candy and popcorn. Large metal frames, empty now, where movie posters would have hung. The green carpet was torn in places, obviously stained. He knew what the place would smell like: the slightly sticky aroma of Coke and sugar. There would also be that scent of expectation, that feeling of living another life, if only for ninety or a hundred and twenty minutes. Of entering a world beyond ordinary. He couldn't get enough of that.

That thrill, that escape, was why he'd started writing in the first place, wanting to create stories of what it was like to be a human being trying to live in a world with meaning. He'd never wanted to lose himself or his family. He hadn't meant to become this man he was now, the one who felt he would die without the success, who had almost sold his soul to find another hit.

He thought he heard his name, but the sound was so soft he wasn't sure.

"Blake." This time there was no mistaking it. He glanced to his left and saw Ella, standing at the edge of the building.

"I thought you might be here," she said.

He walked toward her and she to him until they were both moving faster, until they were together. She buried her face in his shoulder. "I'm sorry."

"It's okay, Ella. It's . . ." He wrapped his arms around her.

"Let me tell you everything, okay?" she asked.

He nodded.

"He wasn't dead," Ella said. "But it seemed like it at the time. He left me . . ."

"So we lied. Both of us. We don't even really know each other. This is absurd to think that we could make something of it. Con artists."

"You're right." Ella took a step back. "I told you who I wanted to be instead of who I was. I lied."

"Tell me everything now."

"It's ugly," she said.

"Tell me anyway."

"Sims. My husband. He left me for my best friend's sister. He's back now—back from the dead, I guess. Remorseful. We're working things out. Trying. My job—mostly I sold shoes at the wedding shop. I've never designed a real dress. I just have some sketches and ideas. It's a dream. It's what I wanted and then I pretended it's what I had. I wanted to stop lying to you. I did want to . . ."

"But you didn't," he said. "Life and death and jobs and husband . . ."

"You kept going . . . too."

"What did you say once? That you can't let the facts get in the way of a good story?" Blake shrugged. "So I guess this is where we say good-bye."

"Why did we do this?" Ella asked. "Why would we keep doing that? What's wrong with us?"

"I swear I thought I was falling in love with you, and not just with the idea of you."

"But it's all just an idea, right, Blake? The falling in love. Something you made up with this story. You wrote me into your work and I became someone else. Not me."

"Maybe under different circumstances, if we'd met without the fake lives, we'd have a chance."

"A chance for . . . what?"

"Us," he said. "This." He drew her closer and placed his fingers under her chin, lifted her face to his gaze. "How it feels when I'm with you."

"I'd like to think so."

"Me, too." Blake released her chin and dug his keys out of his pocket. "Ella, I'm glad he's back from the dead for you. I'm glad I met you. My life is better for it." And he walked away, because it was the only thing left to do.


She stood in front of the movie theater as if there was another way to finish this scene, another act to this story, which should be a romance, not a tragedy. It took her a long while to move, to walk to her own car and drive toward home with her emotions so banged up that she felt them rattle in her chest. She needed Hunter, or Blake, or whoever the hell he was to go home. She needed him to stay. Something felt amiss and yet she now had all she ever wanted. The world of opposites existed at the same time.

Mimi sat on the garden bench, waiting for Ella's return. Ella sat next to her and took her hand. "That was a little crazy. I'm sorry you had to see it."

"You okay, dear?" Mimi asked.

"A little confused, but yes, I'm fine. I mean, look at all I've got. My dress is a *Vogue* finalist. Sims is home. You're here. The dark moments have passed and here we are, still standing. Or sitting on a bench. Or whatever."

"What did *Vogue* say when you called them back?"

"I'm invited to the big gala in NYC this coming weekend. They offered to let me add my name to the dress collaboration. But of course I can't go. I need to stay here. I mean, with everything happening. If by some odd chance the dress wins, my name will be attached and that's enough."

"That's enough?" Mimi asked. "Really? You dream your whole life of having a real wedding dress design. You sketch and draw and devour magazines and books. You do research and read and have natural talent, and that's enough? Whoever told you that crumbs were enough? Who the hell told you that?" Mimi's voice rose, fighting for something Ella was unsure about.

"What? I mean, if I win, it will be amazing."

"Then forget about 'everything happening.' Get yourself a dress. Buy yourself a plane ticket. Go to New York. What are you waiting for?"

Ella closed her eyes. Right. What was she waiting for?

She'd tell Sims she was going to New York.

"Where is Sims?" Ella asked.

"He took off when you did," Mimi said. "I thought he ran after you."

"I don't think it's me he's running after," Ella said. "Not me at all.

"My God." Ella leaned her head back on the bench, tears coming before the words. "This was all just some elaborate idea—the marriage, the house, the true love. I saw how I wanted it to be, instead of how it really was."

"Yes, there is a difference," Mimi said so quietly that Ella wasn't sure she said anything at all.

Ella lifted her head. "Why would I want him so badly? Why did I?" She paused before answering her own question. "Because I believed everything he said instead of everything he did, that's why. The sentiments. God, the beautiful words." Ella slammed her hand on the bench.

It only took five minutes to find them—Sims and Betsy at the edge of the marina's dock. There they were, screaming at each other, hands flailing. The river dashed against the wood pilings, nature in its relentless ignorance of the human drama going on right there. Ella watched the river; she watched Sims and Betsy, so quiet that someone observing her might think she was holding her breath.

How could she have loved him? Was it the life and home with him that she loved or was it Sims she loved? Staring at him, begging his mistress to understand.

Ella was inside her car, but she could see them and she knew what was happening—the pleas and pulls of the conversation. Sims wanted Betsy back. Betsy wanted him to be the man he claimed to be. Good. Upstanding. Decent. But Sims wasn't that man. He never would be. Charming? Sure. Fun and exciting and romantic? Absolutely.

For so long she'd asked who Sims wanted her to be, now she would ask herself who *she* wanted to be.

A release, a surge of energy, rose from Ella's chest. The hole that had been there, the one she thought she needed to fill with him, now filled with something else. Strength and resilience. A sense of her own worth. It wasn't him she wanted back; it was love she wanted. Love.

# *sixteen*

The ballroom looked like it was ready for a wedding, a royal one with all the accoutrements of bliss. White tulle hanging from the walls like the bustle on the back of a dress; sparkles and sequins scattered on the floor and on tables. Even the chairs were draped to appear like the bodice of a dress. Centerpieces reached taller than the crowd, spouting white feathers, silver branches, and orchids the size of Ella's fist.

*Vogue* covers were framed on the tables—pictures of women too perfect to be real. And yet they were. Attendees wore long dresses that rustled when they walked and when the music paused, the rustling dresses sounded like soft rain. There were nervous introductions and hesitant greetings. Both the men and women servers wore full tuxedo with tails and gloves.

Ella hadn't seen Margo yet, and the expectation pulsed in her chest. Now? No, not yet. Over there? No. She'd practiced what to say to her, talked it over with Mimi, made her face into a resolute smile of acceptance and yet she knew, because she knew herself, that chances were that nothing would come out of her mouth. Or she'd apologize when apologizing was the very last thing in the world she should do.

Bridal music (violins and organ, piano and overwrought cellos) vibrated the room too loud as it came over the speakers from the ceiling, from the floor, from the side of the stage. The stage. Ella stared at it. In normal life it was a podium and a raised wobbly platform, but that was the beauty of adornment—it was now a stage for a winner.

Twelve finalists from thousands; that is what Ella had been told. There were three round tables up front to seat the finalists with one guest each. Name tags tented on top of silver plates told the designers where to sit. Mimi lagged behind Ella as she moved through the finalists' exhibit. Each dress design had been printed on silver paper and then sandwiched between plexiglass. The name of the designer was written below each dress. These designs hung from the ceiling and then were anchored to the floor so they appeared like floating and headless brides.

Ella didn't want to look at the other designs. Not yet anyway. She wanted the evening to be over, to know the outcome, to just get on with it. The thrill had faded and now there was only a nervous hum under her throat.

She looked around the room and finally added the last idea to her list, the list of how to get over your ex: *Find you inner strength and ask yourself, Who do I want to be?*

The tables were set with place cards: Mimi, Ella, Margo. One. Two. Three. Ella picked up Margo's place card and switched it with someone across the table. Lila Hammer. That was a nice enough name.

There was her name on the place card. But Ella felt like an outsider. She wore a long red dress from Rent the Runway. She'd had her makeup done by a sales girl at Barneys, where she'd been talked into buying things she'd never use but at the time thought were indispensable for her beauty routine: illuminating base lotion; brush sets for application of everything from eyebrow enhancers to blush; lengthening mascara and lipstick that plumped her lips. When the woman had finished her makeup, Ella looked in the mirror and smiled back at a polished image of herself. Her hair had been coiffed by the hotel's hairdresser. She looked like she was wearing a soufflé on her head. Mimi waved from across the room and Ella smiled back at her.

The lights flashed and the music quieted. It was time.

"Which dress is yours?" Lila Hammer asked as they sat, smoothing out their dresses and sipping champagne.

"The White Diamond," Ella said, and pointed to the display.

"That's a nice name for it," Lila said.

"Which one is yours?"

"The Rosebud," Lila said.

Ella ran her eyes over the display, for the first time taking in all the dresses and designs. She found the Rosebud at the end of the line, a dress that wrapped itself into multiple layers of lace over a tight bodice and ended above the knee with a train that trailed romantically behind. "It's so beautiful," Ella said.

"They all are," Lila said. "I wonder how they choose."

"Wouldn't we like to know?" Ella took another sip of champagne and then saw her—Margo scanning for her place. She wore a white dress, of course, silk and gathered at the waist. Her hair was down and either she'd grown two inches of silken blond hair or had extensions put in for the night. Her lipstick so red that at first Ella thought her mouth might be bleeding. She caught Ella's gaze and nodded.

"Hello, Ella," she said from across the table as she sat.

"Hi, Margo."

"Well, you must be so excited to be included in this evening."

"So must you." Ella turned away, refusing to take the bait.

"You nervous?" Mimi asked with a smile.

Ella turned her attention to Mimi, away from Margo and her comments and red mouth. "Very."

"Oh, look," Mimi said. "Margo is wearing a white dress. Isn't she so creative and original."

"Completely," Ella said, grateful for more times than she could count for Mimi's presence and humor.

The noise level escalated so rapidly that there wasn't space or time for any more conversation. The woman MC rattled off the history of wedding dresses from Queen Victoria to Kate Middleton to Kim Kardashian. She talked about hemlines and veils, about famous designers and the intricacy of designing the right sleeve. Even Ella, taking small tasteless bites of her dinner, knew it was too much—all the explanation and blathering. There was only one thing everybody here wanted to know.

Finally, she said it. "So now on to the winner of our bridal design. It was a difficult decision this year. Our judges had a very hard time."

Mimi leaned over and whispered into Ella's ear, her breath gathering in laughter. "Why do they always have to say how hard it was to choose? Just tell us."

Ella took Mimi's hand and suppressed her laughter.

"Our winner this year will be featured in a full spread, but also each one of you, each finalist will be shown, so in essence, you are all winners." The woman held up an envelope, and then pretending to be at the Oscars or Emmys or anywhere else an envelope was dramatically opened, she ripped it. "And the winner is the Helena, by Alex Linden."

A man, beautiful and tall, wearing a tuxedo—of course—stood up to a loud whooping sound. Clapping and hugging and all the things done at an award ceremony commenced. A speech. Toasting. Mentions of the other contestants. It went by in a blur, colors and words and music blending together in a mosaic, until Ella stood with Mimi to congratulate the winner. But Margo rounded the table before anything else could be said or done. "Ella," she said.

"Yes?"

"This is your fault. The dress, it would have won if you hadn't embarrassed both of us with your claim and your ridiculous need for unnecessary credit."

"My fault?" Ella lifted her eyebrows, felt the makeup on her face like too much lotion, a mask.

"Yes."

"Margo, it is my doing that we are even here. My doing that you are wearing that hideous lipstick and your name is hanging off the ceiling and you get again to wear a white dress. You would never be here without me. And you know that. You know that." Ella stood taller, felt the straps of her high heels dig into her old ankle injury.

"I don't know that."

"I do," a voice said, a voice Ella missed and tried to forget. The voice of someone she thought she knew but never really had.

Ella turned slowly, wanting to believe for as long as she could that it was his voice, that the music and the noise and the chaos hadn't scrambled her memory of it. He stood there, next to her, Blake, in a black tuxedo. He'd cut his hair and it waved back from his forehead. His face clean and shaven, a gleam of scrubbed skin broken with a smile.

"Blake," she said.

Margo stepped away, finally quieted.

"Hi," he said. "I'm Blake Hunter. I've heard about you and your work, and I wanted to introduce myself. I've wanted to introduce myself for a long time." He held out his hand.

His voice, it was a wave that washed over her, and she was off balance, slightly wobbly. Ella held out her own hand, felt it wrapped inside his as he lifted it to kiss the inside of her palm. "I'm Ella Flynn," she said. "It's so nice to meet you."

They stared at each other and the smiles felt like a secret, something to be held forever and never shared with anyone else.

"What are you doing here?" she asked.

Blake nodded toward Mimi. "I heard about an award ceremony in New York and I thought I just might show up to see who won."

"It wasn't me," she said.

"It's always you," he said.

"Is this the ending you would write?" She touched his cheek.

"No. This isn't about a story. It's about you. And it's not an ending;

hopefully it's a beginning. A new one." He drew her close, his hands on her waist and his lips on hers as if this was the hundredth time they'd come together this way, as if this was always the way it should be.

Ella wound her arms around Blake and pulled herself from his kiss to look into his eyes. "Well, I would have written it exactly this way," she said, and kissed him again.

There was a tug, a pull at the elbow, and a voice that said, "I'd like to meet you. I so love your design." Ella looked to the man, the winner, Alex.

"Don't leave," she said to Blake. "Please. I need to . . ."

"I am not going anywhere." Blake stepped back and stood next to Mimi. "I'm here."

Ella turned to Alex and congratulated him. The evening spun out from there. Ella met everyone—the designers, the staff, the judges. She gathered cards and names and numbers, hugged strangers and forgot about her dress and makeup and runner-up status, but what she didn't forget about was Blake, waiting with Mimi.

The room wasn't quite empty when she went to Blake, waiting at the back. He leaned against the wall with a smile and a glass of champagne. Ella went to him and pressed herself against him, held him so close she could feel his heartbeat through the tuxedo and then her dress. She could feel him breathe. "Don't let me go," she said.

"Never again," he said.

"So, love isn't so much an idea now, is it?" she whispered against his ear.

He pulled back from her and wound his arm around her waist. "I don't care if you're a designer or an opera singer. I don't care if you're a widow or Wonder Woman. I care about you. It's *you*. I couldn't forget you, Ella. I assumed I would. I thought that if I just stopped thinking about you or if I never saw you or talked to you again that I wouldn't want you anymore. But I do want you. I want to share everything with you. You . . . you're the one I want to be near, to share my life, to tell my stories. . . ."

Ella placed her finger on his lips. "Words." She smiled. "Now show me."

Blake wound his hand around her neck and kissed her exactly the way she wanted to be kissed. The kind of kiss that doesn't use words to say, "I choose you."

# one year later

---

*VARIETY* FILM REVIEW: *THE ONLY ONE*

The world premiere of *The Only One* in tiny Watersend, South Carolina, provides a marketing bonanza for the summer's best bet for smart counter-programming to a glut of super-hero action flicks. Goodwill abounds for hosting the film's debut at a newly renovated movie theater and the small-town setting ties into the rom-com's unusual backstory.

Most surprising of all, the big hook isn't the young director hot off Sundance looking for a commercial hit to go with his indie cred. And it's not the attractive TV stars whose show-sizzling chemistry is evident in their feature debut. Instead, it's the screenwriter, a rarity at any point in Hollywood's history. But bankable Blake Hunter can say bye-bye to his recent flops with what's sure to be a boffo hit that puts him back on top. . . .

In a signature Blake Hunter move, this film raises the usual questions about love in a fresh style. Is love just an idea that won't survive the harsh light of day, or can it change your life? If you fall in love at first sight, aren't you just falling in love with a fantasy of who that stranger might be? And aren't they doing the same with you? In the past, Hunter would have swept away such concerns with a wish-fulfilling finale. Here, the climax is just as romantic but now it feels genuine and true, a romance that accepts the complexities of real love as one of its rewards, not an annoyance to be ignored in favor of hearts and flowers.

Adults, especially women, are sure to welcome this entertaining, irresistible story that is better than a fairy tale because fairy tales aren't true. If Hunter is the male Nora Ephron, then this is his *When Harry Met Sally.* . . . And if the rumors are true, Hunter may soon follow in that legend's wake by making the leap to writer-director. Studio bigwigs should cross their fingers that his honeymoon proves just as inspiring as Hunter's search for romance.—Reviewed by Mitz

The camera establishes a wide shot to show a quaint town with brick sidewalks and gas lanterns. It looks like a movie set but it isn't; it is Watersend, South Carolina, on a hot summer evening for a movie premier. On the horizon, there is a church steeple and a sunset so beautiful that it appears like a backdrop painted on canvas, all reds and purples and pinks. The storefronts are lit and benches line the streets as if waiting for lovers. The candlelight glow found during that magic hour of dusk hovers over the town, expectant.

The camera zooms in to focus on the crowd outside a vintage movie theater. The marquee is red and bright with the large lightbulbs of the seventies announcing the movie for the night: *The Only One.* Limos pull up one by one and stars step out to wave at the crowd and then pose for a few photos before disappearing into the theater.

Two TV anchors, Tripp Marshall and Abbie Morgan, are talking over the scene until the camera pans to reveal them standing across the street.

## TRIPP MARSHALL, HOST OF *E! TV*:

We are live in charming Watersend, South Carolina, at the red carpet premier for *The Only One*, which insiders predict will be the romantic-comedy hit of the summer. This idyllic small town may seem an unlikely place for the Hollywood elite to converge, but this town isn't just the setting for the movie's premiere. It's also the setting for the screenwriter, Blake Hunter's, real-life romance with a local woman named Ella Flynn, the very same romance that inspired the movie.

## ABBIE:

Yes, Tripp, that's right. We've heard that Blake and Ella met in Watersend when Blake was traveling incognito to do research. He was posing as a history writer so he could discover some love stories about others but wound up discovering a love story of his own.

## TRIPP:

Yes, Abbie, and Blake wasn't the only one telling a few white lies as his new love, Ella, told us in an exclusive interview. But we don't want to give away any more spoilers. So let's talk about that dress she is wearing on the red carpet. It looks like it's a Steele Henry design. Is it?

## ABBIE:

It does look like it, but the word is that Ella designed it herself.

## TRIPP:

Well, that would make sense; she's a wedding dress designer.

## ABBIE:

It's a fun story, and one we can watch unfold on the screen, thanks to Blake.

TRIPP:

The early reviews have been fabulous so far, but of course
we haven't weighed in, have we, Abbie?

Abbie laughs and winks at Tripp, and then the camera moves away
from them and back to the front of the theater, where Blake Hunter
and Ella Flynn are exiting a limousine. He takes her hand and helps
her out of the car before kissing her. They turn and wave to the crowd
and—

"Blake." The first reporter reaches him and holds out the microphone. "Can you tell us—we've heard it rumored that you rewrote the
screenplay after falling in love with Ella. Is this true?"

"Yes." Blake nods and pulls her closer. "Because that's exactly what
love does—it changes everything."

# *acknowledgments*

Gratitude never seems enough for those who influence and support my work. But nevertheless, gratitude is what I have for so many people because this story (and many others) would not exist without them.

My publishing team at St. Martin's Press is incomparable. My editor, Brenda Copeland, keeps me in line, kills my darlings, keeps me laughing, has numerous nicknames for me, and generally makes both my book and my life better. For all those who support us on every level, I am thankful: Laura Chasen, Jennifer Enderlin, Sally Richardson, Jessica Preeg, Marie Estrada, Kerry McMahon, Tracey Guest, and Jeanne-Marie Hudson. To the sales staff, marketing, and publicity—such an extraordinary team behind every single book, and I don't know the half of what they do!

To Rivendell Writers Colony and Carmen and Michael Thompson, I am eternally grateful not only for the space and inspirational place to write—for Percy's Perch and the tiny cottage on the bluff—but also for saving me when I needed saving the most. And also to Amy Greene and Joe Shuster for sharing that time with me, for opening my heart to so many stories, for walking over the natural bridge with me while we tried to find our places in the world.

To Michael Giltz, movie reviewer, award-winning freelance writer based in New York, and founder of the Web site BookFilter. I am so grateful for your expertise. Any errors about the movie industry are mine alone, but anything correct is Michael's doing.

To Bookreporter.com's entire staff, and especially Carol Fitzgerald, I am thankful for your expertise, creativity, and humor.

As always to my agent, Kimberly Whalen, eternal gratitude.

To my writing tribe, I love all of you. What would we do without one another? How would we find our way? To the bookstores and readers and bloggers and reviewers: how can I ever thank all of you? I don't know if there is a way, but I am sending out so much love to each and every one of you. To those who show up at signings and readings, to those who write to me and tell me your stories, my heart is bigger because of you.

To Gregg Sullivan and Caroline Ambuhl at Sullivan and Associates. What a great year we've had. It's been such a joy working with your creative spirits.

To Mark and Cate Sommer, who never give up in encouraging me on every step in every way. Cate, I've used your hilarious "four-star hotel" slip because you always make me laugh even when I don't think I can.

To my friends, so many, who ran to my front door after I plummeted from the Sewanee cliff in an idiot hiking move. And those who sent flowers, food, and love. God, what would I have done but for you? I wouldn't have been able to finish this book without you; I know that.

To those who brainstormed, read early drafts, and let me talk about fictional people as if they were real: Kerry Lunsford-Madden, Lanier Isom, Kathy Trocheck, Mary Alice Monroe, Dottie Frank, and Kate Phillips. And to Kortni Duff: Your eagle eye and kind heart made this story better.

## ACKNOWLEDGMENTS

Always to my family and extended family, because I couldn't and wouldn't do what I do without you. I love all of you, Callahans, Henrys, Burrises, and Cunnions. Every single one of you.

Mostly to Pat, Meagan, Thomas, and Rusk Henry. What a crazy year, right? We did it together, and here we are. I love you.